Ripple

Effect

Ripple

Effect

Hadley Hoover

Happy Reading!
Hadley Hoover

Ripple Effect
All rights reserved © 2011 by Hadley Hoover

Published via lulu.com. See the author's website for global purchasing options: www.hadleyhoover.com.

Front cover photo and book design: www.kendallhoover.com.
Back cover: Original color photo of the Puddle Jumper Trail bridge, courtesy of Nan Reinking. Used, as modified, with permission.

Ripple Effect is a work of fiction. Names, characters, places, or events are the products of the author's imagination or are used fictitiously. Resemblance to actual events, locales, or persons living or dead is coincidental.

ISBN: 978-1-4583-7911-5

Dedication

◆ ◆

To Kendall:
Stones sink—
whether priceless, pleasing, or painful.
But, ah!
Ripples remain—
resilient, lingering as the heart heals
from memories of sinking stones.

Also by Hadley Hoover

◆ ◆

Miles Apart
Uncharted Territory
Hidden Crossing
Storm Path

◆

Off Track

◆

Rough Terrain
Unguarded Edge
Late Harvest
Shifting Shadows
Fallow Fields

◆

Rogue Wave
Shaky Ground
Prevailing Winds

◆ ◆

See details, including preview chapters, at:
www.hadleyhoover.com

Acknowledgements

• *Donna Haslett-Nelson*

Hats-off to you and others over the years for making the Crosby (Divide County) North Dakota Threshing Show such an annual crowd-pleaser. The event's website [www.dcthreshingbee.com] shows much ingenuity as fresh ideas join "old favorites" on each year's program.

• *Rose Howard*

Your insider information in response to my off-the-wall and often fuzzy questions about the Threshing Show was timely, detailed, and terrific. For this and much more, I give you my heartfelt thanks. I look forward to seeing all the action at the authentic Big Ole's Cook Car someday.

• *Bev Jacobson*

When I needed a place for my fictional characters to set up a canopy in Crosby, I could think of no better spot than outside J Co Drug. It is a very enticing store! Your classy style shows in every aisle.

• *Pastor Keith Krebs*

On August 30, 2009, you preached a sermon titled "Ripples." It greatly impacted me (a visitor to American Reformed Church) and so reinforced my title-choice for this novel that I even kept the service program. The Biblical texts (David's story in II Samuel 14:4-14 and Psalm 3:1-8) not only provided a solid foundation for your message, but formed some of the invisible support system for *Ripple Effect*'s storyline.

• *Harold & Rose Van Der Weide*

Thanks for giving me a fast-track education in the joys and technicalities of playing harmonicas. Each time I hear the real Harmonica Band perform, I not only gain additional details but, more importantly, so much pleasure.

• *To all who asked if they'd ever see Blyss and Eddie again*

Here you go . . . Persistence pays!

FRIDAY

CHAPTER 1

Sweat. Perspire. Swelter. Wilt. Drip. Knowing so many ways to state the obvious? Always an occupational hazard for the author sitting on his sticky lawn chair. Heat radiating from street and sidewalk made Zeke Eden one sweaty-perspiring-sweltering-wilting-dripping guy.

Eight-thirty? Skeptical, he verified his cell against the bank's flashing sign. *Already eighty-eight degrees?* "Our coolers have enough ice, Mom; fling some of it at me!"

Haze frowned. "I don't throw things. Certainly not ice."

"Nonsense. The girl known as 'feisty Hazel Anderson' in her rowdier years still lurks inside Haze Eden. If *Hazel* smacked innocent Bess McAvoy back then, can't *Haze*—"

That still-feisty gal (just seventy-some years older) scoffed, "Not so innocent!" but otherwise ignored Zeke and continued checking ice-levels, adding more as needed.

"Here's what I don't get: You swung your six-year-old fist and Bess still likes you. If *only* she'd held a grudge all these years, we'd be basking in air-conditioned comfort in a swanky bookstore now, not sweating in North Dakota."

"Men sweat; ladies glisten. Besides, perspiration is good for us; it cleanses our pores."

"Okay, but while your lady-like pores are glistening, my reamed-out male pores are gushing geysers here in hot-hot-*hot* Crosby. Not out in ocean-breezy San Diego, or mountain-cool Denver, or even up in chilly Anchorage."

She stiffened. "I'll pick places where my friends live over those big-city bookstores—anytime, anywhere. You need to work on getting friends, Zeke. You're a recluse."

"A recluse? *Puhleeze!* Writing isn't a social career. And I have friends." He snapped fingers off his thumb in succession: "Sage *(index finger)*. John and Maggie *(middle, ring)* who are the only editor and agent on the planet who'd ever agree to a tour like this. Oh, and Pudge *(pinkie)* at the gas station; he always waves at me. See? That's four friends." Four fingers waggled triumphantly.

Haze raised a hand in rebuttal: "Sage is your wife *(index finger)*. John and Maggie *(middle, ring)* like how you make them rich. As for Pudge? *(pinkie)* The man waves at statues, Zeke!" Four fingers waggled dismissively.

"Quibble all you want. Point being: I have friends, I have never punched any of them, and I am not a recluse."

Haze resorted to what she did best when trapped: she changed the subject. "Which is better? Stacking the books at zig-zaggy angles like this, or in straight-up piles?"

"No changes for our last event; lined up spines reinforce a title. Quit dodging the issue. *You* hit Bess, so why am *I* suffering heat stroke in North Dakota in July?"

"I didn't raise you to be such a whiner! She deserved a black eye; she said my hair was like porcupine quills."

"I've seen pictures; you did look dangerous."

"Hush; open another box. I swear, no one would dream you have a lick of experience with book-signings. If people don't see plenty of books, they won't stop by."

"Sure they will; our snazzy banner makes them wonder 'What's happening under that canopy? Let's go see!' Don't ever underestimate the power of suspense."

"Oh." Haze fanned her face with her apron in hopes the minuscule movement of air would revive her, or ease the *glistening*. She eyed an ice-filled cooler longingly.

Zeke raised hands in mock surrender. "But this is your gig, Mom. If you want a box opened, I'm on it. See? We box-opening chauffeurs don't whine for long."

"You're hardly merely 'the chauffeur,' and it's hardly just '*my gig*.' Not with both of our names on the—" Her voice dropped to a stage whisper. "Someone's coming! No more complaining, you hear me?"

Mother and son smiled their welcomes, unaware the approaching woman had been watching them from her second-story efficiency apartment since eight-thirty . . .

CHAPTER 2

It's eighty-eight degrees at eight-thirty? Hélène groaned and peered out the window. Every day she checked her bedside clock against the bank's flashing sign, but today something besides time-and-temperature diverted her.

She dropped to a crouch, letting the curtain shroud her shoulders. By craning her neck she could partially see, though not enough to really know, what occupied a portion of sidewalk space outside J Co Drug.

Four metal poles, anchored in buckets, supported a rectangular canvas tent . . . *No, not a tent; is it what's called a gazebo?* She'd seen such open-sided structures used at fairs or yard sales as protection against weather. The odd angle of her view blurred most of the words on a sign tied to the fringed canvas flap. That banner likely explained why the shebang was pitched on Main Street.

Whatever the shelter was called, it shaded a skirted table; whatever it protected was unidentifiable from a distance, but appeared to be books. But were those boxy things coolers? Unlikely if it was books beside them. Not much more was visible: a seated man, and a woman standing by an empty chair. Minimal and mysterious.

The Threshing Show was in full swing out at Pioneer Village, just west of town. It always brought thousands of old-time-machine enthusiasts to Crosby. Even now, she heard steam engines puffing and clicking in the distance. But no one from that crowd set up booths on Main Street. *Maybe it's a booth . . . unless booths require walls.*

Inching forward, Hélène leaned so close to the screen it imprinted a mesh-design on her nose. Her next breath dislodged dust from the wiry weave. She sneezed, then read aloud, guessing at what was imprinted in red letters on the white banner: "S-short-word, ends in an S, too . . .

On in—Huh? Well, *that* makes no sense—*R*-whatever, *C*-something-'LY' and a *K*-word, ending in an 'N,' I think. The sun's glare sure doesn't make reading it any easier."

Hélène shifted to a kneeling position and propped her elbows on the sill, waiting for action to unfold. *Nothing.* It was a trumped-up drama with two dull characters and no hint of plot. *And an audience of one—that'd be me.*

Stage left: The woman idly shuffled items on the table. Hands waving, she spoke to her companion, and resumed reorganizing the objects. *She's either as bored as I am,* Hélène decided, *or too antsy to sit still.*

Stage right: The man lounged at the opposite end of the table, motionless as a mannequin, except for one burst of hand gestures. Legs extended, he was the epitome of relaxed. *The woman amuses him.* Hélène sighed. It had been a long, long time since she had held a man's interest. As for amusing him? *Seems like eternity.*

She let the curtain fall back in place, unconsciously mimicking stagehands' actions to signal a scene's end in live theater. Rising, she looked disinterestedly around the space she never thought to call *home* though it had been her dwelling for many months. Life revolved in a dreary circle: working downstairs, eating-sleeping-*being* upstairs.

She gave the window a fleeting glance. *It's a sad state of affairs when such trifling action on Main Street is more appealing to me than anything within these four walls.*

That admission spurred her to action. Within five minutes she was heading down outside steps to the alley. Turning the corner that landed her on Main Street, she easily read the banner's message: SOUP'S ON IN RAVEN CROWLEY'S KITCHEN. She now knew what it said—and *'On in'* made a little more sense—but one question remained: *Who is Raven Crowley?*

Lingering in the shadows, Hélène felt eyes watching through the plate-glass window behind her. Over the years since trouble landed on her doorstep, she had pursued one goal: *Be Invisible.* She moved to the bricked section of wall beyond the window. From there, a parked pickup's bulkiness allowed her to see without being seen by the unidentified couple across the street.

Well, maybe not *couple* in the usual sense of the word. Noting that the man was considerably younger than the woman, she deduced they were friends, possibly family—though she did not naïvely equate the two relationships. Family could be friends; friends could become like family.

Sometimes.

When the woman leaped from the chair she had occupied for only a moment, a smile dislodged Hélène's frown that, as usual, sprang from dark thoughts about family. The woman resumed fiddling with whatever the table held—*Yes, it's books; yes, she's antsy.* One moment the books were perfectly aligned; seconds later, they formed a zigzag pile. Hélène's gaze drifted to the man who watched the woman without offering her any assistance.

Still not moving, he spoke. The low rumble of his voice reached Hélène, though a passing car's loud muffler blocked his actual words. The woman waved dismissively at him, reshuffled the stack to a straight pile, and tapped each book, obviously counting. Hélène mouthed numbers along with her: . . . *four, five, six* . . .

Yes, it was coolers; but why not keep them out-of-sight below the table? Were these people vendors connected to the Threshing Show, planning to sell refreshments? No, a food-booth wouldn't sell books, not along with messy things like snow-cones, ice cream bars, and cold drinks. And the sign only mentioned soup. *Good grief; a soup stand in July in North Dakota! Are they idiots?*

Curiosity bested her usual caution; she stepped off the curb. The town rarely held much intrigue for her, not even its annual third-weekend-in-July Threshing Show of wide-ranging fame ever snagged or held her interest. For over four decades, vast crowds had flocked to participate in or attend an event that meant little to her.

Hélène didn't understand such enthusiasm. For her, Crosby was just a place to live while she wished life could be different than it was. Her mental and emotional focus clung to Prairie Rose: a village a mere thirty miles away according to the state's atlas, but an unnavigable thirty-million miles away according to her heart's map.

Though careful not to broadcast such a locally unpopular opinion, Hélène cared nothing about antique steam engines, or one-of-a-kind tractors, or restored threshing machines. She couldn't identify one vintage or classic automobile from another. And she didn't care. To her, a car was simply transportation, no matter how authentically it had been refurbished. To her, less conspicuous trumped everything else.

But nothing about this couple's display or their attire suggested any connection to farm implements or vehicles.

Hélène stood between angle-parked cars, waiting for a slow-moving SUV with Ohio plates to pass. Driver and passenger looked exhausted. *They probably drove through the night to get to the Threshing Show.* Hélène was relieved they didn't stop to ask her where to find a motel with vacancies. No such thing for miles, certainly not the Golden Hub Motel; it was full to the rafters. *If they're smart, they're prepared to pitch a tent and camp out.*

Though she'd usually pay more attention to out-of-state visitors, other things now occupied her mind. She was determined to find out what was happening in her front yard, so to speak. *Some front yard,* she thought glumly. *Flowers I didn't plant, dead blooms and weeds I can't pull—and all of it in pots hanging from light-poles on Main Street. The closest thing I have to a yard or garden isn't green and growing, it's asphalt and concrete.*

"You know better than to fixate on everything you've lost," Hélène chided herself. "Find out what this tent-gazebo-booth-thingamajig is about, and then get to work. At least if you learn what's up, you'll have something to talk about besides tractors at the store this weekend."

CHAPTER 3

As their potential customer approached the canopy-shaded rectangle of sidewalk, Haze's smile rivaled the blazing sun. "Good morning! May I offer you a sample of soup? The recipe's included in our new cookbook."

"No, it's too early and too hot for soup. But thanks." A hesitant smile robbed the woman's refusal of rudeness. She exhaled an upward breath. Curls lifted but promptly dropped back to rest on her forehead, so she thrust her sunglasses into her hair to restrain the wayward curls.

Prone to ignore protests when doing so suited her purposes, Haze smiled and filled a small plastic cup from a carafe kept in the cooler. "It's warm, but this may help."

The snared woman eyed the container of frosty, pale green liquid she now held. A cautious sip. "Refreshing!" She stepped back to view the banner. "A cold soup?"

"Yes; it's cucumber. See how simple the recipe is?" Haze tapped the full-color pages in the browsing copy she'd strategically placed for customers' easy viewing. "But first, let's get acquainted. I'm Haze Eden, and this is my son and co-author Zeke. May I ask your name?"

A startled blink, then: "Uh . . . I'm Hélène."

"What a lovely name! Do you spell it with a final 'E'?"

The woman followed her hesitant nod with a prolonged sip, which Zeke suspected was intended to end that line of discussion. But he knew something Hélène-with-a-final-E didn't know: He knew his mother.

"I adore French names!" the undeterred Haze gushed. "Tell me: How many syllables are in your last name?"

"One," she said warily, then added in a rushed clarification: "It's W-I-L-S. Spelled with one 'L'."

"Perfect! Why, Hélène Wils rolls off the tongue like honey off a spoon. Speaking of honey, when you're ready

I'd like you to sample our delicious fruit soup. Zeke and I believe honey blends flavors without overpowering . . ."

It was a pity Haze hadn't gotten into sales until she joined forces with her son to create SOUP'S ON IN RAVEN CROWLEY'S KITCHEN. *She takes to it like a duck to water,* Zeke mused. He could permit the cliché because it was utterly true—though, as an author, he considered it toxic, even if he merely thought it. *Like a duck in a pond, she paddles around customers, creating mesmerizing ripples.*

While Haze engaged Hélène in examining unique features within the cookbook's glossy pages, Zeke opened a box below the table and took out the top copy. The cover-art always made him smile. It showed the hands of an unseen chef (obviously masculine, given the contours of the background shadow) who stirred a steaming kettle with one hand and held a smoking gun in the other.

Hélène took advantage of a rare break in Haze's cheery, fast-paced spiel to ask, "Who is Raven Crowley?"

Like a marathoner poised at the *Ready-Set-Go* mark, Haze inhaled and took off: "Raven Crowley is the hero in Kiel Nede's sixteen mystery-thrillers. Are you a reader?"

Obviously bewildered by what seemed a bizarre shift in subjects—*Weren't we talking about soup?*—Hélène nodded tentatively.

'Yes, I'm a reader' was the correct, if unspoken, response. Haze beamed her approval.

Getting non-readers to care about a fictional character's recipes was up-hill work, and even tougher if they were non-*cooking* non-readers. It had stunned Haze when one such Nebraskan interrupted her explanation of a recipe to ask, "When it says 'add thyme' that really just means 'increase minutes,' right? Like when those peculiar British people spell Smith as S-M-Y-T-H-E?"

Having established that Hélène was both reader and cook, Haze sprinted along. "Zeke and I were elated when Mister Nede gave us permission to create this cookbook. It features the soups Raven Crowley makes when he's not chasing down criminals. Have you ever read Kiel Nede's books?" At Hélène's denial, Haze waved at the window display behind them. "J Co Drug sells them, and your local library likely has the full set. They're *very* popular."

Meanwhile Kiel Nede sat five feet away. It agonized Haze not to say, *"Kiel is right here! Zeke is Kiel!"* But she honored Zeke's original edict: "I need anonymity to be my best. If you're asked what I do, say I'm a writer. Be mum about Kiel, and vague about what your son Zeke writes."

Haze zipped along: "In Kiel Nede's novels, you see that Raven Crowley not only knows his way around a crime scene, but he's right at home in his own kitchen . . ."

Kiel/Zeke masked a smile and turned pages. He knew the facts Haze didn't share: He and Raven had been an award-winning team for three decades. Writing under the pseudonym formed by taking *Kiel* from his given-name Ezekiel and flipping the letters of his surname to form *Nede*, Zeke manned the computer that spit out the best-sellers. Every successive title made Zeke's editor, agent, publisher, and readers eager for what came next.

Each thriller sent the fictional-but-frightening Raven Crowley into dark places where he gave bad guys well-deserved nightmares. In every story, Raven was a loner. In real life, Zeke's privately passionate and publicly business-savvy wife, Sage, kept him sane and social.

But then. Good times screeched to a halt for the Eden family. Kiel Nede's sixteenth book—OFF TRACK—veered much too close to reality, sending them into a tailspin from which they had yet to recover. That's when Zeke lost his zest for dreaming up more bad guys for Raven to pound into the ground.

Wisely, John Lawrence Winthrop of JLW Literary Services didn't let his role as Zeke's editor deprive him of his humanity. As it became evident another manuscript wasn't even in dream-stage, let alone in progress, John didn't badger his star author or complain about the unfairness of the universe. He merely fell silent on his end of that fateful phone call. When he finally spoke, it was gruffly (*kindly* would have been too much for either to handle). "You know how to find us when you're ready."

John's use of *us* was intentional. Maggie was John's wife and Zeke's agent; she excelled in each role. Both men knew who really ran the show: it was that perky, talented gal whose wry humor tempered her dry sarcasm.

Zeke's abrupt withdrawal from the writing world put a serious crimp in the Winthrop-team's financial picture, so it evidenced the genuine friendship the three shared when Maggie's tender heart ruled her razor tongue. She followed John's example and let Zeke set his own pace.

Then one day, like rainclouds drifting over the horizon toward parched fields, a wisp of an idea blew over Zeke's dried-up muse. Like a spring shower, it brought hints of life to the desert. He had considered the idea in jest before—just once, only to himself. Then, even without nurturing, seeds took root and sent up hopeful shoots.

During a routine "keeping-in-touch" phone call, Zeke suggested to John that maybe, just *maybe*, he and Haze could collaborate on a cookbook. Both loved to cook, and whatever they produced usually garnered raves . . .

A cookbook? Digesting that startling notion, John inhaled and exhaled lung-clogging smoke from his ubiquitous cigarette. "A cookbook, hmm?" *Puff, puff.* "You know, Zeke, whenever Raven unwinds after his rampages and gets out the stock pot, I drool even before I know what he's making. A cookbook devoted to Raven's soups would be a huge hit with your fans. *Huge.*"

"It could, but this time the name on the cover would be Zeke Eden, not Kiel Nede. And Mom gets top-billing. Those are my conditions if this is going to happen."

A pause sufficient for several puffs. "Okay. I see. Would you at least allow a tie-in to Kiel, to appease his fans? He could—oh, I don't know, give his blessing, maybe? But we don't need to settle anything today. We can figure out details as we go along. How's that sound?"

And so it was that SOUP'S ON IN RAVEN CROWLEY'S KITCHEN was born.

Maggie rejected numerous book covers until one met her standards. Then she plunged into organizing what she dubbed the "zaniest book-signing tour" of her career. But, despite Maggie's zeal and abilities, it was Haze's stubbornness that determined the *Where*'s and *When*'s the cookbook's author-events would take place.

At a face-to-face meeting in the JLW Literary Service's Kansas City office, Maggie told Zeke with awe swelling her voice, "The next person who accuses *me* of being tough? I'm going to introduce them to your Mama!" Haze smiled sweetly, trying (and failing) to look cuddly.

Mother and son hit the road—literally, because few planes landed near locales where Haze's life-long friends and various relatives lived. Their back-roads tour left national bookstore chains confused about a cookbook inching its way up the bestseller charts while they couldn't get author appearances for it on their calendars.

Haze insisted on at least a full-day event at each place, and she tripled that to match the Threshing Show's schedule. From the start they had bypassed brick-and-mortar bookstores so sitting on a sidewalk outside a North Dakota drug store now seemed almost normal.

All gigs were in non-neon places, like a classmate's Minnesota Iron-Range beauty salon. The odors gave Zeke a blinding headache, but he popped aspirin and scrawled his black-ink stalwart *Zeke Eden* below what seemed like zillions of "happy-pink-ink" *Haze Eden* signatures.

Another weekend, they shared space in a Wisconsin Farmer's Market booth with two former neighbors. Customers walked away with SOUP'S ON IN RAVEN CROWLEY'S KITCHEN and bags of Jim and Pat's veggies, having tasted each variety in the day's soup samples.

What stunned Maggie in her high-rise office was when one weekend's sales beat all previous figures. Handmade signs had pointed the way for miles in all directions to an innovative niece's porch: SOUP'S ON / COME 'ND GET 'ER / BUY A BOOK? / YOU SURE BETTER! / RAVEN SAYS. "I hope Burma Shave views imitation as praise," Zeke murmured.

A bird flying from the REDUCE SPEED warning on the Southern edge of that Iowa burg barely needed to flap its wings to reach the RESUME SPEED sign on the Northern border. But cookbook sales took flight and soared.

The next weekend, Zeke jammed the brakes so hard he almost activated the rental car's airbags outside Haze's favorite sister-in-law's hometown. A billboard displayed the vivid cookbook cover, flanked by the two authors' smiling faces. It truly was startling how large things—like nostrils—seemed against the cloudless cerulean South Dakota sky. Zeke snapped a picture of the startling sign, e-mailing it to Maggie and Sage without comment.

Maggie responded with a wordless text message: !!!!!!!!!!!!!!!!! Seventeen of them. Zeke knew; he counted.

Sage called; it wasn't much of a conversation—mostly hoots from Utah. "I expect more dignified behavior from a hospital CEO," Zeke huffed between her whoops. "I hope you're alone in your office." She only laughed harder.

In a remote Nebraska town, a café-owning cousin featured soups from each of the cookbook's eight categories. They had to extend their stay so the publisher could ship books via overnight express when empty boxes outnumbered full ones. "People will want their books signed," Haze insisted. Apparently she was right; sales never floundered after Day Two's stock was resupplied.

By now, nothing surprised Maggie. "Brutal!" was her comment when Zeke informed her they'd be in Crosby for not one, not two, but three days. "Haze moves gobs of books. I may rethink our usual two-hour signing stints. That, or hire her to help authors with sagging sales!"

Meanwhile, John and Maggie spent several evenings scouring the sixteen Kiel Nede titles, hoping to find something else book-worthy that Raven Crowley might have created besides mayhem and great soup.

CHAPTER 4

Zeke had no need to read the Preface to SOUP'S ON IN RAVEN CROWLEY'S KITCHEN. He had written it at John's behest as a way to incorporate Kiel Nede into the project. But he read it anyway, against the backdrop of an herbs-versus-spices discussion between Haze and Hélène:

> Raven Crowley knows how to unwind: This ominously silent avenger, whom bad dudes and dudettes rightfully fear, retreats to his kitchen. After each encounter that leaves another corner of the world safer than he found it, Raven opens the door to the undisclosed location he calls home. There, away from the madness, he makes soup.

> Always starting from scratch, he improvises as he chops and purees, and finally settles down with a tall cold one while the stock pot simmers. Flavors blend, a pleasing aroma rises, and Raven smiles—something few have seen him do.

> Raven Crowley doesn't smile much. He kills if needed, or maims if such will suffice. I know: I'm the one who created this formidable man, so I understand that nothing calms a savage beast (which fully describes Raven on the job—not when he's wearing an apron) like good soup.

> Follow Raven's example: A bowl of savory soup prepares you for life's next onslaught. Now, for the first time, Raven reveals his recipes, though his other dark secrets remain hush-hush. I give my blessing to Haze and Zeke Eden as they expose the softer side of the toughest guy I know.

> *Kiel Nede*

For years, Zeke's anonymity held because each persona carried a unique visual identity, and because Haze mastered being mum or vague. The shiny-scalped man paging through a cookbook wore a prosthetic foot, though few could correctly guess: *Left or right?* It was a necessary attachment due to his life-changing encounter with an axe thirty-plus years earlier.

For public appearances promoting the mysteries, Zeke/Kiel removed his fake foot, picked up crutches, and donned a shoulder-length wig made from his own Sixties-era hair. Sweating beneath the sun-blasted canvas, bald Zeke was glad he, not bewigged Kiel, was on this tour.

He turned to the Table of Contents. Each recipe listed held memories of hours of brainstorming and debates.

Always the expert marketer, Maggie insisted that they link Kiel Nede's book titles to the soups. "Folks who like the crab bisque may buy VANISHING POINT," she argued—and won. While Haze was all about making people happy, Maggie didn't care if people were grouchy as long as they bought books. But Maggie couldn't—and didn't—discount the financial benefits which Haze's philosophy produced.

John suggested an unusual Index that included seasonings, and even suggested appliances. "Let's say I grow herbs in my window-box in Boston. It'd be nice if I could look up 'chives' and see how many soups I can make, right? Or, if I got a food-processor for my birthday, how handy to know which recipes will let me use it." Haze accepted the tedious job of indexing accordingly.

Sage's input was brilliant: "What if I don't like fish, or I shudder at the thought of tomatoes, but I like how a soup sounds otherwise?" The result was variations of each recipe allowing for preference, price, and availability restraints: *Tired of chicken? Try this with lamb.*

Zeke's initial job was identifying the soups which, at the time of writing each thriller, he had randomly decided Raven Crowley would prepare. He realized anew that John's idea for the cookbook's theme was a winner:

SOUP'S ON IN RAVEN CROWLEY'S KITCHEN
Recipes & Where You'll Find Raven Making Them

Meat and/or Veggie Soups
In *Stick Up* and *Ill Winds*

- Goulash Soup with Beef or Pork
- Mulligatawny with Chicken or Lamb
- Minestrone
- Split Pea with Ham or Sausage
- Vegetarian Senate Bean

Fish Stews and Bisques
In *Vanishing Point* and *Slow Burn*

- Bouillabaisse
- Gumbo with Shellfish
- Cioppino
- Lobster, Crab, or Shrimp Bisque

Chowders
In *Depth Deception* and *Ground Down*

- She-Crab Soup
- Clam Chowder
- Chupe
- Corn Chowder

Cheese Soups
In *Mucked Out* and *Class Act*

- Apple-Cheese
- Tortilla
- Asparagus or Cauliflower
- Beer-Cheese

Cream Soups
In *Double Take* and *Turbulent Tides*

- Tomato
- Mushroom
- Potato
- Broccoli or Celery

Taste-buds now on full alert, Zeke turned the page . . .

Broths
In *Off Track* and *Diving Point*

- Chicken, Turkey, or Beef
- Chinese Egg-drop or Bird's Nest
- French Onion
- Vegetarian or Meat-based Consommé

Chilled Soups
In *Stir Crazy* and *Penalty Box*

- Borscht
- Cucumber
- Gazpacho
- Vichyssoise

Dessert Soups
In *Cloudy Vision* and *Border Dispute*

- Berries or Cherries
- Fruktsuppe
- Ginataan
- Chocolate

He grinned, recalling Sage's "Pick me to taste-test all variations of this one!" when she first saw the final entry.

"Zeke," Haze's voice jolted him from his reverie, "you know Kiel Nede's books better than I do. Which ones would you say his female readers enjoy most?"

Setting the book aside but retaining his smile, Zeke stood. "That depends. What are your interests, Hélène?"

"Interests?" A frown creased her forehead. "I used to like to cook, but I'm alone now . . ." Abrupt inhalation ended further words, but silence shouted her pain.

Alert to others' distress since her family traumas, Haze said softly, "Oh, Hélène! I understand; my husband, Rudy, died last year. We always entertained, and I enjoy cooking, so now I freeze more, or divide recipes. I find it relaxing to spend time in the kitchen. When my freezer gets too full, I just share with neighbors, or invite friends for supper. Are you also a widow, Hélène?"

The responding head-shake became a tremor that spread through Hélène's whole body, affecting even her voice. "Uh, no; deserted, then divorced. Excuse me; I really must go." Her eyes darted, seeking an escape. Zeke sensed only ingrained manners kept the distraught woman from running pell-mell from her persistent inquisitor. "Thank you for the sample." She carefully placed her empty cup on the table.

"You're welcome." Haze tossed the cup, but held firmly to her subject: "I know how hard fresh pain is."

A head-shake. "Mine's not fresh; enough time has passed that—" She inhaled sharply and, on the exhale, straightened her shoulders as if marshaling her stamina. "Sorry; I don't mean to . . ." She bit her lower lip. "How long will you be here? I need time to think about the cookbook. Could we talk about the mysteries later?"

"Yes, of course; we're here the whole weekend," Zeke assured her. A segue from uncomfortable subjects was needed to help Hélène regain composure. The topic wouldn't matter, so the Master-of-Words started talking: "These three days finish our book-signing tour. We're in Crosby because of Haze's childhood friend, Bess Green— you may know her; she's a part-time clerk at J Co Drug. Anyway, Bess arranged for us to come during the annual Threshing Bee. Or is it called a Threshing *Show*?"

She shrugged. "Threshing Show, I guess." Though obviously still on-edge, she lingered, making a stab at civility: "I know it's not very civic-minded of me, but I really don't get involved."

"Bess has told us that, year-after-year, the Show continues to bring crowds to town," Zeke rambled on since his diversionary tactic was getting results. "We've seen many out-of-state license plates—from Canada, too."

"I guess there's nothing like it anywhere else, so much unique, old machinery in one place." A pause, then she looked at Haze. "Yes, I do know Bess; she's always very pleasant to talk to whenever I see her at the drug store."

"She's a sweetie, all right. And I enjoy talking with you! Let's meet again," Haze suggested impulsively. "You can sit with me and we'll chat between customers." Hélène's expression suggested she'd prefer a root canal to being on display. But Haze didn't quit: "Come back and taste our samples tomorrow. And on Sunday we'll feature tempting chocolate dessert soups. So please stop by our canopy whenever you're free throughout the weekend, Hélène."

Canopy; of course . . . Hélène thought. But solving the minor dilemma of what to call the booth-tent structure didn't alleviate distress over the idea of sitting idly by while strangers stared at her. She dropped her sunglasses into place—not only in preparation for stepping back into the blazing sunshine, but also as a standard prop in her continuing efforts to *Be Invisible*. "I'll see how things go," she hedged. "I could be busy, but maybe it will—"

A sudden commotion sliced through the otherwise fairly quiet morning, halting whatever would have followed Hélène's "*maybe*." She shot a worried look over her shoulder while Haze and Zeke searched for what had so abruptly jolted the conversation that seemed to have rallied.

"Oh, no!" Hélène's voice communicated more dread than shock. "Have you met Eddie yet?" She was already backing away from the table.

"Eddie?" was the unintentionally unison query from the two stymied cookbook authors.

The question hung suspended. Hélène was gone, leaving more to confound than to answer the questions swirling through Zeke and Haze's minds.

CHAPTER 5

Cacophony announced the fellow's approach. *Scuffle-skiff-shuffle! Bing-clangity-bang! Whish-swoosh!*

The man was a walking sound-effects machine.

Haze emitted a wordless chirp before her ingrained etiquette masked any other reactions.

Zeke's long-dormant author's-eye-for-detail winked into action as he examined a fellow of indeterminate age loping toward them. It was hard to know where to focus:

Apparel? Ripped jeans gave hints of barbed wire or frequent brawls. Wild gyrations shot sunglasses off his nose to skitter along the pavement. Retrieving them, he laced the hinge-point of the eyewear's lone stem through a buttonhole on his shirt, and poked it through a gash on the other side where a button was missing. If the gash and buttonhole didn't align horizontally, not a problem!

Footwear? One laceless black high-top athletic shoe encased a foot wearing a sagging sock. The other bare foot was stuffed into a holey canvas shoe that had began life as white, but long-since succumbed to gray.

Hair? Eons had passed since anything but rain had dampened the dingy mess and spotty beard. As for shampoo or soap? Even longer. Wild strands loosened from a long brown plait displayed sun-bleached dull hues. The braid ended in a tangle resembling an inverted corn-shock in which birds had nested.

Backpack? Duct-taped bulges tested each zipper's strength. Some objects that were attached to various loops rattled or bounced: a small pan, tin cup, can-opener, and scissors. Other items dangled or dripped: a stained sock, a threadbare hunk of towel, and a plastic beverage bottle minus its label.

Oblivious to their inspection of his person and possessions, the fellow dug through a curb-side trashcan. Finding nothing of interest, he headed for the canopy.

Vapors heralded his approach, sending uninitiated nostrils into a near-sneezing frenzy. A murky cloud of body odor, grease-grime, weedy-field, and gutter-debris stenches hovered.

The man was potency on the prowl.

Whistling snatches of "Pop Goes the Weasel," he leaned back on his heels and squinted up at the banner. That action nearly toppled him off the curb, but he recovered, flailing his arms to maintain balance.

Zeke had visions of headlines if he fell backwards and cracked his head: *Injured Man Collects Millions!* Haze had visions of spills-and-spoils if he fell forward and upset their display table. Each breathed a muffled *"Whew!"* when he stepped forward with neither injury nor incident.

A laminated foggy but official-looking photo ID dangled off a lanyard attached to the backpack's uppermost loop. It flopped over one shoulder and proclaimed this was EDDIE.

Haze wanted to scrub him, top-to-bottom.

Zeke wanted to hear his life-story, front-to-back.

Each crease in Eddie's visible skin held enough dirt to grow several rows of carrots—and his fingernails looked as if he had just finished planting them. Scratching an armpit (easy to do with the sleeve ripped off) he demanded, "Whazzat say up there bout soup?"

Haze's reply was oddly high-pitched. "It's the name of our cookbook: SOUP'S ON IN RAVEN CROWLEY'S KITCHEN."

His nose twitched. "Don' smell no soups." Frowning, he lowered his backpack to the ground. "Ain't never hear'd bout no soups wha' gots raisins innit."

Haze's amused peep could have been much worse. "Not raisins: *Raven.* Raven Crowley is the name of . . ." At that point, she wisely ditched her usual patter and opened the cooler. "Would you like a sample?"

When she placed a plastic cup in his hand, he yelped. "Tha' be co'd! Soups ain't s'posta be co'd! Nuh-uh."

"Taste it," she urged, smiling. "I think you'll like it."

For a guy who had so recently scoped out a garbage can, Eddie's shudder after a tiny sip from a pristine cup struck Zeke as amusing. But he modeled great restraint.

"*Ackk!* Ain't no chicky-noodle, tha' be a fo-sure fac'. Who tole ya it be soup?"

Zeke's restraint failed, but at least his erupting guffaw morphed to coughing, which was more than Haze managed. Laughter bubbling unrestrained, she evaded Eddie's question, "People *do* like chicken noodle soup."

"Then ya oughta jus' makes chicky-noodle."

"We could; but cold soup is good on hot days. Maybe you'll like this one better; it's made from fresh fruit."

Eddie sipped the new sample tentatively. "All-righ', uh-huh! It tas' *zac'ly* like jug wine." He smacked his lips and lurched into a dance.

Dipping and spinning, he sang loudly and off-key: "Yeah-yeah-*yeah*, it be a really fine wine!" His wild gestures sent a chilly red wave swooshing from the cup.

It crossed Zeke's mind that Eddie's last taste of jug wine may have been fairly recent.

Pausing only to lick his fingers (giving Haze her turn to shudder) Eddie resumed swirling and swooping. When the song playing only in his head ended, he skidded to a stop and ran his tongue along the cup's rim in search of stray drops. "It good, but ain't no soup. Nuh-uh."

Biting back a giggle, Haze watched him boogie. As he bebopped back with the empty cup, she resumed her mission: "Let's get acquainted. This is my son Zeke, and I'm Haze Eden."

Eddie stared at Zeke with intense focus; a tic twitched his cheek. Maybe from nervousness in the presence of Mister Clean? He shifted his gaze back to Haze. "Thanks for the co'd stuff, Hazeden. Tha' secon' one anyhows. Jus' dump tha' ucky one." He grimaced at the memory.

"What's your name?" Haze continued, back on-script, though Hélène's heads-up alert and Eddie's dangling ID with his name in plain view made the question pointless.

He clicked his fingers above his head, summoning the answer: Left-*snap*–right-*snap*–left-*snap*. "Eddie."

"That's a nice solid name. What's the rest of your name, Eddie?" Haze persisted.

"Jus' Eddie," he said firmly. His eyes dropped to the tabletop. "Whazzat book cos' anyhows?"

Zeke stepped in to rescue Haze. "Twenty dollars."

"Twen-y *dollah*?" Eddie whistled long-and-low, then threw back his head and howled, revealing a lifetime of poor dental care. "Peoples gets soupcan for twen-y cents! Migh' be squashed, but they still okay. Ya ain't gonna sell *nuttin* if'n it be twen-y dollah for a *book*. Nuh-uh."

As if felled by a blow, he sank to the ground. His legs formed a circle into which he swung his backpack. When he noticed Zeke peering down at him across the table, he ordered sternly, "Don' ya be lookin' at my private privacy."

Duly chastened, Zeke pulled back and cast a warning glance at Haze when she chirped again. She pressed fingertips against her lips. Even so, she sounded like a smoke alarm's low-battery alert.

Backpack zippers unzipped. Eddie resumed whistling *". . . all around the mulberry bush . . ."* Zippers rezipped. He rose and thrust a dented can bearing a 20¢ sticky label into Haze's hand. "Here. Gots can ope'ner, don'cha?"

Having spotted a rusty one hanging off Eddie's backpack, Haze nodded vigorously, hoping he didn't ask to see it. Possession didn't necessarily mean *right here*. She viewed the can with the same tortured look that would have surfaced if Eddie had handed her a snapping turtle.

"Maybe bean soup; paper wha' say gots wet 'nd fell off. If'n ya sells *hot* soup, tha' be good, but," he eyed the once-again zig-zaggy stack woefully, "peoples don' wanna pays no twen-y dollah for no book bout soup. Nuh-uh."

He leaned forward; Haze froze. "Yer nice, Hazeden; it jus' be tha' firs' co'd soups I dinn't like. Now I go see lotta action I dinn't know bout b'fore. See ya later, al-gater!"

As he ambled away, the view Eddie offered from behind was an unwelcome glimpse of pale skin where a left hip pocket used to be. If there was underwear anywhere, it wasn't under-*there*. He pulled a ball-cap from the remaining back pocket and planted it above his braid, turning the brim to the left. Glancing at the sky, he shifted it over his right ear.

Abruptly he halted, mid-street. A car with Canadian plates honked wildly. Waving cheerfully at the panic-faced driver who had so nearly hit him, Eddie took giant *"Simon-Says"* steps back to the curb.

Shifting the cap, he tapped the brim that now shaded his face. "My fren' Harv wha' live in Prairie Rose, he ga' me this hat cuz blue be my bes' thin'. Ya know Harv?"

Shaking their heads, neither Eden dared to look at each other, though looking at Eddie wasn't much better. His cap, with I'M FAR FROM NORMAL embroidered above the brim, pretty much guaranteed they would soon lose control of the volcanic laughter rumbling within their chests.

"Harv say'd, 'Need sumpthin' on yer head or ya gets head cancer.' Head cancer be bad stuff; hairs falls out." He stared at Zeke's bald pate, nodding slowly as if the answer to a stumper had finally been unveiled.

Zeke squirmed beneath such unwavering scrutiny.

"My fren' Harv gots more hats like this, Dude, if'n ya wan' one. Ever'-buddy like blue; ya likes blue, don'cha? Blue hats be like wearin' sky on yer head."

Zeke blended determined head shakes *(No! Don't ask Harv for anything, especially if it matches this!)* with uncertain nods *(Hats prevent cancer?)* which created the whirling sensation of a washer's spin-dry cycle.

All that motion left Zeke-Dude so woozy that fainting seemed inevitable. But he could be dizzy from the whole

Eddie encounter; it was hard to differentiate. He hadn't taken a decent breath since Eddie appeared, so he could very easily be diagnosed as oxygen-deprived.

Clicking his tongue in uneven cadence, Eddie spun off, his gait suggestive of walking on marbles. Zeke watched warily, expecting a tumble that didn't happen.

Eddie had accomplished the rare feat of rendering Haze speechless. Granted, it was a momentary condition, but noteworthy. Grimacing, she slid the *"maybe bean"* soup beneath the table and collapsed on her chair. "Well, *that* was interesting." She pumped a double dose of antiseptic cleanser onto one palm.

"Yooo-hooo!" They turned to see Bess Green coming from J Co Drug and carrying a cooler. "I told them inside that this old lady is taking a break! Do you need more ice yet? Mercy, I hope you aren't getting bored out here."

Zeke grinned; Haze chuckled; then both whooped, much to their friend's confusion. Zeke stood and pointed to his chair. "Sit here, Bess, and visit with Mom. I'm going to stretch my legs, but maybe she can dredge up something interesting enough to share!" He winked at Haze as he pulled out his pen to autograph the stack of books, as was their practice before either took a break.

With studied nonchalance, Haze gazed into space. "Interesting, huh? Hmm, that's a tough one. Let's see; we've sold cookbooks, given out samples; must be something—oh, we met Hélène and Eddie . . ."

Bess' lips gaped—*open-close-open-close*—like a baby bird eyeing a tantalizing worm in mama bird's mouth. Baby-Bird-Bess dragged Zeke's chair nearer Mama-Bird-Haze. Two feathery grey heads dipped close together. The worm wiggled, and then dropped.

Zeke reached under the table for his wide-brimmed straw hat. It wasn't blue and had no slogan, but it was perfect for bald guys who live under Utah's unrelenting high-mountain-desert sun. He'd get the Hélène-Eddie scoop later. Having Haze for a mother guaranteed that.

CHAPTER 6

Having long lacked mental stimulation, Zeke suddenly yearned for action, and that didn't mean merely tailing Eddie. He felt like a chick tapping a crack in its protective shell. The itch inside him matched the sensation that always struck when a new Raven-plot pecked at his brain. *Can it be I'm ready to write again?*

To hear Eddie toss off the phrase ". . . like wearin' sky on yer head . . ." gave Zeke a guilty twinge. He prided himself on thinking of apt comparisons to make his writing sizzle. But when had that last happened?

Walking along the blocks which signs indicated led to Pioneer Village, Zeke heard what sounded like live music coming from . . . *Where? Ah, over there . . .* He crossed a recently mowed lawn, remembering (but ignoring) Eddie's strict rebuke about encroaching on "private privacy."

Reaching a back yard, he took advantage of dense shrubbery's leafy shield. From his hiding place, he drew upon his writer's instincts for observation, mentally bulleting details of the scene playing out before him:

- *Live entertainment! "Camptown Races" played on harmonicas. Fingers tap or flutter. Amazing how breathing sets music free from tiny metal holes!*
- *Eight elderly men sit in lawn chairs on the open porch. They all wear striped brim-caps, bib overalls of the same denim, and faded blue shirts. Red bandanas around their necks match geraniums along the walkway going to the alley and garage.*
- *The slant-roofed porch stretches the width of this 1930s-era house. Painted pillars connect roof and railing. A well-tended flower bed outlines the porch.*
- *Overflowing pots of herbs hang off chains hooked to the porch ceiling. Someone here likes to cook!*

♦ *Lacy curtains—like a lady's hanky tucked into a breast pocket—ride a breeze from an unscreened upstairs window. There must be a fan on inside.*

But lyrics soon replaced bullets in Zeke's mind:

Camptown ladies sing this song: Doo-dah, doo-dah . . .

The song ended. Someone said, "Next, 'Saints Go Marching,' in C." Rapid hand motions switched harps. One instrument served as pitch-pipe, its note echoed seven times. It was a rousing tune; eight feet marked the beat on the porch's wooden floor:

. . . Oh, Lord, I wanna be in that numbah!

Zeke might have escaped unnoticed had not one musician sneezed. Time-out to blow his nose gave the others opportunity to look around, which led to Zeke's discovery. "Bless my soul, we have an audience! Come here, young fella!" *Busted.* At some point, the music had pulled Zeke from the bush's safety zone into plain view.

Young fella? Zeke glanced around, finding no one who qualified. He turned back to the porch and did a quick mental calculation. *A birthday cake to honor all these men would require close to 600 candles, so from their perspective I guess I'm young!*

Smiling, he approached the group. "Sorry to trespass, but your music made me forget my manners. Hi; I'm Zeke Eden." He gave an all-encompassing wave.

An onslaught of names followed: Jake, George, Jesse, Bud, Larry (or maybe Jerry?) plus several Zeke missed.

"You fellows are good; don't stop. I'll be on my way."

"Don't rush off, Zeke. We play better with an audience." Jesse, here," a nod to his left, "clowns around more but it don't affect his playing none. Or so he says!"

Jesse ignored the good-natured gibe. "We take requests. We'd appreciate ideas for new songs," he added hopefully. We're all weary of our repertoire, right, boys?"

"Rep-per-tware," scoffed the man who looked to be the oldest. "Fancy words don't change the fact we're old duffers with too much time and too little talent to do much but blow-and-draw tunes outta our sorry ol' harps."

Sorry old harps? They shine like Mom's kitchen! Zeke bit back a grin as the men released a barrage of details:

"We call ourselves The Harmonica Band. Gives us a little more class, don'cha think, to have a name?"

"Coming to the parade, Zeke? We ride a float."

"Decided we needed matching outfits. You like 'em?"

"Our wives boot us outta our houses and say, 'Go play with your friends.' All but Bud's wife, Retha." A wave toward the screened back door. "She's deaf enough we can use her porch and she never complains about noise!"

"What time is today's parade?" Zeke asked, joining the laughter over the obviously oft-repeated joke.

"None today; Friday's the Tractorcade. Parade's only Saturday and Sunday. We've played every Threshing Show parade for twenty years," Bud boasted.

"Twenty-four," Jake countered.

"Could be," Bud said amiably. "Long time, anyway."

"You ever hear a parade that needs a harmonica band, let us know. We got a van to haul us'n our float."

"Float!" someone snorted. "Two railroad baggage carts chained together ain't much of a float. We bump along like everything else those old carts hauled over the years."

"At least we don't fall off like luggage always did!"

Intrigued by the camaraderie evident in the group's easy give-and-take, Zeke settled on the top step and leaned against a post. "How'd you all get started playing?"

"Trains. Gets lonely on the tracks. Music helps."

"So, you all worked on the railroad?" Zeke managed a casual tone, though *trains-trains-trains* clanged in his head like a railroad signal halting traffic at crossings. Trains had been at the center of the Eden family's miseries ever since he wrote OFF TRACK.

The men's answers spilled out:

"Yup; engineer," at least two replied, one stating firmly: "Steam, not diesel. Hate diesel."

"Worked as a fireman. All of them forty-four long-and-dirty years," came another justifiably proud reply.

"Machinist," two responded, with one adding: ". . . my whole working life. The wife still fusses that my fingernails never look clean. That grease is a bugger."

The grating voice of a life-long smoker: "Brakeman, until my muscles gave out. Hard work, every bit of it."

Another drawled "Brakeman" rode an accent hinting its owner was raised beyond the state's northern border.

A terse "Conductor," echoed authoritatively over other voices and halted the recitation. The reason surfaced midst sputtered laughter:

"George, here, would rather wear his Conductor's hat, but we're all-for-one, one-for-all in this band; that goes for caps, too."

George grinned. "Yup; my days of telling people where to get off are over. We take our orders from Jerry."

Jerry protested, "Only orders I give are what key to play in. We're basically just a bunch of lazy guys; don't have much organization, truth be told."

"Yeah, we're lazy, but George's sister, Lilly, sure ain't! She plays electric piano for us. She's baking pies for her church's food-stand, or she'd be ridin' herd on us today. Lilly keeps us as organized as we get, which ain't much."

"Don't need much," a former machinist said. "We just wanna play harps, not sit around having meetings."

"Good thinking! Please play some more. I'd bet you know a railroad song or two," Zeke said with a grin.

"Do we? Nobody does 'em better," Jerry boasted. Okay, boys: Give Zeke a ride on 'Life's Railway,' key of G."

Work-hardened hands enveloped the eight gleaming instruments. The deluge of memories of his Grandpa Eden singing the song nearly overwhelmed Zeke:

> Life is like a mountain railroad,
> with an engineer that's brave . . .

Pure strains of music drifted over Bud's yard like a distant train whistle streaming across a lonesome prairie.

The two-part harmony filled Zeke's ears, flooded his mind and expanded in his chest until he thought he could hold no more. He closed his eyes to contain the tears that now suddenly clouded his vision. Memories of simpler times, reminders of that good man singing of things he believed, his feeble, yet still-true tenor voice ringing out . . .

> Watch the curves, the fills, the tunnels;
> never falter, never quail . . .

Long-forgotten words seemed interwoven in the music moving across Bud and Retha's back porch:

> Keep your hand upon the throttle,
> and your eye upon the rail . . .

Zeke swallowed hard, recalling the lyrics—wise words he had not heard in decades.

The melody trickled out between stubby, callused, scarred fingers that had kept trains running. Hearts that had known too many lonely nights, too many long trips away from hearth-and-home gave the song a depth and poignancy Zeke had not anticipated. He had expected a jivvy tune, perhaps "I've Been Working on the Railroad," and had primed himself to applaud.

Now, applause seemed sacrilegious.

At a signal Zeke missed—*Or does it always come next on their program?*—they played the hauntingly beautiful "His Eye Is on the Sparrow" all the way through to:

> . . . and I know He watches me.

The notes hung by silvery threads as these final words from his Grandma Eden's favorite song filled his mind. Zeke noted a string of nods moving man-to-man—nods communicating so well that words were unnecessary.

They're all friends with shared or at least similar memories. Maybe Mom's right; I need more friendships like what these men have. It was silly to list Pudge when I could have named Hank; he truly ranks among my friends.

But Hank Bedlow's unusual role in the Eden family made him an unsafe topic for ruminations while Zeke sat on a porch with eight strangers eyeing him, no matter how friendly their welcome was.

So Zeke dismissed thoughts of Hank. Instead he conjured images of the railroaders gathered on Bud's porch making countless long runs with harmonicas for companionship. Each man knew when he reached the end of the line, he'd find soul-mates who understood him and his unconventional life—others who appreciated music's role and ability to give solitary moments meaning, not more loneliness.

Zeke cleared his throat and rose from the step. "What time's the parade? And where is it?"

"Won't be today, remember. Today's the Tractorcade. Probably fifty or more machines will come rumbling into town. You won't have any trouble finding them, even if your ears don't work any better than mine! Parade's one o'clock the other days. Starts at Pioneer Village, goes along Main Street, then circles back to Pioneer Village."

"Not much in the way of parades as you likely think of them," George warned. "No marching bands; just us for music. It's so short a parade, they run it around twice."

"Okay, thanks; catch you later." An eight-part chorus offered varied farewells to their one-man audience.

As Zeke headed back to Haze and Bess, snatches of remembered words from "Life's Railway" interspersed his audible mutterings:

> You will roll up grades of trial;
> you will cross the bridge of strife . . .

"Ain't that the truth?"

> You will often find obstructions . . .
> On a fill, or curve, or trestle,
> they will almost ditch your train . . .

"Been there, done that, and got the scars to prove it." He increased his pace, as if to escape restless thoughts.

But the joys of discovering The Harmonica Band soon outweighed grim ruminations. Crosby was turning out to be more interesting than he had anticipated.

CHAPTER 7

Despite his detour to Bud's back yard, Zeke had not given up on tailing Eddie. He continued toward Pioneer Village, confident that was where he would find the "lotta action" which Eddie "dinn't know bout."

Flashing arrows wouldn't have done a better job than the sounds and smells that guided Zeke: exhaust fumes; horn honks and whistles; coal-smoke plumes; hissing, belching steam engines. Parallel to all this: enticing food aromas, and the undercurrent of human voices, clanging bells, and animals' snorts, stomps, and scents.

Zeke paused to read a sign at the gate:

ADMISSION:
Adults:
$5 per day or all 3 days for $12
(You'll need 3 days to see and do it all!)

High School Students:
$4 per day or all 3 days for $10

FREE Admission for Children
FREE PARKING ON THE GROUNDS

Without hesitation, he pulled out his wallet and exchanged a ten and two singles for a three-day pass. He received a surprisingly thick booklet in return.

"Map's on page three." Task accomplished, the gangly young gate attendant unwrapped a stick of gum and tucked it into his cheek to join the wad already in place, giving the distinct impression of a smokeless chew.

No farm machines were visible from where Zeke stood, but a steady din verified their presence. Thumbing the brochure, he commented, "Oh, good; I see the Threshing

Show has more to offer than machinery. The introductory pages' captions below the photos give historical details about the buildings on the grounds. That's great!"

The attendant jerked as if slapped. *Great? More to offer?* "Machinery's the whole point!" His voice shot to its upper register. "Nobody forks over twelve bucks just to see old buildings!" he squawked.

Okay, got the message! Apparently only odd ducks cared more about history than horsepower this weekend. Giving what he hoped was a manly machine-lovin' nod, he moved along before he uttered anything else dim-witted. As he turned by the Sateren Homestead (so the Page-3 map informed) a genial "Hall*oo*-there!" hailed him.

The greeter, coming at a sprightly pace, may have lost his grip on seventy, but he was fighting off eighty with grim determination. His disregard for the cane dangling off a sinewy forearm mirrored a disdainful hound-dog's demeanor: *"I don't need no stinkin' leash!"*

"Hello . . ." Zeke's curiosity equaled his amusement over such evident spunkiness.

"Looking for the guided tour?" Extending a hand, the man looked Zeke in the eye. "Sparky Johnson. Who are you?" The firm grip and constant motion numbed Zeke's hand while Sparky awaited a response.

It was slow in coming because Zeke was trying to figure out what prompted the tour-offer. *Do I look lost? Did the kid at the gate send out a silent alarm: "Old coot more interested in transoms than tractors is loose on the grounds!"?* Crushed fingers helped him resurface. "Hello; I'm Zeke Eden. What sort of tour would that be, Sparky?"

Sparky scrutinized Zeke like a rancher determining his livestock's state of health. Zeke reflexively clamped his jaw shut. *No way will I show my teeth!*

Shaking his head, Sparky said sadly, "Not really here for the Threshing Show, are ya, Zeke?"

"Not really," Zeke admitted, adding earnestly as he waved the brochure, "but it sure does look interesting!"

"What brings ya here?" He gave the cane a baton-twirl—a whimsical feat at odds with his stern query.

Keeping a wary eye lest Sparky attempt (and miss) a baton toss-and-catch, Zeke opted for honesty, fully aware it sounded wimpy. "My mom and I are on tour promoting our cookbook. We're set up outside J Co Drug."

"A cookbook?" Sparky reared back, frowned, and scratched his chin. "*Hmmph.* Well, come on." He strutted off: a drum major leading his parade of one straggler.

Having decided anything mechanical was surely wasted on a slick-headed city-boy in ironed khaki pants and snazzy golf shirt, Sparky's tour covered only the buildings. His voice rose above the impossible-to-ignore, yet unmentioned engines' drone.

Horses had left calling cards along the path. Sparky dodged them all; Zeke wasn't so lucky. His shoes grew heavier, his posture became more off-kilter with each addition. But he had no time to remedy the stinky problem. He was too busy matching the brochure's entries to Sparky's rapid-fire cane-punctuated recitation:

"Wildrose Mixer Office." *Tap, tap.* "Last totally hand-set newspaper in North Dakota."

"Barbershop's got four chairs." *Tap, tap.*

"Farmers State Bank. Only area bank to survive the Depression." *Tap, tap.*

"Bakery's only open during Threshing Show; good stuff." *Tap, tap.*

"Doc-and-dentist office." *Tap, tap.* "X-ray machine on display came from the old Ambrose hospital."

"Old-man Points' office; self-taught lawyer; colorful fellow." *Tap, tap.*

"Here we go." *Tap, tap.* "Big Ole's Cook Car." Sparky halted by a weathered building with freshly painted railings around a stubby porch. Wide and sturdy steps led to the front door. "Typical cook house for old-time threshing crews." Shoulder-to-shoulder, they silently faced the simple structure. "Whadda ya think, Zeke?"

"Part of history" was Zeke's best offer. Crime, he understood. Cook-cars were black holes in his universe.

"Don't bother the cooks. They've got *no need* for cookbooks. What's the whatchamacallit? The title?"

Miffed that Sparky had already pegged him as a fast-talking door-to-door nuisance, Zeke said stiffly, "SOUP'S ON IN RAVEN CROWLEY'S KITCHEN."

Sparky's wordless grunt showed equal parts of pity and perplexity. *Tap, tap.* Zeke considered explaining Raven, but decided it would only make things worse.

Sparky pointed his cane at the cook house. "Menu never changes year-to-year. It's 'Eat What's Served' at Big Ole's. Fridays, it's meatballs, gravy, boiled 'taters, salad, bread, water, coffee, cookies, ice cream." *Tap, tap.*

"Who eats here? May I?"

"Nope. Only tractor- and threshing-crews. If ya show machines, ya eat free. Every year, around seventy do.

"Really? Seventy. Oh, it's take-out food, right?"

"What? No! They don't all eat at once! Seats ten. Sign in, eat, leave, next group comes in. No loitering, no hats. That's the rules." *Tap, tap.* "Take-out!" he scoffed.

Zeke deftly switched topics. "You say, 'no hats'? Big Ole's doesn't look fussy enough for that restriction!"

"No hats," *tap, tap,* "and no arguing. Workers who don't like the menu or rules can get lunch elsewhere."

"May I look inside?" Zeke didn't want to leave without a visual memory to accompany Sparky's brusque facts.

"I don't know . . . Well, ya did write a cookbook . . ." *Tap, tap.* "But ya can only look through the window 'round back. *No* bothering the cooks," he repeated firmly.

A fiercely rattling air-conditioner (vented through a hole sawn in the door) filled most of what Sparky called a "window." Peering through the narrow strip of glass to one side of the hard-working machine, Zeke spotted a plaque on the opposite wall: CAN'T LIVE WITHOUT COOKS.

A wall-clock showed the time: eleven-ten. *That's why these apron-clad, hair-netted women are hustling.* One set places—*Four to a side, one on each end; yup, that equals ten*—at the oilcloth-covered table. One stirred a steaming roaster; the third stacked plump, obviously homemade cookies on a tray.

Zeke salivated. *Unusual menu, but I'd eat it in a heartbeat!* "Meatballs today; what served the other days?"

Sparky halted pacing to recite: "Saturday's ham stew, glorified rice, bread, coffee, water, cookies, ice cream. Closed Sundays." *Tap, tap.* "Okay; tour's over; duty calls."

"Thanks. You in the parade?" Despite his liveliness, the only duty Zeke could imagine anyone would expect of a fellow Sparky's age was waving from a VFW float.

"Of course! It's the Threshing Show!" he said as if that explained everything.

"When you pass by J Co Drug, look for our canopy."

"That like a tent?"

"Roof; no sides." At the rate Sparky's sparse speech pattern was infecting him, Zeke figured he could bypass the hassle of churning out full-length books and just write READER'S DIGEST condensed versions from now on.

Pondering roof-only tents, Sparky waved his cane, and punctuated his wordless farewell with final *tap, tap.*

Humbled by his failure to impress Sparky in any way, Zeke felt he needed to investigate more of what the Threshing Show offered. *After all, it is why Mom and I are in Crosby this particular weekend.* He patted his pocket. *And I have a three-day pass, so why waste good money?*

He followed steady rumbles and intermittent rattles to the far edge of the grounds. There he found men perched on vibrating machines, while seeds and chaff (or *whatever*—he could only guess) danced on sunbeams.

Frequent rowdy cheers interrupted the demonstration that held the crowd's attention. Zeke was clueless as to what spawned such delight, but he clapped whenever others did. Normally he wasn't the clapping type, but at this point he would try anything if it helped him blend in.

His encounter with Sparky shamed him over how little he knew about planting and harvesting crops, farming, raising livestock. *What a hard way to make a living!*

For all practical purposes (his Utah garden's haphazard productivity hardly qualified as *practical*) he was ignorant about the gamble against soil-sun-wind-moisture-frost-and-critters that transformed seeds into a life-sustaining harvest. Of course, he read about humans' attempts to alter the course of nature-gone-awry, but his smaller scale fight against Mother Nature was not much different than battling Haze. *Guess who usually wins?*

He inhaled air that was ripe with horse-odors, grease, straw (*Or is it hay?*) and dust. Squeaking belts, clanging chains, and protesting ropes echoed above multiple engines' clatters and clacks. Golden streams poured from chutes on shaking contraptions, adding the clean smell of various grains and a smoky pungency to the morning air.

It all spoke of a way of life and forgotten time that had left no footprints in Zeke's history. He was sobered by skills he had never mastered—knowledge that put food on his table and gave SOUP'S ON IN RAVEN CROWLEY'S KITCHEN the right to exist. Farmers could do just fine without him and his books, but without them, he was nothing. *"CAN'T LIVE WITHOUT COOKS"? They should add "OR FARMERS" to the end of that truism!*

Leaving Pioneer Village, Zeke's pondering featured hard-working folks whose workday was not governed by a clock, but rather by daylight or weather. *Make hay while the sun shines, and worry all night about that hay and a host of other things when it doesn't.*

What with his ruminating about *tap-tapping* Sparky, and digesting all the cook-car details, and wondering about Eddie's whereabouts, Zeke had much to contemplate on his way back to Haze and their canopy. But he did take time to find a sturdy stick with which he scraped those ranch-country horses' all-too-generous gifts off his no-longer spit-shined shoes.

CHAPTER 8

When Zeke had moved from Bud's backyard back to
the sidewalk, The Harmonica Band's sprightly version of
"Be Kind to Your Web-Footed Friends" had set a steady
tempo for his stride. No one was aware another listener
lurked on the opposite side of the house from where Zeke
had hidden.

If the second gatecrasher to the Band's rehearsal had
stopped whistling at song's end, he might have escaped
detection. That not being the case, eight heads mimed
puppets swiveling toward belated strains that matched:

. . . you may think that this is the end—well, it is.

"Who's there?" Bud called out.

No response.

George may have retired, but his Conductor's *Do-
what-I-say-or-else* tone still worked: "Show yourself."

A gangly figure appeared. "Hey!"

Recovering from the shock that accompanies most
first encounters with this stranger, Larry grumbled, "Has
the parade been routed past your house this year, Bud?"

"Shuddup, Larry," Jesse said mildly, pointing the
newest interloper to Zeke's vacated spot. "Have a seat."

The men watched a human beanpole reel across the
lawn—dipping, spinning, clattering, clanging. Reaching
the steps, he shrugged off his backpack and unwittingly
mimicked Zeke's posture and position against the post.
Despite being quick and sparse, these actions sent
pungent odors wafting toward eight twitchy noses.

Restraining comment (though arched eyebrows along
the row communicated plenty) Jerry kicked things back
in gear with: "Okay! Next, it's 'Polly-Wolly-Doodle,' in C."

Music faltered when their visitor pulled out a mouth
harp of questionable age and condition and joined in. He

missed some notes, came in late on others, added a few that came nowhere close, and frequently erupted with hoots and knee-slaps. His interpretation was something the band had not yet tried: *Do your own thing!*

Then the stranger audibly gulped; grabbing his pack, he leaped up. Arms waving wildly, he fled with the speed of a pollen-dusted man chased by swarming bees.

Each musician ceased playing as he realized the latest addition to their band had dropped out as abruptly as he had joined. George fell out at:

> . . . Fare thee well, fare thee well, my fairy fay . . .

Jerry exited at:

> . . . I'm going to Lou'siana for to see my Susyanna . . .

Two more slacked off somewhere around:

> . . . Oh, my Sal, she's a maiden fair, sing Polly Wolly Doodle all the day . . .

Only Jesse remained to play the accompaniment to:

> . . . with curly eyes and laughing hair . . .

Stillness descended, broken only by the chairs' creaks.

George spoke first. "What got stuck in his craw?"

"Guess 'Polly-Wolly Doodle' offended him, somehow."

"He played it from the start, so he knows the song."

"He was on-again, off-again, but not a bad player."

"Think we oughta drop 'Polly-Wolly' from our rep-per-tware?"

"I ain't married to it . . . It sure sent him flying off."

"Do we skip it until we figure out what's up?"

Foreheads furrowed as minds reviewed the unsung lyrics, searching each phrase for possible problems:

> . . . Oh my Sal, she's a spunky gal . . .

Seemed innocent enough, right?

> . . . I jumped on a gator, thought he was a hoss . . .

Nothing wrong there; nothing at all. Or was there?

Finally Bud stomped his foot on the porch floor and said with heightened emotion and stout resolve: "It's a silly song. Nothing bad about it; we're gonna play it."

"Now *that's* talking sense!"

"Just cuz someone runs off doesn't mean it was the song that got him riled up."

"Coulda been he needed to pass gas and didn't want to offend us!"

"Might have helped; whoo*ee*, he was odoriferous!"

"Big word, but he did set off a powerful stink!"

Bud ended the guffaws when he blew as loud a sound across blow- and draw-reeds as human breath achieves. It had the impact of the noon whistle to cease both the contemplating and the joshing.

But, like water still sputters from a hose after a faucet is turned off, a few thoughts required airing at the song's end: "Anybody ever seen that guy before?"

"Nope. Not him, not Zeke, either."

A snort. "No comparing the two of them! Zeke's normal; this other guy . . . well, don't mean to judge, but does he strike anyone as, to put it bluntly, a character?"

Nods all around, with one fervent: "That's for sure."

"He'd make a good scarecrow. Say now, Bud: Stand him out in your garden and Retha won't have to flap her apron to chase birds away from the tomatoes!"

"He reminds me of the silly bobble-dog on Doreen's dashboard when she's doing sixty on a gravel road! *Boing-boing-boing*! Looks like he got springs put inside him where he oughta have muscles!"

"Yeah, touch him on the head and he'd bounce forever!" An octet of laughter erupted.

"Could be he's here for the Threshing Show."

"Doubt it. Didn't look like he'd know machines. But I have seen him before, just don't recall when or where."

"Maybe on 'America's Most Wanted'?"

"Nah; he ain't dangerous; I 'spect he's just peculiar."

"Whatever, Crosby isn't the town it used to be," Orville said ruefully. He thumped his harp against his thigh, dislodging spit that had sneaked past his lips; he frowned at the resulting dampness. *He surprised me so much that I forgot to swallow!* "It's a changing world we live in."

Jerry straightened his shoulders. "Old guys like us can't do much about that, but we can work on 'In the Good Old Summertime' harmony. Whadda say?"

Just like that, The Harmonica Band was in business again, their repertoire unchanged. In the northern-most corner of western North Dakota, eight bewildered-but-resilient retired railroaders positioned their prized harmonicas once again. At the signal, they began to play a pleasant tune with skill gained and polished while passing many lonely hours over many long years.

The music rising from their harps resonated in their minds as clearly as if each heard it being sung:

> . . . Strolling through the shady lanes
> with your baby mine.
> You hold her hand, and she holds yours,
> and that's a very good sign
> that she's your tootsie-wootsie
> in the good old summertime . . .

A nice song, the musicians thought as each closed his eyes and reminisced about girls he had known in bygone days—but mostly about the woman he loved who shared his name and life. Each man let his part in the music drift like a daydream.

Yes, indeed: a fine song that shouldn't offend anyone . . . unless some gal got her nose out of joint over being called some fellow's tootsie-wootsie.

CHAPTER 9

Zeke's return to Main Street found Haze in a rare (for her) *"Move along; you annoy me!"* mood. The culprits were a family of five: haggard mom, vacant-eyed dad, hot-wired twins, and a toddler desperate to escape her stroller. One boy tormented his sister with a feather of suspect cleanliness while the other jerked the stroller back-and-forth along an invisible track.

Dad stared into space as if the disaster unraveling at his feet played on The Big Screen, thus completely beyond his control. Mom, obviously long immune to bedlam, just raised her voice above her offspring's swelling chaos.

Each forward thrust of the stroller bumped one sand-filled bucket, making the canopy lunge. Precious shade shifted with each hit. Backward jolts made the girl's pigtails whips against her face, producing more squalls.

Haze shot Zeke a pleading *Do something!* glance while educating the mother, "Buy the best quality good-sized stock pot you can afford . . ." Or did Haze glare at him? Glance or glare, her look was desperate.

Zeke recoiled. *Me? How would I know what to do?*

Neither parent intervened; the rocking-and-rolling, tickling-and-tormenting continued. Then a blood-curdling shriek from the stroller kicked Zeke into action faster than his worries over the canopy's impending collapse. Bravely he planted himself between bucket and stroller.

Warrior-like, he awaited the four-wheeled Weapon of Destruction's inevitable assault on his real and prosthetic ankles. Suddenly rescue arrived from . . . *Hollywood? Hawaii? Heaven?* Forgetting potential injury and his unfulfilled goal of saving the canopy, Zeke ogled a lei-draped, leggy, lusty Vision. The Essence of Dreams. He fought against blinking, afraid of missing even a second's glimpse of undeniable, unutterable . . . *health.*

"Aren't *you* a treasure!" the exceptionally healthy Vision cooed. One might assume she spoke to the agitated toddler. But *noooo*, she had eyes only for Zeke: blushing, dizzy, gulping, dazed, nervous Zeke.

"Hello," Haze said icily from somewhere in the firmament. The voice Zeke had known from birth barely registered. His brain (despite all it acknowledged to be prudent) busily categorized the amazing combination of The Vision's considerable feminine attributes:

- Bottle-green eyes like twin crystal pools, skillfully outlined and shaded in luminous hues borrowed from nature's palate
- Petal-soft lips form an heart-shaped pout that frames pearly teeth
- Shapely legs emerge from a wispy skirt and end in kiss-of-death high-heeled sandals
- An angelic voice with sensuous undertones: a veritable lexicon of sultry sounds
- And, peeking at him each time the lei shifted, an amazing pair of . . .

At this point of his assessment, Zeke—the author with millions of words in print in dozens of languages—could not adequately describe The Vision's . . . uh, *endowment.*

Mammary glands? Too clinical.

Breasts? So mundane!

Orbs of Wonder covered the topic well, though the concept of covering-well didn't extend to the translucent fabric straining against those orbs' considerable thrust. Zeke's blush blazed like his worst sunburn and, living on a high mountain desert, he knew sunburn.

He heard Haze talking, but her voice barely penetrated his cloud of wonderment—though it did register in his foggy brain that Haze had switched gears entirely with her advice to the mother: "Have you tried adding sage? Zeke and I think sage is wonderful . . ."

Sage? There's no sage in today's samples . . .

Fate intervened when one twin urgently needed a bathroom. The frantic child hopped, clutching his crotch. Like a sailor sighting harbor after a rough voyage, Haze jabbed her index finger toward the park.

With the family gone, The Vision (according to Zeke; The Vixen, according to Haze) stepped up to the table. She paged through the browsing copy with slender fingertips painted a delicious color: *juicy peach.* A peachy fingertip tapped lush peachy lips. Zeke barely breathed.

"I own a bookstore in Prairie Rose." The silken voice trapped Zeke like spider webs waylay unwary flies. "I sell gently used books and reasonably priced new titles."

Bookstore owner! Zeke's heart leaped. *Kindred spirits!*

"This is a lovely cookbook. Do you happen to have any damaged copies? Ones with bent corners, ripped pages, broken spines? I'd love to make a deal with you."

Zeke instantly wondered how much damage he could do if he kicked a box under the table. *Whadda know? Damaged books! Let's make a deal!*

"If we do, we return them to the publisher," Haze said quickly and adjusted the perfectly fine stack of books.

Haze: 1.

Brazen Hussy: 0.

Zeke? Not even on the playing field.

Pulling a trick from her sleeve (had the gossamer blouse with its plunging neckline and strategically placed darts boasted more than flimsy straps) the Brazen Hussy stole Haze's best line: "I'm Blyss Hathaway. Are you," she glanced at the cookbook's cover, ". . . Haze Eden?"

Haze's jaw tightened; she nodded curtly, showing none of her usual eagerness to make new friends.

Zeke thrust out his hand. "Hello, Blyss! I'm Zeke."

"Oh," Blyss exclaimed, "the other author! And a chef— I *adore* a man who cooks. I'm *thrilled* to meet you!" She held his hand as one would a precious jewel. He swayed as a current short-circuited his nerves when her other hand rose to tuck ginger-hued curls behind a delicate ear.

Beneath the table, Haze gave Zeke one hard kick on his flesh-and-bones shin. It hurt worse than what he had feared from the stroller. He flinched.

"A special feature of our cookbook is that you can check the Index for specific herbs—like sage—and select a recipe accordingly," Haze said, pushing the cookbook toward Blyss. "Try sage, under S. S-as-in-spouse." The Vixen slowly released Zeke's hand. *Was that a squeeze?*

Sage? Spouse? Sage! Yes, sage-the-herb was indexed under S, but Sage-the-Wife was in far-off Utah . . . and Zeke-the-Mesmerized-Moron was in paradise . . . *No! Not paradise; I'm in skunk-on-the-road trouble.*

Blyss flipped pages to reach the Index; Haze tapped her foot. *Tap-tap.* Just like Sparky's cane. If Haze held the cane, she wouldn't merely *tap-tap*. She'd aim right for Zeke's fickle heart and *poke-poke.* He flinched again.

Muttering "Excuse me . . ." he fled, leaving Haze with The Vision of Loveliness . . . *No! Temptress! Trollop! Okay, that's a bit dramatic, but she is assuredly not someone I, a happily married man, should be drooling over.*

He stumbled toward a shady spot at the end of the block and blindly punched "1" on speed dial. *That's right, you numbskull; Sage is your Number-One Everything.*

Sage answered on the first ring and listened—which was really her only option since Zeke's talking speed soon hit-and-held at a breathtaking ninety miles an hour:

"Ho-boy, Sage, this Threshing Show is some big-*big* doings! Big-big-big! Why, the only 1911 Quincy Tractor still known to exist is *right here* in little Crosby, North Dakota? Yes, it is! Right here."

"You don't say?" Sage drawled, and leaned back in her office chair, grinning. "Only one? And right there. Wow."

Zeke frantically paged through the Threshing Show brochure. "Yeah; it's really something! The Tractorcade arrives pretty soon; it starts at Noonan; that's a town nearby. Gotta see that—the tractors, not Noonan. Pretty impressive, huh? Imagine witnessing something like fifty tractors *putt-putt-putting* at a snail's pace to beat the band. Oh! Speaking of bands, wowza! There's a *very* cool Harmonica Band. Sure do wish you could hear 'em—"

"Since I'm such a fan of harmonica music, right?"

Missing obvious irony by a country mile, Zeke gushed on: "It's eight amazing fellows, but they're only part of all that's going on. I tell you, this is one happening place!"

"Sounds like it would have to be 'tractors, and thrashers, and bands—oh my!' for little Dorothy. Not 'lions, and tigers, and bears.' Or are there wild-and-wooly she-bears in Crosby for Dorothy to marvel over?"

A pause. "Dorothy?"

"You know: Wizard-of-Oz Dorothy."

"Huh? Why are you talking about The Wizard of Oz?"

"Sorry; never mind. You were saying . . .?"

"It's . . . doggone it, Sage! You made me forget what else I was going to say. Anyway, it's appalling how little most people know about threshing. Not that long ago, even kids knew how a thresher works. I don't; do you?"

"I'm on that sorry ship of the uninformed right with you, Zeke. 'Appalling' doesn't begin to describe us," Sage agreed heartily. "It's abysmal. Inexcusable." She loved it when Zeke squirmed. After similar calls from other book-signings, she knew precisely what triggered The Squirms.

"The Little Devil Hart Parr's really impressive! It's one of only three such threshers known to exist. Amazing, huh?" Zeke paused, squinting at the brochure's tiny picture, trying to verify that it actually was a thresher, not something entirely different, but equally unknown to him. *Why didn't Sparky give me the run-down on machines, not his "Here's-this, here's-that" tour? I can figure out the buildings from the brochure!*

Sweetly from Utah: "What color is it?"

Snippily from North Dakota: "What color is *what*?"

"That Little-Devil gizmo-thingy."

Zeke frowned at the brochure—every column inch in black-and-white. "Uh, it was built in 1916 so the color's pretty faded. And it's very dusty here, you know."

"Must be a clue. Look for green, red, blue, or orange paint chips. Under a fender?" Sage suggested helpfully.

Being nowhere near the actual machine, Zeke could only fudge. "Well, it all blurs after a while, to be honest. It's just one of many impressive things here, I tell you!"

"Hey, I'm impressed with how much you've learned. She must be quite something."

"She?" Zeke trembled; his fist crumpled the brochure. *Ho-boy. Deep trouble. What gave me away?*

Sage piled innocence high and spread it thick as axle grease. "Aren't machines usually referred to with feminine pronouns? Don't guys say *'She* runs fine,' or *'She's* a real honey'? Wow, Zeke, this She-Devil, I mean Little Devil, must be something special if you noticed her."

"*Oh!* The Little Devil Hart Parr!" His palpable relief planted an acre-wide smile in Milford. "Yeah, I guess."

He wisely switched from machinery to music. Sage caught a break in his rapid monologue about velvet-lined harmonic cases and perky tunes to ask in a voice rich with wifely concern, "Is everything okay, Zeke? You sound harried, or winded. Are you feeling all right?"

"I'm more than okay, better than all right. I'm super! Everything's fine. No: better than fine. Dandy-swell-fine!"

"Let me talk to Haze; I want her to check your forehead for fever." *That's a good one, Sage!*

Silence from North Dakota.

Sage smothered her phone to enjoy a hearty chuckle while Zeke worked himself into a full-body sweat.

"Sorry; no-can-do. Mom's busy with a customer, and I'm, uh, away from the canopy. I wanted to be alone to talk to you." *Like anything I've said couldn't be broadcast over Pioneer Village loudspeakers.* He felt about two feet tall: yes, twenty-four inches of wretchedness for being so reckless, so foolhardy as to think Blyss offered anything better than the true ecstasy he shared with Sage.

His beloved's voice interrupted his self-censure with unnerving calm: "Tell Haze I'll call her later."

Uh-oh. "I'll, uh, do that. Yeah; okay, sure thing . . . Remember: I sure do love you, only you, Sage; only-and-always you." He was sadder than sad, madder than mad over slip-sliding into stupidity and flip-flopping over folly.

"You betcha."

It revealed the depth of Zeke's woes when he didn't retort, *"Did you just say 'You betcha'? That's not how the Milford Valley Community Hospital's CEO talks! 'You betcha'? Does Pudge need to come across the street from the gas station to feel* your *forehead?"*

Sage's well-tuned marital sensor had no reason now (nor had it ever in thirty-plus years) to *twing* like a Geiger Counter. Thus, after Zeke's call she didn't fuss, didn't fume, didn't fret. But she did laugh so hard her sides ached and her mascara ran in muddy rivulets that left spots on her blouse. Good thing it was an office day.

After she'd recovered and changed into a blouse she kept in her office closet for just such emergencies, she told Zeke's framed photograph on her desk, "She must be a knockout. Poor Zeke! Missing your flat-chested wife, while trying to ignore a bold flirt's astounding *ba-zooms!*"

Haze was alone when Zeke returned to the canopy. "Did Blyss buy a cookbook?" he asked casually.

Haze scowled.

Too late, Zeke realized the mere utterance of that name had him skating on thin ice in the frosty lake of his mother's disgust.

"Yes," was her crisp reply. Without another word, she signed a dozen books and stomped off toward J Co Drug.

She was gone a long, long time. He had sold nearly all the pre-signed cookbooks before she sauntered back, still grim-faced and stiff-lipped. She—who glowed over each sale—merely shrugged at this news.

"Are you upset about something?" Zeke asked as calmly as his pounding heart allowed.

"Should I be?" came the sharp retort.

"No! I had a nice talk with Sage," he said, desperately trying to remember any news from home, if asked. *Nada.*

"You'd better hold precious memories of Sage more tightly than blame-fool illusions of Blyss." *"Blame-fool"* was shocking language coming from Haze—the wash-your-mouth-out-with-soap kind of shocking. Her chilly tone reminded Zeke of rebukes for his adolescent mischief and youthful indiscretions. He knew she wasn't talking about sage-the-herb or bliss-the-state-of-harmony.

Haze fussed with books; Zeke tightened canopy ropes.

It was awkwardly quiet for two people who loved each other deeply, even after multiple weekends of constant togetherness that would have sent many mother-son combinations into either catatonic comas or all-out war.

"Sage wants you to call her," he finally said meekly.

"Already did." Sage may have laughed from start-to-finish of the call, but Haze wasn't done being irked.

She drained coolers; he emptied trash into a curbside barrel. Books sold. Bess replenished ice and samples.

Finally Zeke broke down. "Mom, I was a fool, but it's not permanent. Sage and I talked, and I'm sane again."

Haze knew life would be pretty miserable unless they put this behind them. If Sage wasn't upset with Zeke, she shouldn't be . . . *But he can stew a while longer.*

Three frail nuns (two leaned on canes, one pushed a walker) appeared wearing habits—something Zeke hadn't seen in years. "We're sisters by birth *and* profession!"

Mother and son were pressed to guess which tottery sibling was oldest. Samples, sales, questions, answers. Zeke wore a fake smile, wishing he were home with Sage.

Why did I decide Raven cooked to relax? Any other hobby would mean no cookbook, no dangerous Blyss encounters. Raven could have been a whittler, making toy soldiers or little birds . . . that'd be much safer than soup!

CHAPTER 10

Maggie would be thrilled to hear that the black-garbed sister-sister trio shuffled from the canopy to J Co Drug to purchase their first Kiel Nede mystery-thriller. Zeke hoped the nuns had either good hearts or good insurance. Raven (outside his kitchen) and the feeble elderly could be a bad combination. Zeke had enough on his conscience without Death by Fright for three Women-of-the-Cloth.

He opened a bottle of water from a cooler beneath the table and handed it to Haze. When she accepted it—and her nod indicated she knew it was not merely a beverage, but a peace offering—only then did he open another for himself. "No one's here now but Henny Penny and her foolish son Chicken Little. Let's sit and have a chat."

Smiling tremulously, she sat. "Well, Chicken Little, Henny Penny has Eddie-and-Hélène tales to tell."

"Figured so. Begin with Hélène; that saves the best for last, like dessert."

Haze cocked her head. *He knows chasing a two-bite candy bar in her see-through wrapper is madness. Especially when a lifetime supply of the world's best chocolate wrapped in pure gold waits for him in Utah.* Even so, she chided, "Hélène's story is not boring."

"Didn't mean to belittle her. But what I really want to hear about is Eddie, so start clucking, Henny Penny."

"Well, Hélène drove into town one day and stopped at the quilt shop." Haze waved down and across the street to where colorful children's blocks painted on a wide front window spelled out the store's name: Quilt Blocks. "She asked the owner if she was hiring."

"I thought you said her story wasn't boring? Woman comes to town, needs job, asks around. Please excuse my yawns! Let's talk about Eddie."

"No, this is all important background."

"Ah, *background*. Could you pick up the pace? You know: get to the good stuff before I doze off."

"Hush! Turns out, she wanted to work for cash." Haze's eyes widened over tight-O lips. "Suspicious, hmm?"

A shrug. "So? Many people work for cash."

"She also needed a place to live, and told the quilt-shop owner—I forget what Bess said her name is: Jenny, Ginny, something like that. I'll call her Jenny. Anyway, she—Hélène, not Jenny. Or is it Ginny?—Hélène couldn't afford much rent. Long-story-short . . ."

Zeke exploded with: "Thank goodness!"

A glare. "Long-story-short . . ."

"You already said that."

"You interrupted."

"*Long-story-short*, Jenny—yes, that's it! See, I used a memory device I saw in a magazine . . . or was it on TV?"

Zeke glared.

"I visualized her as a little bird, like the Swedish Nightingale Jenny Lind—I know *she's* not a *bird* but . . ."

Zeke growled.

"*Okay!* Jenny hired Hélène and let her move into a tiny upstairs apartment in exchange for lower wages."

"The drama, the tension! I see now where my story-telling DNA comes from. I'm practically sitting on the edge of my chair. Do go on!" He batted his eyelashes.

"I'll never finish this story if you don't quit interrupting. A customer could show up any minute and then you wouldn't know the most suspicious part."

"Listening . . . baited breath . . . eager ears . . . blaa-blaa-blaa, et cetera, et cetera, et cetera."

"You are *not* a good listener! In fact, you're rude."

"My list of offenses grows longer: recluse, rude," he stopped short of adding *roaming-eyes Romeo,* "and now a non-listener. Yet you associate with such a reprobate!"

"Are you done with all this smart-aleck sass and the annoying alliteration you tend to toss around?"

"You're pretty good at '*annoying alliteration*', yourself!"

"Just listen; don't talk! Hélène goes nowhere that anyone can get to know her—not to church, clubs, or people's homes; she's a loner. She even races through the grocery store!" This obviously ranked highest on Haze's *Go-Figure* list about Hélène. To Haze, grocery shopping offered better entertainment than an ocean cruise.

"So the woman doesn't live to squeeze the Charmin or shoot the breeze. Not everyone wants to chat with every Tom-Dick-or-Harriet like you do. Didn't you notice her panic when you asked about her name?"

Huffily: "I was being friendly."

"What if *friendly* scares her? I suspect most people invite Hélène various places only to fuel gossip. Can't say I blame her for turning them down. Remember how people we hardly knew suddenly wanted to be our best friends during our crisis? If Hélène experienced anything similar, I'm not surprised she avoids them."

A frown. "I suppose it's possible, even in a nice place like Crosby. But she could be hiding something."

"Everyone is. Including us, if not airing our family's dirty laundry counts as 'hiding something.' And I don't run around saying, *'I'm the real Kiel Nede!'* so that's hiding something, too. Even Eddie does it. Remember how he wouldn't tell you his last name?"

"Oh! Eddie! Now he's an entirely different mystery. Hélène appeared and stayed, but Bess says Eddie has come-and-gone without warning for years. Rumor is, he rides the rails to get here. Just like a hobo in the Great Depression! It's a wonder he's still in one piece."

"I doubt he hops trains when they're moving, though that could explain the sorry state of his clothing and possessions, and his jitters! But he seems content with his life. Any idea why he *does* come here?"

A smug smile. "He's looking for rides to Prairie Rose."

"Really? What's with this Prairie Rose? First we hear it's where Blyss owns a store, and now you say Eddie—"

Haze's wagging finger cut him off. "*That woman* is off-limits in this discussion."

"Merely commenting, not discussing. What's up with Prairie Rose? That's all I'm asking."

A scowl underscored her words: "It better be. Back to Eddie: He stands by the road with his thumb out until someone takes pity on him. Even so, he only accepts rides if he can ride in back, which means pickups and such."

Zeke chortled, propping his feet on a box beneath the table. "Wise decision! A driver could faint from the smell if Eddie sat inside! But why Prairie Rose?"

Eyebrows arched high, she said, "Because," adding a long pause for maximum effect, ". . . *his son* lives there!"

Zeke's jaw dropped. "Eddie's a dad? Whoa. Didn't see that one coming. Does the kid's mother live there, too?"

"Nobody has ever seen her; apparently she rejected the baby at birth. How Eddie managed to bring an infant from Chicago to Prairie Rose is unknown, but he did—*and* he'd already picked out who he wanted to raise him! So, what do you say about *that*?"

"Gaping holes suggest less mystery with Hélène than everyone thinks, and more with Eddie. Hélène seems new to truth-hiding, so her secrets will eventually surface. But Eddie's an old hand at maintaining his aura of mystique. Plus he has street-smarts that Hélène lacks."

Haze turned somber. "They need help finding normal lives, Zeke. I suspect it's *find*—as in first time around—for Eddie. But for Hélène, it's more *regain* normal. She doesn't seem to have lived a solitary life as long as Eddie has, and certainly not as rough-and-tumble a life as his."

"They may like their lives the way they are. People do define 'normal' or 'ordinary' based on experience."

"No one could prefer living like either of them does, at least not if they've ever had a glimpse of a better life," Haze said sadly. "I'm sure Hélène has, and I could help her get back to it. But you'll have to be the one to reach out to Eddie. He needs you, Zeke."

Zeke's feet hit the ground with a thud. "No way, José!
We are not getting involved with strangers who give no
indication they want help.   We haven't exchanged
addresses, or shared holiday dinners, or shown family
photos—we've met them: period. We're strangers. Got it?"

"But I felt a connection with Hélène," Haze protested.

"You feel connections to utility poles, and teenaged
boys with acne!   Remember how you called the utility
company to report a sagging pole on a country road? And
how you suggested to that zit-plagued grocery bagger that
if he decreased fats and sweets, it could help his
complexion?   You're a kindhearted person, Mom; you
could win the Mother Teresa Award for compassion!"

"I didn't connect with the family that was just here,"
Haze said morosely. "I was so upset about *Ms Hussy* that
I didn't reach out to that young mother who is obviously
in over her head with those little terrors."

"Nothing could help them, unless a more alert family
adopted the wildcat twins and their howling sister! Those
parents gave up on discipline long ago, and now they're
saddled with the consequences."

"They're just normally active boys. I know; I raised
two. Oh! Why did I call them 'terrors'? That was unkind."

"Little boys equal terrors. I was one, so I know."

A sigh. "I really want to help Hélène."

"We're leaving Crosby soon. Any help she needs is far
beyond what you could provide in such a short time."

"If only she could connect with people who are willing
to be her friend, no strings attached. People like Bess."

"Bess is a lovely person, and Hélène enjoys talking to
her.   But if there were any connecting points between
them, don't you think they would already be friends?"

Silence.   "Maybe Hélène needs a go-between to get
things moving in the right direction." A slow nod. "Yes! I
could be the needed link between her and Bess."

Zeke groaned. "It's like watching an accident about to
happen and knowing nothing I can do will prevent it.

You're not going to give up, are you, Mom? You have every intention of intruding on Hélène's—what did Eddie call it? Her 'private privacy.' I'm right, aren't I?"

"I'll take my clues from Hélène when I see her again," Haze said primly. "You give some serious thought to how you can help Eddie."

"Have you heard a word I've said? I don't want to help Eddie! There's enough going on in my head without letting him and his vast and varied plights move in. This is our final book-signing weekend. Soon I'll be home in Utah, hundreds of miles from Eddie. I am not going to tell him 'Pack up your troubles in your old kit-bag and life will be dandy' because I don't believe it myself."

"Ah-*ha*! You admit he has troubles."

"I was quoting song lyrics, not assessing Eddie! Name someone who doesn't have trials and tribulations galore. That's life! I have troubles enough without taking on a homeless guy's accumulated miseries."

Haze's eyes narrowed to slits—never a good sign. "I don't know how you expect to sleep at night, Zeke, if you won't at least try to help a man less fortunate than you find a better life."

Zeke limited his response to a growl, which made no promises but did slam the door on his verbal protests. He knew from a lifetime of being Haze Eden's son that he had neither heard nor seen the end of her CRUSADE TO HELP EDDIE AND HÉLÈNE LIVE BETTER LIVES.

Two hapless individuals on the brink of becoming unwitting victims of a full-fledged Haze campaign:

Poor Eddie.

Poor Hélène.

Zeke knew he might as well add *Poor Zeke* to that list. If Haze was thinking such thoughts about two strangers, her son would not fall far down a list best captioned: "FOLKS ABOUT TO FALL PREY TO HAZE EDEN'S DEVICES."

CHAPTER 11

Zeke needed to put some distance between himself and all discussion-debate-disagreement with Haze about helping Eddie. He also needed to talk—really converse, this time—with Sage. *Listening would be good, too,* he humbly admitted. He returned to the shady corner of the block and speed-dialed "1" for the second time that day.

"Hello, Love. How are you?"

"Blissful."

Silence from North Dakota.

Soft burbling laughter from Utah.

"Mom blabbed, huh?"

"Yup. How are you?"

"Happy that you're still talking to this doofus husband of yours."

"There you have it: We're one happy couple. Life's good."

Fervently: "I can hardly wait to see you."

"Seeing you is *soooo* not all that I'm eager to do . . ."

A cleared throat in Crosby. "Mmm-*hmmm.* Will you meet my plane? Actually, it's such a late flight I'll just rent a car and drive home from the airport."

A breathy pause in Milford. "Say when, and I'm there."

A grin in North Dakota. "How will I recognize you?"

A purr from Utah: "Look for a human of the female persuasion wearing a skin-tight blue dress. Your careful, intimate investigation will reveal a motel room key tucked into her *not-considerable-at-all* cleavage."

The particularly astute author standing on a street corner knew the utterly sensuous hospital CEO sitting in her office didn't own a skin-tight blue dress . . . And that's not all this author-also-husband knew. He was one-hundred-percent certain his unchanging definition of true love said nothing about cleavage.

The cleavage-challenged wife in Utah knew that's what her husband believed from the tips of his toes (five real, five prosthetic) to his heart (fully human) and head (bald or wig-wearing) which made up stories but never, *ever* wavered from truth in matters of heart and soul.

And he knew whatever transpired after he and his savvy-CEO–sexy-wife crossed the threshold to whatever motel room that tucked-away key opened, it would make any delay in getting home well worth the wait.

After all, home really is where the heart is.

"Ask for late check-out," he said hoarsely. "And we'd better hang up now."

Coyly: "Oh? Why?"

"Anyone who listened to national news not so many years ago knows that pretty gals who own skin-tight blue dresses can get in one big mess-o'-trouble just talking on the phone. Even if they're only talking to a guy like me who doesn't lead a major nation and whose face isn't on TV every night. It's Trouble, I tell you. Trouble with a capital T that rhymes with B for blue *and* D for dress."

She laughed: a low, husky sound which got his blood pumping so hard that he felt like a woodpecker was doing full-bore drilling inside his chest.

"Trouble?" she teased.

"Yeah; trouble."

"Sounds blissful."

A groan. "You're not going to let me live down my momentary lapse of sanity, are you?"

"Not when it gives me a chance to wear my favorite blue dress."

Moments later, he leaned against a light pole, counting his blessings. Was it only his imagination, or did the breeze carry a tune?

When a man loves a woman . . .

CHAPTER 12

A piercing blast erupted; Haze jumped as high as if she'd landed on a whoopee-cushion. "Noon whistle," a local resident standing in line explained with a shrug. "Live here long enough and you don't even think about it."

Their ears still ringing, Zeke and Haze resumed business. Curiosity and free samples kept people interested long enough for Haze to begin her patter, and they stuck around because she was Ms Congeniality.

Zeke heard enough conversations to realize people regularly scheduled club outings, family get-togethers, or class reunions to coincide with the annual Threshing Show. One customer wearing a CROSBY CLASS OF '66 T-shirt exclaimed, "Oh, here's The Goose!" as she exchanged a credit card receipt for a bagged book and sped off.

The Goose? No need to wonder for long. Looking up, Zeke saw a string of open-sided yellow, blue, orange, and green wooden cars that, according to a sign on the red caboose, ferried people at no charge between Pioneer Village and Main Street. An appropriately attired jovial engineer yanked a bell's rope above the miniature train's white-painted engine. Braking in front of J Co Drug, he called out, "Watch your step, folks!"

Good deal for all, Zeke mused. *We should give that fellow a complimentary cookbook for helping our business!*

Midst the hubbub, Haze trilled, "Hello, Hélène!"

Zeke felt a swell of empathy for the woman standing outside Quilt Blocks. Offering only a weak smile and limp wave, she dashed back inside. For anyone else, her hasty exit would have been a solid hint it was foolhardy to believe a couple conversations could turn a scared hare into a bold lioness. For Haze, it only heightened the challenge.

Then Zeke noticed Eddie had backed a man wearing greasy overalls up against a pickup and was gesticulating wildly. *If Mom's right, he's trying to negotiate a ride!* The captive shook his head resolutely, fumbling for the door handle in an obvious *Gotta go* signal. But not to worry; for all his eccentricity, Eddie wasn't confrontational. With an *Everything's cool, man!* wave he stepped back.

Zeke watched the pickup owner sag with relief as Eddie moved along. He could imagine the conversation at the man's supper table: *"Today that Eddie fella stops me outside Hardware Hank and asks if I'll drive him to Prairie Rose! Like I'm gonna forget all about the hose clamp I went to town to buy. Whadda I look like, a taxi driver?"*

While he understood the man's relief, such thoughts didn't rest easily in Zeke's mind. Haze had shaved them to a prickly point.

He counted change into a customer's palm, realizing too late he'd returned an extra dollar. This would never happen at regular book-signings in stores. There, all he did was sign *Kiel Nede*; clerks handled the finances.

It didn't fix things, but even so Zeke pushed the blame off on Haze. *It wasn't enough to insist on this goofy book-signing tour. Oh no—you had to suggest we add helping Eddie and Hélène to our madcap duties! We are neither psychologists nor social workers, you know, Mom.*

Even as he greeted their next customer, the gentle answer he knew Haze would give thrummed in his head like a wire brush on cymbals: *No, Zeke, but we* are *fellow travelers, two people trying to survive a sometimes painful, always haunting journey. Just like Hélène, just like Eddie.*

It wasn't Haze's fault that when Zeke looked at Eddie and Hélène he saw only complications.

It was Gull's fault.

Gull. Gulliver Swift Eden: the son Haze wished she could redeem.

Gull. Gulliver Swift Eden: the brother Zeke wished he could reject.

CHAPTER 13

Bess finished her half-day shift at J Co Drug after the noon-rush and came out to the canopy where Haze and Zeke were reorganizing after their own hectic hour. "We sure are selling Kiel Nede books in there!" she said.

"Glad to hear it. You ladies have earned a reward." Zeke pulled bills from his wallet. "Here; hop on The Goose when it rolls around again and go tour Pioneer Village. I can handle things here for the afternoon."

Haze started signing books even as she protested feebly, "Oh Zeke, are you sure? What if it gets busy?"

He winked at Bess. "I think I can manage. Sign faster, Mom; pretty sure I hear The Goose coming."

Zeke did just fine. After all, he did have more than a lick of experience with this book-signing business. At least his counterpart, the hairy one-footed Kiel Nede, did.

He was enjoying a momentary lull when he noticed Hélène exiting Quilt Blocks. *Oh my, and crossing the street . . . making a direct approach to the canopy. Lucky for her, Mom's gone.* "Hello, Hélène," he called out.

She stepped up on the curb. "Hello. No one's in the shop now and I can see the door from here, so I came over to ask if you have time to talk about the mysteries."

"If this is your break, Hélène, then you should sit down." Zeke waved at the empty chair. "Mom and Bess are out at Pioneer Village, so rest a bit. I'm holding down the fort and, as you can see, our fort's pretty quiet now. It's a very good time to talk about Kiel Nede."

"I'm here to buy a cookbook, too."

"Happy to oblige, but don't let Haze's high-octane sales pitch push you into anything you don't want or need. When she's revved, it can be a little overpowering."

A quick smile. "I won't. I really want one."

"Okay then. Now: a word of warning about Mister Nede. He's a pretty intense writer and his hero, Raven Crowley, isn't someone to mess with. In fact, soup is the only relaxing thing about Raven. I'm not sure how much nail-biting action you want from your leisure reading."

"There's nothing nail-biting in my life. Maybe if a book revved *me* I'd have the gumption to do something, not just . . . Sorry; didn't mean to digress. Which title is first in the series? I prefer to start at the beginning."

They talked books for a while; then Hélène glanced at the bank's clock. "Before someone needs me back at the store, I'd better buy the cookbook. What does it cost?"

Zeke grinned. "Since you're the person who alerted us to Eddie, you'll have to promise you won't give the same response he did to the same question!"

"Which was?" Hélène asked with the first laugh Zeke remembered hearing from her. "I can only imagine!"

"At the risk of sounding like either a gossip or a snob, I'll tell you." By the time he'd described the encounter, Zeke had heard several more laughs from Hélène. *Maybe this is what Mom hopes to do for Hélène: dig deep enough to help her find joy in little things.*

"I find it amazing that Eddie was just one of two interesting people we met today who mentioned Prairie Rose. It must be quite the town. The other person was Blyss Somebody-or-Other."

Joy-in-Little-Things died a sudden death.

"Blyss Hathaway." While the bank-sign's temperature reading remained steady, beneath the canopy it grew instantly chillier with Hélène's question: "What was your impression of her?"

"Enticing . . . if you like her type," Zeke hedged.

"Most men do." Carrying her copy of SOUP'S ON IN RAVEN CROWLEY'S KITCHEN, Hélène left a garment of happiness behind as if she'd never donned it for one brief encounter with joy.

And Zeke felt like a jerk.

CHAPTER 14

"What did you say to her?" Haze demanded, hands on her hips in classic Upset-Mother style. "You must've said something offensive to make Hélène race away."

Why'd I tell Mom anything? Raising his hands as if in self-defense against verbal attack, Zeke protested, "I merely asked about Prairie Rose in connection with Eddie. Since Hélène had warned us about him, I figured he was a logical topic. It's not like we had a lot to work with, conversation-wise, you know!"

"It can't be Eddie. What else . . . Oh!" Her eyes narrowed. "You mentioned Blyss, didn't you?"

A nervous tic flicked his cheek. "Only said her name, hoping Hélène would talk about Prairie Rose. You know: a neutral subject to pass time. But something set her off."

Tight lips; a nod, then: "Talking about Blyss did it."

"How can that be? I can't see the two of them having anything in common. Ever."

"Bess and I had a good talk out at the Threshing Show. She says anytime Blyss is anywhere in sight, Hélène splits: *Poof!* She sees Blyss, and she's gone. Prairie Rose is close enough that it happens regularly— Blyss showing up in Crosby, I mean."

"Did you two even look at anything in Pioneer Village? If I'd known all you were going to do was gossip, I'd have sent you to the park where you could tittle-tattle for free!"

"We saw plenty. Big noisy machines, lots of people— some who've come by our table here. Interesting historic buildings. And horses. So many horses." She frowned, examining the soles of her shoes. "A person can look and talk, you know." She opened a tube of lipstick, applying it flawlessly without a mirror—a feat Zeke had always admired even when, as now, it was clearly a delay tactic.

She pressed a tissue against her lips. "Now, where was I? Oh right: Blyss and Hélène. Hélène either hates or fears Blyss. Bess says neither response makes sense to most people, but she knows differently. Blyss is a chameleon."

"Chameleon? Hardly the word I'd pick."

"How we saw her today?" Haze leveled a pointed stare at Zeke. "She won't look like that if we see her again. Bess says she could be anything. Like a chameleon. She constantly changes. Hair styles, clothes, how she acts. That shows an unbalanced mind, I think."

"Isn't 'unbalanced' a bit harsh? Maybe she has a natural bent for the theatrical, or has a big wardrobe."

"No, she's wicked."

"Come on! Wicked? *Too forward*, I'd agree with, but—"

A cautionary finger-shake: "Bess calls her a 'man-eater.' Blyss showed up, all the way from California! And she ruined a twenty-five-year marriage in Prairie Rose."

"Idle talk. Maybe not the California bit, but 'ruined a marriage'? That's hearsay: gossip's sneaky cousin."

"Listen to this: the man met Blyss on the Internet and took off for California. Later, he left there and *then* Blyss showed up in Prairie Rose looking for him, but he was in coma after a horrible car accident! He'd lost his ID so one at the hospital knew who to notify." Her eyes grew so large that Zeke figured if eyes could pop out of a head, Haze was on the brink of making medical history.

"So he married Blyss and they live in Prairie Rose?"

"No! His wife divorced him, *and* Blyss dumped him!"

"Too many big gaps in this soap opera, but the guy's not blameless, even if Blyss *is* a shameless flirt. The guy ditched his marriage vows the first time he logged on looking for love in all the wrong places, as the song goes. She owns a store so, to be fair, there's likely more substance to her than our first impressions."

"Well, I heard enough to know that Blyss is dangerous from the get-go. But there's even more to this story, better than what I've begun to—" She sighed. "Oh, bother! Here comes someone who probably wants to buy a book."

Zeke grinned. "How nervy to assume that just because we have samples galore and cookbooks on display means we actually would like them to buy something!"

It was fifteen minutes before Haze resumed her story: a quarter-hour of twitching, fast-talking, samples, and selling three books. The second customer's shadow had barely shifted when she said, "Okay; ready for the best part? I told you Hélène is hiding something and she is!"

He clapped. "A victory for our silver-haired sleuth."

"Scoff if you want, but hear this: Bess said Hélène is that man's wife. Yes! The man Blyss followed back to Prairie Rose is Hélène's two-timing ex-husband! What do you think about *them* apples?"

"Too much coincidence; no 'them apples' about it. It's either gossip or speculation."

"Nope; it's facts. The man's name is Frank Wilson and he's divorced from a woman named Helen who skipped town without leaving a trail." She gave a *See?* type of nod. "Leap ahead a few years: a stranger comes to Crosby, calls herself Hélène Wils, with 'one L' she says. Wils is only two letters shy of Wilson. Now, isn't *that* suspicious?"

"Maybe a woman really named Hélène-with-a-final-E, last name Wils-with-one-L, decided to live in Crosby. But I'll play along. Wouldn't you think she'd pick something completely different than her real name? Or at least use *Wills*—with two L's—for a new surname instead of always having to tell people 'It's Wils—spelled with one L'?"

"Too many quirks of fate. Guess I'll have to ask her."

"Ask Hélène? You've got to be joking! Promise me you'll leave well-enough alone and mind your own business. We'll sell cookbooks for a couple more days, and leave town without causing a ruckus, okay?"

"Maybe she really *wants* to talk about things. I'm the perfect person for her to confide in for the precise reason that we *do* leave Crosby very soon. She'd be happier if she had something like a short-time friend—someone she won't face again. I qualify—I'd listen, and then vamoose."

Zeke buried his face in his hands and groaned.

Haze breezed along, ignoring his distress. "I won't force it but, given the chance, I *will* talk to her."

He looked up.   "Whew! There's hope, then. That chance is unlikely because she already bought the cookbook, and we talked about Kiel Nede books." He raised clasped hands skyward. "Thank you, God!"

"Don't be sacrilegious, Zeke."

"I mean it sincerely. I'm eternally grateful Hélène has likely made her last trip to our little canopy where Someone Who Shall Remain Nameless—though we *both* know who she is, hmm?—seems determined to hand out psychology along with samples."

Haze hummed tunelessly behind pursed lips as she smoothed invisible wrinkles from the tablecloth.

Zeke persisted: "We're qualified to do soup samples, Mom; we wrote the cookbook. But psychology? Not competent at all. No training, no diplomas, no licenses. That's how people get sued. We stick to soups and books, we're okay; otherwise we're swimming with the sharks."

Haze paused, looked at the stack of books, grabbed her "happy-pink-ink" pen and started signing as if it were a race she was determined to win.

Watching this inexplicable flurry of activity, Zeke shook his head ruefully. "You know, we could both catch pneumonia from the breeze you're creating."

Haze said nothing, just kept on signing.

Zeke sighed and silently addressed the woman just doing her job across the street: *If you know what's good for you, Hélène-Whoever-You-Are, stick to Quilt Blocks' side of the street until you see our tail-lights heading out of town. If you venture over here, you're on your own. I've done all I can to prevent the inevitable.*

CHAPTER 15

Zeke had just opened the weekly issue of THE JOURNAL when Haze clicked her tongue. "Why, this pocket could rip right off!" She loosened her apron, thrusting it at Zeke.

The stitching looked fine to him.

"I'll be back," she trilled.

By the time Zeke had absorbed and analyzed the situation—*Rips need mending; mending requires thread; a quilt shop sells thread*—Haze was already opening Quilt Blocks' door. Nothing he could do at that point would rescue Hélène or stifle Haze.

It was tough to focus on local news while he awaited calamity's first wallop. Would ensnared Hélène's wails against bold Haze bring police running to her aid? Would an enraged Hélène send a defeated Haze hurtling out the doorway like ammo fired from a cannon? *Will I need to fork over big-bucks to pay my brash mother's bail?*

Zeke had written many complex plots, but this one stymied him. He rarely knew what to expect from Haze, and (unless one believed Haze's sensational biography) Hélène was a flat character. Whatever was unraveling in Quilt Blocks had one instigator and one innocent victim. Being Haze's target was always fraught with risks.

Eons passed before Haze returned.

Zeke had no fingernails left. Between customers, he clipped-clipped-clipped until he was down to nubbins. He even eyed the shoe hiding his nail-producing foot. *No.* He was certain Emily Post wouldn't approve. His mother might be breaking rules willy-nilly, but—*Oh-oh; here she comes, and strutting like a conquering hero.*

"So, did you get your pocket sewn back on?" Sarcasm dripped from each word. He set aside the newspaper; he would flunk if ever quizzed on its contents.

"Oh Zeke," she giggled, "even you aren't so naïve as to think that's why I went over there!"

He watched her put change from her pocket into the money box. "Well, duh." *Even me? Sticks and stones . . .*

"We had a nice little chat," she volunteered.

"I don't want to hear about it."

"Of course you do!"

"No, I don't. Not one word. I feel sorry for Hélène."

"You don't need to. She thanked me. And hugged me."

"Thanked *and* hugged you? My-my-my; you must feel like a million bucks."

"No, Mister Cynical. She didn't *specifically* thank me, and I hugged her first, but she didn't *not* hug me back."

Mister Cynical snorted.

A pause, then: "I told her what my name really is."

Miming the Hear-No-Evil monkey, Zeke pressed his hands over his ears. "Don't want to hear about it."

She grabbed his hands and slapped them together in emphasis: "You will listen"—*clap!*—"and admit"—*clap!*—"that sometimes what I do works out fine." *Clap!* "Okay, so first I bought thread, and then I borrowed a needle."

He pulled away. "Needle and thread you didn't need," he said, adding peevishly, "and dangled a lie which led her down a path she'd never have chosen on her own."

"Necessary evil," she quipped. "and I *did* stitch around my pocket, even though it wasn't loose. A white lie, yes, but it got me in, right? And it gave her a sale. While I sewed, I casually asked to see the copy of SOUP'S ON IN RAVEN CROWLEY'S KITCHEN that you sold her."

"For what possible reason did you need to see that?"

Haze smirked. "Sometimes I sign books too quickly, which I did before I went with Bess to the Threshing Show. I always wonder if, in my haste, I sign *Haze Eden* or *Hazel Eden.* That's the truth, and that's what I said."

Zeke grunted his grudging admiration. It was a clever way to introduce a tricky subject that had no way under God's blue sky to come up naturally.

"I explained how your dad shortened Hazel to Haze, though I skipped the part about Rudy telling me 'Haze fits you since you can be so *hazy* sometimes.' Then I told her that since my middle name is Louise, when I combine my nickname and my middle initial, *'Haze L'* still spells my given name. All this led right into asking what her middle name is." A dramatic pause; a smug smile. "Oops, I forgot: you don't want to hear any of this."

"For crying out loud!" Zeke slapped the table; a pen leaped and rolled. "What's her middle name?"

Wiggling eyebrows. "Guess."

Jutting jaw. "I won't play your games."

"Guess," Haze insisted.

He stared at nothing in particular, thinking.

She fidgeted like a kid at a circus: Will the aerial artist fall? Will the tiger lunge? *Will Zeke take the bait?*

He bit: "Edith. Esther. Eleanor. Any name that lets her add an 'E' to Helen and presto! She becomes Hélène."

"Elizabeth! Helen *Elizabeth* Wilson was married to Frank for twenty-five years. After he deserted her—that Blyss mess—she didn't want anything to do with him, certainly not share his name anymore. But she didn't know how to change her name without a lot of expense and fuss. That's when she got the idea to do what she did." She took a prolonged swallow from her water bottle.

"Go on." His tone bordered on *crabby*.

Recapping the bottle, she crowed, "You're hooked! She figured out *Hélène* when she signed her middle initial too close to her first name. Just like what works for me! After she figured out which direction those funny little marks go over two of the E's, it was a done deal."

"How did the 'Wils-with-one-L' part happen?"

"She was paying for groceries and stopped to talk to the clerk right when she about to write 'O-N' after W-I-L-S. I love this part! She said she was feeling pretty *off* about Frank, so she left the *'on'* off of Wilson and bingo! She had her new name: Hélène Wils."

A clever way to "off" Frank without committing a crime! Zeke thought. "There remains one sticky issue. For many years Helen Wilson lived thirty miles away and likely shopped or visited friends in Crosby, right? Doesn't it seem unbelievable that *only Bess* suspects Crosby's elusive Hélène Wils is one-and-the-same as Prairie Rose's jilted Helen Wilson?"

"No; Hélène looks completely different than Helen. She's twenty pounds lighter; wears contacts, not glasses. Different hair style and color; that part was easy. Helen was a hairdresser; she and Frank owned a barber-beauty shop. Quilting was Helen's hobby, which qualifies Hélène to work at Quilt Blocks. Oh, she drives a nondescript car and tries to be invisible if she sees people from her past."

"Like Eddie? She sure raced off when she saw him."

"Yes; he makes her nervous when he stares at her."

"Eddie aside—and Hélène may be overly sensitive—it's well known that most people aren't very observant. I'd recognize a thinner or fatter, tanned, black-haired *you*."

"Sure; we're related; no one here's related to her. She usually leaves during the Threshing Show to avoid people who knew her before. But the store owner is in charge of her church's food-stand this year so Hélène has to work."

"Guess you're right; quite the drama going on here." Watching Haze chew her lip, he asked, "Is there more?"

A jerky nod. "Hélène said when her life fell apart, she hated Frank. That's when I told her about Gull."

Zeke's breath caught in his throat like sandpaper on lace. "You did *what*?"

A gulp. "I told her about Gull. Not how you fit into the story, that's your business, but—"

"Why? *Why* tell her anything?" he interrupted harshly.

Gone was triumphant-in-success Haze. The woman avoiding Zeke's eyes folded her apron into tight accordion pleats. "Because," she whispered, "just like I am for her, Hélène is someone I won't see again. I need to talk about Gull, Zeke . . . but you won't, so I picked a stranger."

CHAPTER 16

Thanks to his Grandma Eden's oft-told Bible stories, Zeke knew about Joshua's battle. Seven trips around the city of Jericho, and the walls tumbled. Seven words— *'You won't, so I picked a stranger'*—cracked the fortress guarding Zeke's heart. It crumbled, just like Jericho.

"I need to take a walk, Mom," he said hoarsely.

A jerky nod. "Go ahead. Bess will be back soon after delivering her pies to the church's food-stand."

Zeke signed a dozen books and gave Haze only a thin smile in wordless farewell. He waved off The Goose engineer's invitation to jump on board. Reaching the Threshing Show grounds, he showed his pass, bought lemonade, and commandeered an empty picnic table.

All around, people laughed. The Threshing Show was a joyful place for everyone but Zeke. Old men joked and chewed tobacco, spitting putrid streams on the ground.

Zeke sipped lemonade and wished he could stop the constant internal replay of Haze's words: *"I need to talk about Gull, Zeke . . . but you won't, so I picked a stranger."*

"Hey, Dude! Where Hazeden be?"

Zeke made no effort to disguise his groan. *Everybody sing: "If it weren't for bad luck, I'd have no luck at all . . ."* He watched Eddie leap the fence. *What? No authorities to arrest gate-crashers? They're probably off laughing with all the rest of the hyenas wandering the grounds.*

"Haze Eden," Zeke said sharply. "Two words. Haze is her first name; Eden is her last name. Got it?"

Eddie swung a leg over the table's opposite bench and landed with a thud. His backpack gave him a distinct Hunchback-of-Notre-Dame look. "Uh-huh; tha' be wha' I say'd." He nodded, repeating: "Where Hazeden be?"

Resignedly: "Working at our book table."

Staring into Eddie's eyes, Zeke experienced an unnerving sense of seeing intelligence where he least expected it. *More than street-smarts.* He looked away.

Children played tag; teenagers seemed determined to defy the law of nature that decrees two objects cannot occupy the same space, no matter how pressed together they might be. Laughter formed a soundtrack for it all.

"Why she there 'nd ya be here?" Eddie persisted.

"I wanted to be alone for a while," he said pointedly. *Pointed* was wasted on Eddie.

A stub-tailed dog roamed; the rope his owner likely assumed still secured him to a car bumper or post, instead dragged behind him, leaving a trail in the dirt.

Eddie watched the dog's meanderings and laughed. "Tha' dog in big trouble, huh?"

Zeke shrugged. "I guess. How about a lemonade? My treat." *Throw money at a problem and make it go away.*

"Nuh-uh; lemonade make my mouth itch-like."

"Get what you'd like, then." Zeke tossed two bucks on the table. Anything to get back to Table-for-One status. *Spending time with Eddie is the last thing I want.* Haze's voice bugled: *". . . reach out to Eddie; he needs you, Zeke."*

Guilt robbed Zeke's lemonade of all pleasure, leaving only the sourness of *itch-like* in his mouth.

"I likes 7-Up," Eddie said hopefully, eyeing the money.

Zeke nodded. *Goodbye, two bucks; hello, solitude.*

"Thanks! Be righ' back, Dude. Uh-huh."

Goodbye solitude, goodbye two bucks.

Eddie returned and dropped the change—a nicked quarter, and one shiny dime—by Zeke's drink. "Ya gots a truck?" he asked, plopping down again across from Zeke.

Zeke stared at coins he hadn't expected to see returned. *Amazing.* "Yeah, at home. Why?"

A burp and a grin. "Tha' don' zac'ly help, Dude! Gotta gets ride to Prairie Rose to see my kid."

"Tell me about your son." Too late Zeke realized that for someone supposedly just hearing about Eddie's dad-status, knowing that *kid* meant *son* represented too much pre-knowledge. But he needn't have worried; Eddie didn't.

"He be Justin Edward Larson. *Justin* for Mister Justin wha' live in New York. *Edward* be sumpthin' like *Eddie*." He tapped his chest proudly. "*Larson* for Cate 'nd Luke wha' be his mama 'nd daddy nows. I calls him Lil' Eddie."

Zeke zeroed in on one piece of solid information in the mish-mash: "And your son lives in Prairie Rose?"

"Uh-huh. With Cate 'nd Luke."

"How old is he?"

A squint. "Old-like; but he not be old-like—" Eddie ceased slurping to point the straw's dripping end at Zeke.

Old Zeke grimaced. "I meant *your son,* not Luke."

"Oh." A sly grin. "Lil' Eddie be eight. Tha' not zac'ly *lil',* but he short-like. His firs' mama dinn't eats good, 'nd she done drugs. Cate cook good. *Her* soup be *hot.* Luke gots groc-y store so it be plen'y food alla times. Uh-huh. Lil' Eddie be real happy 'nd smart 'nd polite-like."

"When's the last time you saw him?"

"B'fore Hal-aween." Momentary sadness quickly gave way to sheer elation. "Hey, maybe he not short no-mores! It be bad winter 'nd I dinn't see him at Cris-a-mus, or his birt'day cuz they go'd see some big ocean."

"So you're pretty eager to see him again, hmm?"

"Tha' be whys I as't bout truck. Ain't foun' no-buddy wha' live there 'nd gots truck wha' be goin' home t'day. They workin' alla days 'nd sleepin' in tent ever'-night."

Or so they say. Zeke watched Eddie flick the bottom of the cup; when crushed ice hit his tongue, he laughed.

An idea crossed Zeke's mind, which he instantly discarded. But some ideas don't take rejection without a tussle. This one reared up and jabbed holes in Zeke's conscience. *Tap-tap. Poke-poke.*

Zeke wiped suddenly sweaty palms on his pants. The words he knew he should say stuck in his throat. Instead, he opted to divert the conversation: "What's a typical day like for you, Eddie? Tell me about your life."

The door slammed shut on Eddie's gusto; his eyes narrowed. "Why ya wanna know tha'? I don' run from no trouble. Nuh-uh. I jus' wanna see Lil' Eddie."

"No reason, except I'm always interested in people I meet. That's how I am: a curious guy."

Eddie tilted his head and stared mutely at Zeke for a nerve-wracking moment. Zeke shifted under the scrutiny. *No wonder Hélène's nervous around Eddie. It's like he sees right through me.* Then Eddie yanked the lanyard over his head and flung it across the table. "Read this."

Zeke complied calmly: "The bearer is a licensed homeless person given privileges by the city of Chicago to work in Union Station within restrictions stated in . . ." He sped-read the rest of the proclamation's legalese. Now equally interested and confused, he returned the laminated ID. "What sort of work do you do there?"

"Helps peoples."

"You help people. Do, uh . . . what?"

"Stuff. If'n peoples fraid-a stairs wha' moves—them ex-ca-laters—I takes 'em wheres alla elevators be."

"That's helpful," Zeke said encouragingly.

"If'n I hears peoples talkin' bout eatin', I says, 'Wha' food ya likes?' If'n they say'd 'Mex-can' or 'Chinese' or go'd like this," (he raised both palms) "I says, 'Hotdog? Ham'bugger? Pizza?' or 'Didja eats bref-fas' yet?' if'n they lookin' sleepy-like."

"Then you show them to where they can buy food?"

"Uh-huh. Mos' peoples wha' drags big suitcase be from far-aways; they don' knows bout alla diff'rent foods. I helps carry stuff if'n they breathe *'huhuhuhuh'*-like."

"That's good." Zeke wondered if he would ever entrust his luggage to someone like Eddie, but instantly chastised himself for such prejudiced thoughts. *If the Chicago Port Authorities sanction the homeless to do a job, who am I to judge?* "People must appreciate your help, Eddie."

A shrug. "I gets tips, 'nd sells maps wha' shows alla street. But I don' sells no-buddy *no junk*. Nuh-uh."

Zeke aimed for a neutral tone. "Do you earn enough doing all those helpful things to pay for a place to sleep?"

"There be lotta way to gets money, Dude! I al-'ays picks up ever' loom-num cans I sees. Tha' be good money. But in Union Station, don' never gets in *no fights* bout cans. Sum-buddies do; not me. Nuh-uh."

Zeke processed this deluge of details; questions galore remained unvoiced as Eddie continued, "No-buddy 'lowed to panhandle or sleeps in Union Station. Tha' be a law."

"I see. So, is there a shelter close by the station where you can sleep and keep your stuff?"

Eddie stiffened. "I keeps my stuff righ' bys me alla-times." Absentmindedly he pulled his backpack closer.

Zeke had almost tacked on *". . . or a mission?"* to his query, but suspected it might insult a working homeless person. But now, Eddie's response raised an incredulous question: "Everything you own is in your backpack?"

Eddie ignored him, concentrating on rapidly melting ice chips. Evidently he was done explaining his life, though one head-jerk may have been a nod, not jitters.

Zeke thought about the closets and dresser drawers in his restful Utah home—all crammed with clothing suitable for varied weather and diverse activities. And the well-equipped laundry to keep those clothes presentable.

He remembered—longingly—quietness surrounding that home, and the peaceful view of mountains, not bustling crowds or noisy city streets. Yes, like Eddie, he heard trains—but they belched and rumbled several miles away, not disturbing the tranquility one iota.

He saw his inviting kitchen full of food that not only sustained but enhanced life to the point of "I can't eat another bite." When had Eddie last felt full? Had he ever enjoyed a nutritiously balanced, flavorsome diet with choices—and tasty leftovers for late-night snacks?

He thought about shelves of books, two televisions, recorded music, the workshop: all for his and Sage's personal pleasure. And ample leisure time to enjoy it all.

He saw the office where everything he needed to earn a very good living was at his disposal. And nothing was held together with duct tape.

He thought about beautiful, loving, attentive, wise Sage. Unlike Eddie's unnamed messed-up *girl-fren'*—his son's mother—Sage took good care of herself.

He looked at the ragged pack: heavy, stuffed, bulky. *How long could I survive on what fits in a backpack? How long would I remain sane without Sage to love and nurture me, to laugh at my jokes, to understand my silences, to give my life purpose? Would I be as content with my life as Eddie is with his if government decrees, spelled out on an ID hanging off a lanyard, defined my identity?*

Zeke saw a dented can of "maybe bean soup" as clearly as if it sat between a famous, wealthy author and a self-reliant homeless man. *I gave Eddie two dollars and thought that was generous. He not only gave Mom and me a can of soup representing a day's food for himself, but returned change from the money I'd given him in hopes of making his disappear. Those coins would have bought more damaged cans with 20¢ stamped on sticky labels.*

Thoroughly chastened and ashamed, Zeke dusted off the idea he had all but stomped into oblivion just minutes earlier. If he didn't act quickly, he'd lose the opportunity because Eddie seemed primed for flight. *That,* Zeke could understand. He was on the verge of running, himself.

Balanced on the slippery edge of sanity, he dove into the deep end of risky business. "Give me an hour, Eddie, and then come see me on Main Street. Someone with a truck will drive you to Prairie Rose," he promised grandly.

Eddie's grin was as wide as the horizon; in North Dakota, that's saying something. Too giddy to sit still, the ragtag but happily whistling man bebopped away.

Guilt-laden thoughts notwithstanding, all the way back to the canopy, Eddie's spit-shined tablemate, with those unexpected loose coins jangling in his pocket, mumbled, "What did I just do?"

CHAPTER 17

The problem with Doing The Right Thing (especially when the Do-Gooder secretly hopes The-Powers-That-Be will intervene and release the impulsive Do-Gooder from reckless promises, or at least ensure those pledges won't backfire) is that Fate has a truly wild sense of humor. In reality, Providence, Fortune, Destiny—whatever name one assigns The-Powers-That-Be (Grandma Eden's voice pricked Zeke's conscience: *"Ahem! You know it's God, Zeke!"*) must enjoy watching impetuous altruists flounder, desperately wishing to retrieve words they spoke in haste.

Even as Zeke walked along mumbling, he knew Fate-Fortune-Destiny (*Yes, Grandma: it's God*) had beamed on him via Eddie's grin. He wasn't all that eager to tell Haze what he'd done. She'd get all teary-huggy-gushy and say *ad nauseum*, "Oh Zeke, I knew you'd do the right thing!"

The muttering kept pace with his gait: "I'm no hero, not a social worker, hardly even a Boy Scout. Just a regular guy hoping to get his pesky mother off his case."

By the time he reached the canopy, he was a man with a plan. Yes, he was still a man who had blurted out something he really hadn't thought through, but he wouldn't go back on his word, even if it meant stepping outside his comfort zone. It was a good plan:

- Tell Haze all about it; deflect her guaranteed-to-be-verbose and unwarranted praise
- Ask Bess who owns whatever trucks are parked along Main Street; then locate the driver and offer him big-bucks to make a sixty-mile round trip with a smelly passenger riding in back
- Enjoy a leisurely dinner with Bess and Haze, and then make tomorrow's soup samples.

Zip-zap. A man with a plan is a happy man. *Uh-huh.*

And what a good plan, considering a crazy idea had started it all. A fine plan, really. Zeke felt much better about himself as a human being, in general, and a good son, in particular.

"Guess what, Mom?" he announced with a modicum of humility, though pride threatened to sweep *humble* away until not one crumb remained. "I'm helping Eddie."

She beamed. "I told Bess . . . well, never mind. It's your story, so start talking, and don't skip any details."

"You know the saying, 'If Mama ain't happy, ain't nobody happy'? Well, get ready to be one happy Mama, Haze Eden, because your son is Doing The Right Thing. I'm paying Eddie's way to Prairie Rose. He wants to go there to see his son and, like you said, he insists on riding separate from the driver. So what I'm going to do is locate someone who owns a pickup and pay for their gas and their time for the hour or so it'll take, round-trip."

Step One of the plan? *Check.*

As predicted, Haze got all teary-huggy-gushy while Zeke recounted his activities since he'd left her. "I'm so very proud of you, Zeke!" *Yup, one happy Mama.*

On to Step Two!

"So, Bess," Zeke said, feeling mighty fine, "who owns all these?" He waved at the impressive variety of vehicles nosed up to the curb on both sides of Main Street. It was, after all, North Dakota *and* the Threshing Show so there was a profusion of pickups in the mix.

"Well . . ." Her gaze slowly traveled the path of his gesture.

"Start here." He pointed at the closest one: a Dodge Ram with an open bed. Just what the Do-Gooder needed to accomplish his good deed.

That's when Zeke's good plan—no, make that his practically perfect plan—fell apart. Shattered, even.

CHAPTER 18

It seems the Dodge Ram's owner had recently survived a heart attack. Drive Eddie to Prairie Rose? "Don't even ask," Bess said firmly. Doctor's orders were clear and stern: *"No stress."* Eddie could stress a healthy man.

Next in line, a Chevy with racing stripes and, yes, a locked steel toolbox in the bed, but still room for a passenger. *Oh-oh: Michigan license plates.* That'd never work. Eddie wasn't the kind of memory Crosby's Chamber of Commerce strove to create for visitors this weekend.

The Toyota Tacoma belonged to the owner of the business the truck faced. "Billy can't close the cafe just so you can keep a promise," Bess insisted. "Not with all those hungry people." Yup; a line was forming outside.

As for the red-hooded F-150 with its black driver's door, green passenger door, and badly dented fenders? The kid slouched behind the steering wheel (trying to look cool) had a restricted permit. Bess bought eggs from his mom and knew he could drive on the farm or to school. Sneaking to town matched neither, so forget it—though Caleb (like any young driver) would leap at the chance. *Paid to drive sixty miles? Almost worth getting grounded!*

A Chevy with a gun rack mounted above the back window had a flat tire. "Parked there all week." Disgust underscored Bess' words. "It should be fined and towed."

Zeke rolled his head back on his shoulders and moaned. Eddie would show up any minute and . . . *And nothing.* Every visible pickup—or otherwise appropriate vehicle—in a two-block, both-sides stretch was discussed and dismissed. Rational reasons for "no" abounded. Zeke grew more distraught by the minute.

It was a veritable *Water-water-everywhere-but-not-a-drop-to-drink* disaster with vehicles galore, in every possible condition from factory-new to "How's a wreck like that hold together?" All makes and models, not one of which helped accomplish Do-Gooder Zeke's Big Plan.

"Hmm. If you got it running, I wonder if my brother's old pickup would make it to Prairie Rose," Bess mused. "I think the keys are in my kitchen junk drawer."

Being the mannerly sort, Zeke remembered Bess was his mother's friend. He gnawed his cheek rather than blurt out, *"Couldn't you have mentioned your brother's truck, oh, let's just say . . . forty-five minutes ago!"* Was septuagenarian Bess finally getting even with six-year-old Hazel Louise Anderson for that black eye? Did delayed revenge taste mighty sweet to Bess *nee* McAvoy Green?

He counted silently to ten. *One-I-pinch-her, two-I-poke-her, three-I-punch-her, four-I-bite-her . . .* Reaching *ten-I-smother-her* without acting on any such abuses, he asked with what he considered commendable composure: "Uh, Bess, where is your brother's truck? Out at his farm?"

"No, it's in my garage," she said calmly.

His forehead furrowed. *Can senility occur so abruptly?* "Really?" As he scratched his chin, he wondered how to challenge gently. "Uh, I don't think so, Bess. Last night your car was on one side and I pulled into the other. Pretty sure I neither hit nor *saw* a truck in the process!"

Bess laughed merrily. "Of course you didn't, Zeke; it's parked in my detached garage that faces the alley!"

His relief was palpable; no one likes to witness mental demise. "Good, good; I didn't know about another garage. Thank you!" *I still have no idea why we had to discuss every pickup parked on Main Street before you remembered one in your own garage, but hey! That's just overly critical, impatient me.*

"You're welcome. By the way, no one's driven it for quite some time, but I'm sure you can get it running."

So, don't get giddy yet, Zeke. "Was it towed to town?" A sinking feeling: *The plan was I find a ride, not drive . . .*

"No, my nephew drove it right into the garage."

"Well, there we have it. One pickup, ready to roll—and just in time, because here comes Eddie."

"Hey, Hazeden! 'Hey, Dude! Hey, store-lady!"

"Hello, Eddie," Haze responded. "I'm glad you had a nice talk with my son *Zeke*." Zeke could have told her that, just as she was now-and-forever *Hazeden*, Eddie had rechristened him *Dude*; but she'd still try to fix things. "My friend *Bess*, who works at J Co Drug, is loaning *Zeke* a pickup for your ride to Prairie Rose."

If Eddie wondered why the whole world knew his business, he gave no indication this breached his privacy. He spun around and pumped both fists in the air. "I be gonna see my kid, tha' be a fo-sure fac'! Uh-huh."

"Okay, Eddie," Zeke said, interrupting the ensuing wild song-and-dance, "we'll meet right here at five-thirty, okay?" He pointed at the bank's clock. "You keep an eye on the time, I'll be back here with the pickup, and then we're off to Prairie Rose to see your son. Five-thirty," he repeated for good measure.

"Cate al-'ays feed me supper, so tha' be good time."

Zeke turned to Bess. "It's also good because it means I'll be back here in time to eat with you and Mom. If it's only thirty miles to Prairie Rose, I should be back at your house pretty close to six-thirty, seven at the latest."

"No rush," she assured him. "Haze and I will prepare tomorrow's samples while you're gone. It's a cold supper, anyway. I'll go home now and make sure the truck is cleaned out. I haven't looked at it even once since Paul drove it here. Oh, you might need gas."

Eddie left in one direction, Bess headed in another, and Haze and Zeke kept busy until they closed up shop. While Haze packed the day's unsold books and other supplies, Zeke dismantled the canopy, and dragged the four buckets to a spot beneath the drug store's windows where they would spend the night. Together, they stowed boxes, coolers, lawn chairs, and canopy in the rental car.

Back at Bess' house, Zeke carried coolers into the kitchen. "I'm off," he told the two chattering women who were already busy in the kitchen, "or I will be once I get the keys to the truck."

"They're in the ignition," Bess said. "By the way, I called my brother and he says it's fine that you use the truck. It should be driven every once in a while, anyway, to keep it in good running condition. You're doing both of us a favor because I'm scared to death," she patted her chest as if to calm a racing heart, "of driving a truck, and he's too old to drive now. And my nephew has his own vehicles, so there you have it: you're helping all around!"

"Have a great time," Haze said, beaming. "You're a good man, Zeke. I'm so proud of you!"

"Don't hurry; nothing bad will happen to our supper if you're late," Bess reassured him. "Oh, the truck is parked in the North side of the garage, closest to the sidewalk. I took the padlock off that door for you."

"Thanks so much for everything," Zeke said. He kissed Haze on the check and playfully loosened her apron strings. "See you ladies soon," he added, dodging her swat.

One happy Mama.

One belatedly kindhearted son now personally helping his less fortunate fellow man—which, Zeke had to admit, was even better than his original idea of passing Eddie off to someone else.

One perfect plan.

Life was good.

CHAPTER 19

Halting the nameless tune he whistled, Zeke huffed, "Haven't seen this kind of door in a while." He pushed the heavy wooden garage door sideways along a protesting metal bar that ran the width of the garage. It reached the rail's end and bounced off the other side's locked door.

Late afternoon sun illuminated half the dark building.

Late afternoon sunbeams danced on rusted fenders.

"Whoa! Haven't seen one of these in, well, *forever*." He stared at a steel-bumpered pickup that last knew anything close to *better days* about the time he'd graduated from college. Maybe since he'd started shaving.

The newest thing about it was a hardly new camper shell. *Totally empty side-window frames*, Zeke noted, circling the vehicle. Climbing inside, he realized the window between cab and shell was also missing every bit of glass. Thick spider webs, laced with fossilized spiders, crisscrossed the gap in pathetic imitation of a screen.

"Let's review," Zeke suggested to the image staring at him from the pitted rearview mirror. "I'm sitting in the truck Mr Methuselah drove when he took Mrs Methuselah to the prom. It may or may not start; it might or might not be insured. Do I want to think about that? I do not."

He noticed a greasy rag by his feet and used it to clear spider webs from behind his head. Tossing it over the hump on the floor, he resumed his monologue: "I'm about to drive a guy I really know very little about to see a child who may not even want to see his dad. Way to go, Zeke; great plan!" He cocked a finger at the mirror; his tongue clicked the requisite pistol-shot.

He reached for the key (in the ignition, just as Bess had promised) and turned it. Several *errr-errs-errr*'s and a stuttering death-rattle resulted, followed by an eerie silence. Then, without warning, the engine leaped to life with a lion's roar. The truck shook; Zeke's teeth rattled. Gingerly, he touched the shuddering gear shift, coaxed it into reverse and stepped on the gas.

All the horsepower from the straight-six engine that growled beneath the truck's hail-pocked hood shot the driver and his suspiciously malicious vehicle straight out of the garage as if they were merely Tinker Toys.

Zeke hit the brakes, which of course killed the engine, just seconds before he would have either destroyed or been mired in a thicket of lilac bushes. Leaves were all he could see in the wobbly side mirror or the murky rearview mirror. Maybe the bush hadn't escaped damage, after all.

Leaning his forehead against the quivering steering wheel, he waited for his pulse to slow. It pounded loudly in his ears; he winced. He pressed one hand against his heart. "Jackhammering" was what rescuers should tell 911 when he was discovered. Would he be found by morning? Where was the nearest cardiac care center— with a helicopter?

Woof!

Zeke jolted as if electrically shocked: *not* what an erratic heart needed. The side mirror was missing a screw so it dangled freely, providing a cockeyed view, mostly of the pot-holed alley. As it swung, the mirror also revealed random glimpses of a laughing dog leaping beside the truck. *Yes, a laughing dog, just like Daisy in the Dagwood comic strip.*

"You wouldn't be so amused if I'd squashed you flat," Zeke muttered, then: "Why am I talking to a dog?" Cautiously he turned the key again. He cranked the gearshift, gripped the steering wheel in proper ten-and-two position and stepped on the gas. The truck was in motion. Granted, it was slow motion, but it was moving.

Automatically he lowered the visor, and shook his head ruefully. "What a clueless nitwit! *You* are this garage door's only automatic opener and shut-er." He shifted into neutral, climbed out and heaved the door back into place, gaining a splinter in his palm in the process.

The dog went crazy, leaping high in the air to welcome his new playmate. The truck's engine chugged, ready to take out everything in its path. At that moment, *everything* included Zeke, one crazed dog, and a garage.

Mission accomplished (the dog outside the garage, not in the truck—no easy feat, Zeke discovered) he navigated the truck along the alleyway in low gear and reached the street. He flicked the turn signal. It fell off.

The driver's window was already down, albeit in a lopsided position about two inches above the bottom frame. But this was good since the handle used to roll the window either up or down was a razor-edged nub.

Being a law-abiding citizen, Zeke dangled his left arm out the window, ready to signal all turns. The two inches of visible window dug into his arm and made it tingle—a sure sign it would fall asleep soon. "Oh, yeah; life's just getting better by the minute," he groused at his vibrating reflection in the truck's rearview mirror.

Shifting gears required that he steer with his knees. But at a jerky ten miles an hour (*Does the speedometer work? Good question*) did that infraction really matter?

Spewing gassy fumes and dropping bits of itself like Hansel and Gretel's breadcrumbs to mark a path, the truck attracted a fair amount of interest. Small-town etiquette required a response, but *how humiliating* if folks recognized him as the canopy-guy from Main Street. Averting his eyes, he gave each waver a brisk nod instead.

He swerved to miss bicycling children who followed him, collecting screws, who-knew-what-all, even a mud-flap: junk left in his wake. "At least I don't need to stop and collect my litter. See, Zeke?" he mimicked Haze's perkiest tones. "There's some good in every situation."

He tried to look unfamiliar when a rug-shaking woman gawked at him from within the dusty clouds swirling around her. "Keep flinging that dust, lady," he muttered. "Nothing to look at here, nothing at all. Just a Do-Gooder-Wanna-be with rocks for brains."

He bypassed even nodding at one lawn-mowing man whose stare he preferred to interpret as sheer awe at his derring-do, rather than: *How far does that bozo think he's going to get in that bucket of bolts?*

By the time he reached Main Street, Zeke figured phones were ringing all over Crosby:

"Didja see?"

"You won't believe . . .!"

The only way it wasn't true was if anyone who hadn't seen or heard him passing by was either busy out at Pioneer Village, or a housebound blind and deaf mute.

He braked in front of J Co Drug just as a mangy alley cat used one of the canopy's sand-filled buckets for her litter box. "Stop that!" He hit the pickup's horn. It stuck; endless deafening *ararkkk-ararkkk-ararkkk*'s blasted the evening calm before he could pound it into silence.

The cat kicked up a mini-sandstorm and stared defiantly at Zeke: *"Come closer and let me scratch your face, Angry Horn-Honker."* She hissed, whipping her tail like a sword. *"Take your pick: cat-scratches or cat-pee?"*

"Hey, Dude!" Eddie yelled, bounding into view. His backpack flopped around; anything that could clang, did.

"Hey, Eddie," Zeke responded wearily. He stepped out, pausing only to shake his fist at the flat-eared, contemptuous cat still perched in the bucket. "You win, Cat. *For now*," he snarled and stalked back to where Eddie stood gazing in wonder at the camper shell.

"This be like a lil' house, huh?" Eddie rubbed the camper's door knob with something verging on reverence.

"I guess so. But it'll get too windy in there for you. All the windows are knocked out. Besides, I doubt if it's even legal for a passenger to ride in the back of a pickup on the highway, whether you're inside a camper, or not."

"It be wheres I rides." Eddie's jutting chin said *"End of discussion"* as clearly as any voiced words.

"Well . . . okay." *I hope every Divide County law officer is busy at the Threshing Show.* Zeke opened the camper's door; it was missing a hinge which was now likely the proud possession of a bicycling pint-sized scavenger.

A second hinge showered rust flakes on his pants and shoes before it fell apart; the sound of metal hitting pavement seemed unnecessarily loud. He looked around furtively, expecting to hear a booming: *"Hands up, Mister! That does it. I'm ticketing you as a litterer and menace to the health and safety of our fine citizens."*

Zeke eyed the remaining hinges suspiciously. They now bore full responsibility for holding the door close enough to latch. Having hung around the two other disreputable hinges, they'd likely picked up shoddy habits and now awaited the perfect time (*Like right by the Highway Patrol's hidden spot on a curve?*) to mimic their former companions' bad examples. Zeke envisioned an airborne camper door surfing the North Dakota breeze.

"Aw-righ'!" Chortling, Eddie tossed his backpack inside, knelt on the bumper, and crawled into the shell. He was a kid on Christmas morning; Zeke was his Santa.

Santa-Zeke stuck his head inside, getting his first glimpse of what lay within. What with his shock over the truck's outer condition, he hadn't given thought to the camper shell. Obviously Bess' brother had used it for more than just protecting whatever supplies he hauled.

Eddie dug through a bushel basket and, exclaiming over each find, pulled out a shabby blanket, a stiff and stained rug, and one pillow with more lumps than fluff. "This be a fine ride, Dude! Uh-huh."

"Whatever," Zeke mumbled. A rope to secure Eddie to the truck's frame as they careened down the highway probably would have been a wiser accessory to supply than padding. *Ticket-time,* he thought glumly.

When he passed the side window, Eddie was already leaning against the wall where cab and shell connected. With rug and blanket beneath him, eyes closed and head propped on the pillow against the recently spider-webbed window frame, Eddie personified peace. "A fine ride."

Zeke climbed into the cab, jiggling into a hollow which previous drivers' posteriors had formed in the seat. An obstinate spring poked places he wished it didn't, but that was the least of his problems. *Oh, yeah; a swell ride.*

Lurching along, garnering odd glances and amused headshakes, Zeke settled into a reasonable facsimile of someone who had figured out what he was doing by the time he reached the highway. *If they only knew . . .*

Wind whistled everywhere. It gusted through the camper, rushed through the cab, whistled shrilly at fifty miles an hour (with the speedometer fluttering more than functioning, fifty was only a guess). Whatever the figure, it was the speed at which the truck performed best, if shiver-and-shake can truly be considered best.

He remembered Bess saying, *". . . keep in good running condition . . ."* and snorted. *When did that last apply?*

Five minutes outside of Crosby, Eddie yodeled in Zeke's ear, "Thiiiis beeee aaahhh niiiice truuuuck, huuuuh?" Zeke whipped his head around to see if Eddie was pounding on his chest while talking. *Nope.* All those warbles were courtesy of an extremely bumpy ride.

"You doing okay?" Zeke hollered back, easing off the gas to lessen some of the roughness Eddie was enduring with amazing nonchalance. *Well, compared to a boxcar, I guess it is smooth.* "Sure you don't want to ride up here?"

"This my bes' thin'. Uh-huh," Eddie shouted.

When first Zeke missed seeing Eddie's pillow in the mirror, he panicked. *Did he fall out?* The door rattled, but was neither flapping open nor missing. *Whew.*

Then he heard a loud snore. *Wow; have I ever been so tired I could fall asleep in a battered pickup whose springs have lost their will to spring?* "I would never survive being Eddie," he confessed to the wind.

The truck shook; Zeke drove; the wind howled; and Eddie slept.

CHAPTER 20

Ten miles later (strictly an estimate with the odometer trembling at an unlikely 112-mile reading, unless it had circled the count-cycle several times, which was a distinct possibility) Eddie reappeared behind Zeke. Arms propped on the empty sill, he yawned. "We aw-mos' there?"

"Beats me," Zeke bawled into the wind.

"If'n ya stays on same road as al-'ays, we gets there," Eddie assured him. "Hey, Dude, do ya gots kids?"

Whatever happened to segues? Zeke shook his head.

"Why not?"

Zeke's shrug should have been a sufficient answer.

"Why not?" came Eddie's repeated query. "Ya gots a woman, don'cha?"

"A wife; no kids," Zeke shouted.

"Ya likes kids, Dude?"

"Some I like, some I don't."

A grin. "Ya gonna likes Lil' Eddie. He be good kid."

"I look forward to it." Understatement of the day.

"Do yer woman likes kids?"

"Some kids, she does."

Eddie chortled.

They chugged along; Eddie "moo'ed" at cows in fields. Mid-moo, he scooted to the window and tapped Zeke's shoulder. "If'n ya had kids, maybe ya not be sad-like."

Wind cranked up to ear–piercing decibels: an expected result of increased gas-pedal pressure, which was solely due to Zeke's shock. "Sad-like?"

"What?" Eddie yelled.

Zeke bellowed, "I am *not* sad-like!"

"Uh-*huh*. Ya al-'ays ack *real* sad-like. Like sumpthin' chomp at yer insides wheres ya don' gots long 'nuf arms to swat it."

Zeke's grip on the wheel tightened. He knew first-hand about those *chomping things*.

"Do ya gots sum nuther job b'sides sellin' tha' book with Hazeden?"

"I'm a writer," Zeke shouted back, startling a flock of fence-sitting birds. "I write books," he added at full-bellow. *What's with this? Mom can't breathe a word about me, but it's okay for me to blare personal facts out across the prairie? Could've left it at "I'm a writer" but I haven't written a word in months, so is that even true?*

"They big books?"

A nod.

"Wha' they bout?"

"Criminals getting caught. Made-up stories."

He rolled his eyes. "Ya gots sum nuther *real* book, or jus' tha' book bout soups wha' cost twen-y dollah?"

"Only the cookbook; the others . . ." skipping the intricacies of publishing, Zeke finished with, "are done."

"Ya gonna be broke, Dude. *Bad* broke."

"We're okay."

"Huh." Eddie whistled tunelessly before shouting in Zeke's ear, "Peoples whats buys yer books, they hafta knows how to reads good, huh?"

Zeke chose his response carefully but wondered, *When what's said is blared, does sensitivity matter?* "A person who doesn't read well could have a hard time."

Lips pursed, Eddie nodded. "I don' reads good," he hollered. "Mos'ly jus' papers wha' peoples dumps."

"That's good. Reading anything improves our minds."

"My fren' Pete al-'ays roll his eyes, like this, when I keeps alla papers I finds."

Zeke caught a demonstration of Pete's disdain in the rearview mirror.

"Nows I gonna tells him, 'Readin' be m-provin' my min' jus' like findin' yer new shoes be m-provin' yer feets'!"

Eddie's laughter was contagious as the pickup followed the road's yellow dashes. During a lull in their shared merriment, Zeke yelled, "Who do you hang out with in Chicago? Girlfriend? Sister? Brother?"

"I gots lotta fren', but not no girl-fren'. *Nuh-uh.* Lil' Eddie's firs' mama? She be nuttin but trouble. Nows I stays far 'way from alla girl whats wanna be my girl-fren. Uh-huh. My fren' be guys wha' gots same job as me at Union Station. Hey, Dude, ya gots a brudder or sistah?"

When will you learn? Don't ask questions you don't want coming back at you. "Just a brother," Zeke shouted.

"Where he be?"

How much farther is to Prairie Rose? "In Utah."

"At yer house?"

"No."

"Close bys yer house?"

"No; several hours away."

"Tha' crazy! If'n I gots a brudder, I lives righ' bys him. Uh-huh. Tha' be a fo-sure fac'. It why yer sad-like; cuz ya don' lives bys yer brudder, huh? He write books, too?"

"No."

"What he do?"

Gulp. "Uh, nothing much."

"He gots a job?"

Heart pounding and with a lump the size of a Utah boulder clogging his throat, Zeke yelled, "He's in prison." Since the trial, Zeke had never said those three words together, let alone blasted them across the land. *The wind's pulling out secrets like a magnet collects iron filings.*

"Uh-huh." The rearview mirror showed Eddie's nod in gray-tones. A pause, then: "Tha' be why yer sad-like?"

"I guess." *Wow; open a door and the confessions fly.*

"I know'd ya be sad-like. It be good reason, sure-'nuf, Dude." He clasped Zeke's shoulder with a touch so light and quick it might have been imagined had not warmth remained. "Tha' be why ya writes big book bout bad guys, huh? Cuz yer brudder in prison?"

Stunned by Eddie's physical gesture of sympathy, Zeke blinked rapidly, telling himself: *It's dust, not tears.*

"Since he got arrested, I've only written the cookbook. The others were written before he, uh, went to prison."

"Ya *sure* ya ain't broke, Dude?"

"Positive."

"Peoples wha' lives in houses with toilet and doors wha' locks gotta reads good to keeps livin' there, huh?"

Brief puzzlement preceded Zeke's *Ah-ha* moment. "Knowing how to read helps people earn enough to rent or buy a place to live. Some people might pay rent to a family member, or work in exchange for rent, or be a caretaker for a business. Or the government—"

Protest hissed in Eddie's throat even before words spewed. "*Nuh-uh.* Gov'ment man say'd if'n we don' tells our names, we goin' to jail. I don' tells him *my* name!"

He spun off to a side window, giving Zeke time to contemplate this new information from his tight-lipped passenger. *I'm sure it's a problem, especially for anyone living off the government's grid. How many like you are out there, Eddie? How many struggling, homeless—but otherwise self-sufficient and justifiably proud of it—people who can't break through the system?*

Even the wind couldn't drown out Zeke's conscience, which spoke in Haze's voice: *"You'll have to be the one to reach out to Eddie . . ."* He cleared his throat, but guilt can clog an airway quite solidly so it wasn't an entirely successful attempt. *And the guy she expects me to help just reached out and literally, physically touched me . . .*

Coming into view ahead, seven feed-storage units bore painted letters that spelled out P-R-A-I-R-I-E R-O-S-E: one letter to a silo, one word to a line. Zeke slowed down. "Here we are," he shouted through the space behind him, now completely void of glass and Eddie's face.

Not a moment too soon. So much for confidentiality! It may be easier than baring my soul on a psychiatrist's couch, but it's certainly not a form of therapy I plan to pursue, ever again. You're not alone, Eddie, in guarding private privacy.

CHAPTER 21

Eddie cheered the news of their arrival loudly. He scooted, crab-like, from one side of the camper shell to the other. His excited greetings and pronouncements turned heads: "Hey, Petey, it be me: Eddie! Uh-huh!" and "Look, Milton! It be Eddie, ridin' inna lil' house!"

Along the streets, from yards and porches, people waved and called back. Either Eddie was some kind of celebrity or Prairie Rose citizens greeted everyone with abandon. *Shades of Pudge*, Zeke thought as he also received curious glances accompanying friendly waves.

Eddie thumped the outside of the camper. "Go inna this alley, Dude. Cate's Café be righ' there. Stop! I go sees if'n she here." Eddie had opened the camper's door, jumped out, and hopped onto the café's loading dock before the brakes screeched to a complete stop.

He banged on a doorframe. "Hey, Cate! It be Eddie!"

"Eddie!" The screen door flew open. A slim woman, whose snowy hair surely belied her age, burst through and grabbed Eddie's hands. Their reunion was joyous; they spun in a wild dance on the elevated cement pad.

Then, as if he'd blown a fuse, Eddie stopped, bent over, and peered into the pickup. "Dude! This be Cate!"

Cate and Zeke reached the front of the truck at the same time. She didn't comment on the hissing radiator; in fact, she didn't even give the old truck a glance. Extending a hand, she said warmly, "Hi, I'm Cate Larson."

"Hello; I'm Dude to Eddie and his ride to Prairie Rose, and also known as Zeke Eden." The engine ticked like a bomb; the camper door swung, creaking-and-croaking, on the remaining hinges. *Such a proud moment . . .*

She grinned. "Eddie's ride, but also one of the authors of SOUP'S ON IN RAVEN CROWLEY'S KITCHEN, right? Served your corn chowder today. Big hit! Heard you'd be in Crosby, but couldn't get away. That's life for a simple, small-town café owner. So I ordered a copy on-line."

"Always good to hear from a satisfied customer . . ."

"I doubt you remember everyone who comes to your events, but Blyss Hathaway showed me her signed copy. Will you sign mine, too, even if I didn't come to Crosby?"

"Sure," he agreed, all the while thinking: *Any male walking the earth who claims to forget Blyss is lying!*

Eddie's patience ended. "Where Lil' Eddie be?" Zeke welcomed anything that erased Blyss from his mind, even if it interrupted compliments for Raven's corn chowder.

"Luke and I need to work late today, Eddie, so he ate supper at the café and is playing at a friend's house. I'll call and have him ride his bike back here. Meanwhile, how about something to eat? The special today was meatloaf, and there's enough left for two sandwiches. Zeke, one has your name on it if you can stay."

A supper with his name on it also awaited him in Crosby, but Zeke really wanted to meet Justin. Eating would fill the waiting-time. "Thanks; I'd enjoy that."

Cate wiped her face with her apron. "You know, it's so nice outside and so stuffy inside, I bet you'd like a picnic in the park. I'll have Justin meet you there instead. Now, excuse me while I make that call and pack your suppers."

Eddie didn't seem to find the offer unusual, though Cate obviously knew he didn't handle *indoors* well. The ease with which he sat swinging his feet against the loading dock hinted that he'd eaten Cate's "real good food" out here during previous visits to Prairie Rose.

Despite Zeke arriving in a pickup so decrepit as to peg him only slightly better than destitute, Cate's shifting the picnic from the alley to the park showed that her sensitivity to Eddie outweighed any need to impress Zeke.

Seeing Zeke head for the truck, Eddie protested, "No-buddy drive to the park, Dude!" So they left the truck behind the café and walked. They opened the bag (for which Cate had refused Zeke's money: "I never charge anyone who brings Eddie to see us!") and found hefty sandwiches on thickly sliced homemade bread. Fresh fruit, carrot sticks, made-from-scratch cookies, bottled water, and chips completed the menu. Considering there had been no "Incoming-Eddie!" warning, Cate deserved high praise. *Simple, small-town café owner? Ha!*

Zeke set his sandwich aside long enough to call Bess. "Don't hold supper for me; I'm eating in Prairie Rose."

Eddie gulped his food and scanned the park, taking no time to talk, though Zeke made stabs at conversation. "Do you come to Prairie Rose often, Eddie?"

"Uh-huh." Eddie was halfway through his sandwich; Zeke had eaten two bites.

"Seems like everyone here knows you."

"Seem like," Eddie agreed, opening his chips and eying the other bag, ready to pounce if no one laid claim.

Zeke considered dangling potato chips as bait to get better answers than were forthcoming. "What do you do when you come to Prairie Rose?"

"I be with Lil' Eddie lotta time. Gonna eat yer chips?"

"No; would you like them?" Apparently so. "Do you stay at the Larson's house when you come here?"

"Nuh-uh; I guard Mister Justin's store." Sprays of juice squirted each time he bit into an apple.

Zeke thought *Guard?* but limited his query to "Mister Justin has a store here?" Instead of clarifying, Eddie's answers had only increased the confusion. "I thought you said he lives in New York?"

"Uh-huh. He be rich, but he real nice." Another bite.

Give up, Zeke! "And your son is named after him?"

"Uh-huh." One final bite and the core was history.

Zeke blinked. *He even ate the apple core?* He tried again: "So . . . a little boy in Prairie Rose is named after a man who lives in New York." Anyone else would pick up clues this wasn't a declarative sentence, but a wide-open question. Eddie merely tossed grapes in the air, cheering each time he successfully caught one in his mouth. Some missed the mark, but if he found them, he ate them.

A more direct approach was obviously needed. "How'd you meet Mister Justin, Eddie?"

"We be here same time."

"Oh, I see! He *came* from New York, but he *lives* here?"

"Nuh-uh. He here *sum-a-time*, not alla times. Me 'nd Mister Justin, we *kind-a* here. Ya want tha' b'nana?"

Zeke would have donated blood (to say nothing of all available fruit) to get to the bottom of this bewildering account. But that wouldn't happen until Eddie claimed all items in sight. Zeke slid the untouched remainders of their supper toward his food-focused tablemate.

Despite diligent watching (true, even with Eddie's consuming interest in edibles and Zeke's pondering how life's mysteries had increased, not depleted) the sound of playing cards whipping against bike spokes caught both picnickers off-guard. "Hey, Big Eddie!" A joyous greeting came from a red-cheeked boy pumping pedals on a full-sized bike. "You came!"

"I came!" Eddie shouted back, leaping up. Food was forgotten. "Look-it ya, Lil' Eddie! Ya growed!"

The bike fell with a clatter; its wheels spun as Justin leaped through space to fling his arms around Eddie's waist. Eddie hugged the boy just as tightly, and then broke away and bent over as if preparing to lift him. "*Ooofff!* Ya gots too big for this any mores, Lil' Eddie!"

"That's what Daddy says, too! He told me 'Big Eddie will think you're a different kid the next time he sees you!' Did you? Or did you know me right away?"

"I know'd who it be the minute I see'd ya pumpin' that bike like ten big-bad dogs be chasin' ya!"

Justin's giggle was infectious; Eddie caught the bug. Their reunion made what Eddie declared "a whole-lotta-happy" in the Prairie Rose town park.

"Can you stay real long, this time, Big Eddie?"

"Maybe," Eddie said with a sudden air of mystery.

At least I'm not the only one getting dodgy answers from him! Zeke thought, wondering what was behind Eddie's light-on-details, heavy-on-suspense response.

"I wish you could stay forever, Big Eddie!"

Eddie's look gave nothing away. "Gotta sees wha' yer mama 'nd daddy says bout sumpthin'. If'n they says 'okay,' we gonna have a big a'venture! Uh-huh."

"What's our adventure?" the excited boy demanded.

"Won't tell ya; not less'n they says it be okay."

Justin pouted for a moment but his face showed the split-second he remembered: *Manners!* He extended a small, gritty hand. "Hello, Sir." He met Zeke's eye. "I'm Justin Edward Larson. I'm sorry I ignored you."

"Hello; I'm Zeke Eden. I drove, uh—*When in Rome, do as the Romans?*—Big Eddie to see you. Glad to meet you, Justin Edward Larson. Don't worry, I don't feel ignored."

Justin's grin revealed a set of the oversized front teeth all kids endure when their baby teeth fall out. He said with unblinking seriousness, "You can call me Justin. I only said my whole name so you'd know who I am. Big Eddie calls me 'Lil' Eddie.' It's a nickname," he added.

"Big Eddie said you're named Justin after—who is it?"

"Mister Justin Campbell-Lampman. He lives in New York. We like him lots, don't we, Big Eddie?"

"Uh-huh; he rich, but he ain't stuck-up."

Still uncertain how to process a rich New Yorker with links to Prairie Rose and the Larson family—or, even more baffling, tie-ins to Eddie—Zeke stuck with known facts: "And your middle name is Edward, after Big Eddie."

"That's right. See, Big Eddie brought me here after I got born so Mama and Daddy could have me." The simplicity made sense to Justin, so no need to expound. Zeke wondered how much the boy really knew.

"And your last name is Larson, like Luke and Cate?"

"Before Mama married Daddy, she was Cate Jones. Then she turned into Cate Larson. That happens to girls." He cocked his head. "Are you married, Mister Eden?"

"I am. My wife used to be Sage Crowley; when she married me she turned into Sage Eden." Zeke was enjoying this exchange more than any in recent memory.

Justin covered his mouth with both hands and doubled over. "That's funny!" he sputtered around a spate of giggles. "See, 'sage' is an herb Mama cooks with sometimes. But that's not the funniest part! Mama just got a new cookbook." Laughter surged again. "She helped me say a name on the cover and it was Crowley—like what you said your wife's name used to be!"

Eddie crowed, "I tole ya Lil' Eddie be real smart, huh? He figure stuff out, 'nd he read good, too."

Meeting Eddie and Justin (*The kid knows herbs!*) caused a fellow to rethink long-held, oft-spouted ideas about intelligence, genetics, environment, opportunity: all things now doing battle with Zeke's preconceived assessment. He had dug no deeper than face value. *Admit it, Zeke; you're a snob, even with a brother in prison.*

How many people had called out greetings by name, not just *"Howdy"* to Eddie as they drove into Prairie Rose? Zeke had lost count; it was more than *he* got back home.

And Cate's welcome wasn't faked. She was probably more germ-conscious than most people in town, given her occupation, yet she had grabbed Eddie's hands without hesitation or cringing.

And what about Justin hugging Eddie, burying his face against him? Only love, acceptance, and seeing beyond the obvious could accomplish that. *I've never even touched Eddie, never patted his shoulder like he did mine, or offered a handshake*, Zeke admitted sheepishly.

"Let's go home, Big Eddie," Justin was saying. "I want to show you the tire swing Daddy made for me."

Zeke could leave now. He had delivered Eddie: promise fulfilled. A check-mark on his Perfect Plan. He had met Justin: a goal accomplished. But having seen Cate, he wanted to meet Luke—the man who didn't balk at raising a boy who could turn out like Eddie.

CHAPTER 22

With Eddie doing fancy footwork on one side of Justin's bike, and Zeke trotting along on the other, they made an odd trio navigating the streets of Prairie Rose.

Justin talked non-stop. He interrupted his recitation of who lived in each house—"Mrs O'Dell's oatmeal cookies always taste like paste!"—to stop and study Eddie.

The boy frowned, and honked the bicycle's air-horn to add authority to his firm words: "You need a haircut, Big Eddie. Let's go see if the barbershop's still open."

Zeke froze. *From the mouths of children?*

"Hokey-dokey," Eddie said cheerfully.

"I bet you haven't cut your hair since you were here last time!" Justin scolded, sounding more like a mother than a little boy as they circled back to Main Street.

Last time? Zeke promptly adjusted his previous estimate of elapsed time since plaited hair met shampoo.

"Hooray! The light's still on!"

Eddie and Justin raced ahead; Zeke paused to examine a damaged sign on the building they approached. Obviously the tag-end of a business name, it now only read D CURL. *Whatever's missing, it's a weird name for a barber shop,* Zeke thought, stepping inside.

Eyeing his visitors with less enthusiasm than behooves a businessman, the somber barber muttered something indiscernible. *Somber* became *glum* with the boy's cheerful pronouncement: "Big Eddie's back, Mister Wilson, and you get to cut his hair!"

Mister Wilson . . . Frank Wilson? As in Hélène's Frank Wilson? Zeke stared at the sullen barber and tried to see what was so enticing that Blyss Hathaway had left California for him. *It must be something only a woman can appreciate, because Frank is hardly a babe-magnet.*

Eddie hopped into the barber's chair while Justin climbed into the vacant companion-seat on the opposite side of the room. *Hélène's side*, Zeke realized. Facing the two traditional shop-chairs from a bench beneath the window gave Zeke ample opportunity to set a scene:

- Frank and Hélène (*No, she was Helen back then*) work side-by-side in this shop all the years of their marriage

- Frank decides Helen isn't enough woman for him; he finds Blyss by devious means, and believes the myth that her name will match his expectations; he dumps his wedding vows and picks up empty promises of *va-va-voom*

- Helen, on the run, transforms into Hélène. Blyss becomes The Other Woman. Frank, on the down-side of a bad decision, shows his true colors as The Fool

- Based on the number of chairs lining the windows, it must have been a busy place but now seems lifeless: two dead light bulbs; old magazines in the rack; dusty bottles and jars on the beauty-shop side where a cloth-draped pedestal hair dryer tilts eerily over a chair

Approximately twelve feet separated the barber- and beauty-shop sides. It seemed too wide a chasm for two sadder-but-wiser, lonely people to ever cross again.

Zeke fervently wished that right now he could squeeze Sage and whisper words for her ears only.

Justin resumed his chatter. "Mister Wilson, why don't you make Big Eddie look just like Mister Eden?"

The scowling barber turned toward Zeke. "That you?"

A nod. "I'm Zeke Eden, Eddie's ride to Prairie Rose."

"Where are you from?"

What's this? We're playing Twenty Questions? "Utah."

Frank's eyebrows met over his nose. "What were you doing in Utah, Eddie?"

"Not be in Utah; gots ride from Crosby like al-'ays."

"What are you doing in Crosby if you're from Utah?" Frank challenged Zeke.

Zeke wished he dared retort, *Meeting the woman you cuckolded?* Instead he answered vaguely, "Well, it's the Threshing Show, you know," punctuated with a shrug.

Frank spun the chair around to face his customer. "You're a mess, Eddie. I'm gonna shave you down to your scalp, and this shabby beard goes, too."

"Tha' be good! I gonna looks *zac'ly* like Dude!"

"Dude?" Frank groused. "Who's Dude?"

Zeke would've preferred to punch, not educate, Frank but he merely said, "It's Eddie's nickname for me." Frank's grimace communicated feelings better left unsaid.

Sending his chair into a spin with one foot against the counter, Justin crowed, "Big Eddie, you'll look like Mister Eden's twin! Oh! May I use your phone, Mister Wilson?"

As Zeke tried to wrap his mind around being Eddie's twin, Frank *harrumphed* grudging acquiescence. Justin hopped down and stretched to punch numbers in a wall-hung phone. "Hi, Mama. This is your son, Justin. We're at the barber shop and Mister Wilson's making Big Eddie look like Mister Eden! Can he cut my hair like that, too?"

Zeke gulped.

Frank nearly nipped Eddie's ear.

Eddie grinned.

"G'bye. I love you." Hanging up, Justin told Frank, "Mama says 'okay,' but she says I should ask Daddy, too. May I please use the phone again, Mister Wilson?"

Frank nodded nervously—if *pale* indicated nervous.

Justin dialed and repeated his message. After all the "Yeah! He's right here!" and "Mister Eden gave Big Eddie a ride," and several "Okay! Thanks, Daddy!" exchanges, Justin hung up, chortling, "Yippee! We can be triplets!"

"I gots plen'y money," Eddie said proudly. Zeke figured payment was the least of Frank's worries as they both eyed the accumulating hunks of stiff hair on the barbershop floor. He suspected Frank would not merely sweep the shop tonight, he would burn the clippings.

Eddie emerged from his encounter with Frank's scissors and razor beardless and sporting a stark white cap of slick-shaven scalp. Justin bounced off the barber's chair looking like a model for the Smiley-Face logo.

Zeke grudgingly felt a bit more favorably toward Frank when he brusquely refused Eddie's inadequate and seriously wrinkled five single bills in payment. But that act of kindness (if that's what it was, not fear of cooties on Eddie's money) didn't outweigh Zeke's disgust and anger over what the barber had done to ruin his own marriage.

Three nude-headed males walked out of D CURL and through the neighborhood (*Which*, Zeke thought, *could readily serve as the set for "Leave It to Beaver"*) where Justin's startling next plan for Eddie awaited: a bathtub.

Zeke marveled at the small boy's powers when Eddie showed no embarrassment at giving over decision-making about his hygiene to an eight-year-old. *Must be standard activity whenever Eddie shows up . . . If so, he should come more often!*

"While you're taking a bath, Big Eddie," Justin said matter-of-factly as they climbed the steps to his house, "I'll wash your clothes like Mama does. Give me the stuff in your backpack, too." Zeke restrained a grin. *I hear Cate's voice and wisdom echoing in those words!*

Eddie gamely unzipped his pack (*No "private privacy" warnings for Justin*, Zeke noted) and handed over an assortment of items that looked more appropriate for Cate's rag-bag than her washer. He tossed everything he'd been wearing through the doorway as the tub filled.

After the bathroom door closed and Eddie's off-key singing commenced, Justin confessed to Zeke, "I'm just a little kid; I don't really know how to wash clothes."

"We'll figure it out," Zeke assured him solemnly.

And they did.

Chapter 23

Cate and Luke arrived home to find three sleek-headed males exploring the wonders of their back yard. The washer load had been shifted to the dryer. A well-scrubbed Eddie (no longer as *tan* as previously) now wore a robe Justin had provided for him from Luke's closet.

The boy was pumped: "Mama! Daddy! Big Eddie wants to take me on an adventure! Please say 'yes'!"

A stunned Zeke listened to Eddie propose that Justin accompany him back to Crosby. "If'n ya says 'okay,' we gonna sleeps inna tha' lil' house on Dude's truck. Uh-huh! T'morrow, Dude drive me 'nd Lil' Eddie back here."

Zeke gulped, but instantly relaxed as he realized, *No parents will agree to such a wild idea. I don't even need to protest about Eddie reorganizing my schedule!*

Luke stuck out his hand towards Zeke. "I presume you're Dude? Also known as Zeke Eden, Cate tells me." He smiled broadly. "Welcome to Prairie Rose, Zeke."

"Thanks," Zeke managed, still curious how the couple would respond to Eddie's goof-ball proposition.

"May I, Daddy? Please, Mama? It'll be fun!"

Cate caressed Justin's hairless head. "My goodness; I haven't seen your head this bare since you were a baby!"

She's stalling! Zeke realized. Hope flapped its wings.

"What do you think, Luke?" she asked. "Can we manage without an eight-year-old sleeping under our roof tonight?"

Hope plunged to earth like a bag of bricks.

"I don't know, Cate . . . We're pretty fond of him."

"It's only for one night!" Justin protested. "And there are pictures of me all over the house!"

"It's up to Mister Eden," Luke told Justin. "He did us a favor in bringing Big Eddie here." He turned to Eddie. "We'll drive you to Crosby whenever you want to go."

Yes! Grabbing the *out* offered, Zeke said, "The truck I'm driving is borrowed." *Did Luke catch the subtle hint of: As in, not mine to continue driving or let people sleep in?* "Which reminds me, I better take off." Allowing the implication someone awaited the truck's return would undergird Luke and Cate's final decision of *"Sorry. . ."*

Haze's voice *poked-poked* his conscience: *". . . do the right thing."* He wasn't qualified to hang a DO-GOODER sign around his neck yet. He cleared his throat. "I'm not sure about the legality or safety issues with riding in a camper shell. It may be different for adults, but for a child?"

Luke and Cate exchanged glances. Justin planted himself in front of them, but sent pleading looks at Eddie, who was only too glad to come to his rescue.

"Dude never tha' busy," he said breezily. "Hazeden sell books by herse'f if'n he ain't there, tha' be a fo-sure fac'. Uh-huh. Truck be good sleepin' place. T'morrow, me 'nd Lil' Eddie sees machines 'nd horses, 'nd watch parade. We eats hot dogs, 'nd 'splores stuffs all day."

Justin's pleading gaze would have melted a heart of stone. Neither Luke nor Cate qualified as stony hearted.

"Give us a few minutes to get acquainted with Zeke, Justin, and then we'll make a decision," Cate said, turning to Zeke with a grin. "Not that we consider you suspicious! I imagine you'd appreciate some time to make your decision, too."

Wise woman, good mother, Zeke thought.

Luke turned to Eddie: "What with Justin's excitement, I haven't said a decent hello to you. Wonderful to see you again. It's been too long!" Justin's two dads shook hands.

Luke draped an arm around Eddie's shoulders. "I've got some things tucked away in a closet that you might like." While Eddie and Justin waited on the porch swing for Luke's return, Cate took Zeke over to her herb garden.

"Luke's bringing out a backpack, a few clothes. Not new, just better shape than what Eddie has now," Cate confided softly. "I'm not sure how you know Eddie, but we try to help him out a bit whenever he comes here."

"I don't really *know* Eddie; he sort of fell into my life."

She grinned. "That's Eddie in a nutshell! We know him quite well, though he still has so many unrevealed facets. But that's his right; we trust him completely. He survives a tougher life than we can imagine. Even so, he's not dangerous or devious. He's a kind man, honest, and even-tempered. The only thing he's fierce about is Justin. Eddie would give his life for that little boy. That's our lasting connection: We all love Justin."

"So you're saying you're okay with his proposition?"

"Absolutely; Luke is, too. Eddie and Justin often go off on adventures. But it's your call. If you want to leave alone, we understand and we'll get Eddie back to Crosby."

"Okay." Doubt shaded the word. "Unless you know more than I do about North Dakota laws and regulations, their adventure's on. I'm happy to drive them back here."

Cate smiled broadly. "You're a good man, Zeke! Have a seat on the porch while I pack a few things for Justin."

"I'm sorry about the . . ." He rubbed his hair-free pate.

"You know the saying: 'The only difference between a good and bad haircut is two weeks!' Justin will have hair again by the time school starts."

Luke returned, carrying a box. "Eddie, our dryer wasn't kind to your clothes. Maybe you can find things in here to replace what got damaged," he said.

Zeke saw SAVE FOR BIG EDDIE in a childish scrawl on the box. He also noted nothing—not a shirt, nary a sock, no pants—had made it from the laundry room to the porch.

Bald-headed, cleaned-up Eddie is a shock to behold, Zeke mused as he leaned against a porch post to watch Eddie gleefully remove *private privacy* from the old beat-up pack. The equally bare-headed Justin assisted.

Digging through this new bounty, Eddie selected an armload and headed for the garage. He emerged, his eyes bright with joy, sporting gently used clothes. Leaping the steps, he pointed to canvas high-tops. "See, Dude? New shoes be m-provin' my feets!"

Back to looking through the box, he discovered a pair of sunglasses with both stems intact. He tested the eyewear with a little jig, delighted when they stayed on his nose. "Now I be new all over! Uh-huh."

Cate retrieved anything that had been in the old pack which looked like it ever touched food; she ferried it off to the kitchen. Zeke heard running water and knew Eddie's dishes would return to the porch thoroughly scrubbed.

Justin had held off begging, but when it looked like Eddie's retrenching was complete, the boy's tolerance for delay ended abruptly. Luke arched an eyebrow at Cate, asking a question and receiving her answer in the unspoken language married couples often share.

"Well, Justin," Luke drawled, "isn't it time that you, Big Eddie, and Mister Eden leave for Crosby?"

Rendered speechless by such good news, Justin flung himself into Luke's arms. Twisting free, he sped off to pat Cate's cheek and assure her, "I'll come back, Mama. I won't go to Chicago with Big Eddie. I promise."

Eddie's glee said that time with Lil' Eddie trumped socks without holes, shoes that matched and fit, and clean everything else. It even beat Cate's good cooking.

Zeke focused on blinking back inexplicable tears.

Twenty-four hours earlier, he didn't know Eddie.

Twenty-four hours earlier, he'd been a guy who kept his nose out of other people's business because he didn't want their noses in his.

Twenty-four hours earlier, Zeke Eden was a different guy than the one now walking with Luke to retrieve a borrowed wreck-of-a-truck from the alley behind the café.

A church bell chimed the quarter-hour. "Nice sound. Melodic, not jarring. Almost soothing," Zeke said.

Luke agreed. "It reminds me of Pastor Tori; she's the minister at our church—where the bell is. She calms hurting, lonely or confused folks, just like that bell does. She knows how to reach people where they are."

Like Hank? To halt such memories before they could overwhelm, Zeke launched into an impromptu and brief—though unrequested—autobiography as they climbed into the pickup. *I'm only giving an account of my merits to assure Luke that Justin is safe with such an upstanding person as I am, despite this truck's suspect appearance!*

But Luke's ego-rattling response to the account was simply, "If Eddie trusts you, that's good enough for Cate and me." With that, Luke stepped out of the truck.

Huh? If Eddie trusts me? In Zeke's experience, no one listed the homeless as character references. He could just envision Eddie's recommendation:

DUDE BE OK. HE JUS' SAD-LIKE. UH-HUH.

Standing back from the flurry of activity in the yard, Zeke examined Eddie with new curiosity based on his shock over Luke's comment. The man holding a replacement backpack filled with good things was the person whose opinion counted most for Luke and Cate.

Amazing. He obviously had much to mull over. *Why does Luke think Eddie trusts me? Is the mere fact that Eddie showed up with me sufficient basis for trust?*

Wearing a smaller pack, Justin hugged his parents. He clutched a sleeping bag and pillow as he assured Luke the two five-dollar bills were safe in his shirt pocket. "See, Daddy? I'll snap it shut like this after I buy things," he promised, adding earnestly, "I won't get robbed."

Luke took charge of getting Eddie and Justin into the camper shell, which Zeke privately considered a good idea. *Maybe seeing a nearly useless door and no window glass will give him a clue this isn't such a good idea!* But no such luck; Luke didn't comment on rusted or missing hinges, and Cate leaned through a glassless window to exchange noisy kisses with Justin. *Who are these people?*

Armed with the Larson's home and business phone numbers and the realization that sometimes a person's life can do a complete turn-around in twenty-four hours, Zeke climbed behind the wheel of a pickup that could decide any minute it had gone its last mile. The seat groaned beneath him: a sentiment he shared.

"Got enough gas?" Luke asked, sticking his head in the driver's side window. He squinted at the dashboard. The gas gauge, as untrustworthy as everything else about the pickup, pointed below the quarter-tank mark.

"Hope so," Zeke said ruefully, "because I bet nothing's open this late, right?" *Maybe the fact I neglected to take care of that will change your mind about sending Justin off with me?*

Again, no such luck. Luke slapped the driver's door. "Wait a second." He jogged towards the garage, returning with a five-gallon funneled can. "Mower gas. Now I have a good excuse for an overgrown lawn until I remember to refill the can," he chuckled as he removed the gas tank's cover. "Call if you get stranded."

How the rest of the night would unfold didn't seem to bother any of the other players in this drama. As Prairie Rose disappeared behind them, Zeke mused that it wasn't up to him to solve the problems of the world. *Messing with strangers like Eddie can get problematical. Meeting strangers like Luke and Cate can be bewildering.*

His passengers' laughter and constant talking (though few words were distinguishable to Zeke since he was not the intended audience) drifted across the dusky prairie as the horizon swallowed the sun in one final gulp. *Today was complicated, convoluted, knotty and, yes, I admit, packed solid with good stuff that's been missing in my life.*

He still didn't know what he was going to do with Eddie and Justin when they reached Crosby. Luke and Cate may not be worried, but he was: *Does letting Eddie and Justin sleep in a camper inside a dank, dark garage count as Doing The Right Thing?*

CHAPTER 24

A whispered "Whew!" was Zeke's heartfelt response to discovering Haze and Bess had retired for the night by the time he returned. They should be; it was close to ten o'clock. He found a note taped to his bedroom door: *Hungry? Leftovers in 'frig. First one up turns on coffee.*

Having submitted to Justin's fervent plea for an "outside adventure," he hoped he wouldn't regret parallel parking the pickup in the alley instead of inside the garage. But facing a heavy, creaking garage door—twice— in the dark didn't appeal to him, so he had reluctantly agreed. He frowned at the splinter still wedged into his palm and wondered where Bess kept her needles.

Justin had tiptoed inside with Zeke and used the half-bath just off the kitchen before turning in for the night. Zeke decided not to entertain worries about the implications of Eddie's refusal to use the inside facilities.

After showering (and, to his relief, finding tweezers and ointment in the medicine chest) Zeke peered out the bedroom window that faced the alley. He opened it a few inches, thinking, *If anything happens—like, God forbid, sirens screaming, lights flashing, and official commands to "Come outta that camper with your hands up!"—I'll hear, and hopefully get out here in time to intervene . . .*

Lying in his comfortable bed, thoughts about Eddie's rug, skimpy blanket, and lumpy pillow—and Justin with only a sleeping bag cushioning him from the pickup bed's hard floor—pricked at his conscience. But he wasn't the irresponsible party; not really. *I can't believe Luke and Cate permitted this insanity! Granted, I "don' gots no kids," as Eddie would say. But if I did, I sure wouldn't be as casual about things as Justin's parents are!*

What if the dog he'd almost hit earlier in the alley roamed all night? Discovering an occupied camper parked in the dark alley could set off a full-fledged dog-alert: *"Come one, come all. Let's howl: wooff-wooff-a-rooooo!"*

The alley was dark. Spooky-dark. Would Justin sleep a wink? Would he cry out from nightmares?

Night sounds drifting through the open window were neither sirens nor canines running loose. It was still too early for nightmares which, Zeke admitted, might not come. Shrubs brushed against the window screen in a soothing tempo; a bird choir cooed; a distant car backfired; gentle laughter wafted from a porch or yard. Then . . . *a harmonica? Even if someone in The Harmonica Band lives nearby, I doubt he'd play outside this late . . .*

When realization struck, Zeke groaned louder than anything coming from the alley. He leaped out of bed and peered into the darkness. It had to be Eddie playing; it sounded close by, and no one else was around. If this was a lullaby for Justin, it wouldn't last long. He listened and easily identified the melody . . . *Peace in the Valley? How can Eddie play this song with such feeling?*

I'm tired and weary, but I must toil on . . .

That part Zeke knew Eddie understood. But if the refrain summarized the homeless man's beliefs, Zeke wished he could say the same with any degree of conviction:

. . . There will be peace in the valley for me—
No more sorrow and sadness or trouble, I pray . . .

Peace was a less frequent visitor lately in Zeke's Utah valley than Sorrow, Sadness, and Trouble.

Eddie played and no dogs howled; no neighbors shouted "Shut up, out there!" Rather, sleep soon blessed two adventurers in their haphazard accommodations. And the pensive man (who had more pressing things to contemplate than *How did Eddie get a harmonica?*) finally turned away from the window and crawled back into his bed in Bess Green's guest room.

SATURDAY

CHAPTER 25

Zeke was first-up, which made him the designated coffee-starter. He did so, relishing the quiet . . . a quiet that lasted until the kitchen door banged open in jarring whacks against the wall, shuddering on its hinges.

Pale-faced in a chenille bathrobe and wearing a crown of pink foam rollers—one dangling over her ear—Bess clung to the doorframe. "People! Dog! Camper!"

A logical explanation to calm the distraught woman demanded a lot of anyone in a pre-caffeinated state. This accurately described Zeke, so he opted for Haze's system of dodging topics: "Did you wake them up?"

Breathing hard, Bess shook her head and fumbled for a chair, gasping fragmented details: "Heard noises." The droopy hair roller now bounced to her lap, sliding unheeded to the floor. "Saw crazy dog, so went out to check." She patted her heart briskly. "Quite a scare!"

To think I had a chance to run over that critter. Zeke eyed the gurgling coffee pot with a sense of desperation. Being a gentleman, he interrupted the brewing cycle and gave Bess the first cup. Fear gripped him when she said, "The police can deal with this!" Coffee in hand, she left.

Zeke moaned, longing to be anywhere that had no alley, no camper shell, no beat-up pickup, no Eddie. This NO-NO-NO-NO quartet sang in Zeke's head like a recording stuck on replay. *Peace in the valley? In your dreams, Mister Do-Gooder.* He reached for the pot.

"It's you! I expected to see Bess. That coffee smells wonderful. Be a good son; pour some for your mother."

Zeke sighed and handed Haze his finally filled but still unsipped cup. Was he destined to go through life without ever tasting coffee again? "Here you go; poured and ready." He managed to smile as he handed it over.

She eyed him shrewdly. "Looks like you need caffeine administered by IV, not merely by the mug! What time did you get in last night?"

"Sort of late; ten-ish."

She blew across the cup's rim. "Well, our lives return to normal after this weekend. It's been extra tiring for you, flying home between signings and back to Rochester, and then driving us to the next . . . What on earth—?"

Zeke halted the stream of coffee filling his cup; drops slopped on his hand. A sense of impending doom descended as he realized precisely why Haze was suddenly silent. *The alley. Forget polite sips; this demands gulps.* He winced as coffee burned a path to his stomach, but he risked an even bigger swig. *Get it while I can.*

Haze strode to the window facing the back yard. "Why is that pickup parked in the alley?" she demanded. "It wasn't there last evening; I know that for a fact, because Bess and I sat on the porch until bugs drove us back inside. Mercy! A dog's leaping around in the truck! Now it's outside—no, it's inside again. I bet it has rabies!"

Evasion only wasted time if Haze was in hot pursuit of answers. Zeke did the calm-down hand gesture. "It's the pickup I drove to Prairie Rose." Coffee slowly cleared his mental murkiness. *I could have at least parked in front of the garage, out of view from anyone in the house. All this morning mayhem is because I didn't want to mess with the garage door. Stupid, stupid, stupid!*

"What about the dog?" She spun around. "Please say you didn't bring a rabid animal back from Prairie Rose! I'll just have to call animal control. Find a phonebook."

Stick with the truth, nothing but the truth . . . just skirt around the whole truth about what else is in the truck. "The dog lives somewhere around here," he said vaguely.

"Very strange," Haze murmured.

You ain't seen nothin' yet.

Footsteps approached. Dressed for her day, a much calmer Bess greeted them cheerfully: "G'morning Haze, and belatedly to you, too, Zeke. Breakfast is coming shortly, but before I start that, I need to take care of—"

Haze and Zeke's eyes followed her gaze as it zeroed in on the kitchen door's slowly turning knob. No banging the wall this time, only an *errkk!* Creaking hinges: a heart-stopping spook house sound. *Errkk!* Six eyes saw the door creep open as if nudged by a breeze. *Errkk!*

Feminine gasps echoed when a small hairless head peeked around the partially opened door. The eyes in that startling head were at door-knob level.

Lively eyes moved from one slack-jawed woman to her wide-eyed female companion at the table. Relief flooded those searching eyes when they landed on a familiar male face. "Hi, Mister Eden! May I use the bathroom again?"

Zeke nodded. Two gray heads swiveled. First they tracked the child's path to the half-bath; next they landed on Zeke. Unvoiced questions outshouted the burbling coffeepot.

Expecting to hear a duet of "Did he say '*again*'?" Zeke pursed his lips and waited. *Newton said, "For every action, there's a reaction." Did I really expect to escape undetected?* But parked pickups and potentially rabid dogs were long-forgotten; the implications of "again" were of no concern.

"That little boy's completely bald!" Haze blurted out, but hastily lowered her voice to a stage whisper: "Cancer! He lost his hair during chemotherapy!"

Zeke stared at his mother with mind-numbing disbelief. Before he could connect the dots from *I-see-bald* to *The-child-is-dying*, their hostess had joined the swelling madness.

But her whispered query revealed shock in a different vein: "Is *that* who I saw in the camper? I came this close"—her two fingers were definitely close—"to calling the police to arrest a sick-and-dying child?"

Zeke shook his head furiously, but neither woman noticed that, nor did they heed his urgent "He's *not*—"

Apparently The-Truth-from-Someone-Who-Knows was merely a pesky fly. Haze waved his protests away, nodding in advance agreement with her own opinions: "I bet he got that dog from the Make-a-Wish people. It's what they do, you know. They give dreadfully sick kids their hearts' desires and boys always want dogs."

Zeke tried again: "No! The dog lives across the alley. Tell her, Bess. It belongs to your neighbor with the lilac bushes, doesn't it?"

Bess wasn't worried about dogs, rabid or not. "The man in the camper could have kidnapped him and they're on the run. I'm calling the police! They'll put the poor child in a foster home until they sort things out. Meanwhile he can receive the medical attention he—"

Zeke slapped the table; cups rattled and coffee sloshed. "Calm down, both of you, and let me—"

But there'd be no calming down at Bess Green's house for a while, not with a face plastered against the window and a body casting a long shadow over the spotless kitchen floor. The women yelped in unison.

The fastest way to reach the window would have been to leap across the table. Being a mannerly fellow whose worst offense, to date, was transporting unrestrained persons in a questionably safe vehicle, Zeke settled for rounding the table at a good clip. He pushed aside the curtain, revealing the source of the alarming shadow.

Haze stared and gripped her coffee cup.

Bess stared and clamped a hand over trembling lips.

The bathroom door opened; the bald boy ignored them and greeted the shadow, "Hey, Big Eddie!" He skipped over to the window and placed his hand within the outline of the adult-sized hand pressed against the screen.

Man grinned; boy giggled; women gaped. Zeke wondered if he had never met two individuals as easily delighted with life's simple joys as Big Eddie and Justin.

"That's Eddie? *Bu-bu*-but Eddie has—" Bess stuttered, waving her hands around her head in giant squiggles resembling octopus legs. *A realistic and reasonable depiction of Eddie's former appearance*, Zeke thought.

Haze rose from the table and opened the window. "Eddie? Eddie! What happened to your . . ." *Your head? Your hair?* She did a quick self-edit: "I mean . . . to you?"

"Hey, Hazeden!" His hands cupped around both eyes and his face pasted against the screen, Eddie peered into the kitchen. "Hey, store-lady! Me 'nd Lil' Eddie look jus' like Dude. Uh-huh!"

"Lil' Eddie?" Bess and Haze chorused and faced Zeke.

He sighed; the day was heading downhill at a dizzy speed. "Mom, Bess: meet Justin Edward Larson. 'Little Eddie' is the nickname that Big Eddie," Zeke jerked his thumb at the shadowy figure in the window, "gave him."

Questions abounded, but thankfully Bess doffed the inquisitor role and donned her hostess mantle: "Come in, Eddie; I'll feed you and Justin, is it?" A toothy grin accompanied a nod. "I'll make us all a nice breakfast. Come in," she repeated when Eddie didn't move.

"Nuh-uh; out heres be my bes' thin'. B'sides, Lil' Eddie's Mama pack us real good bref-fas'. Come on, Lil' Eddie, it be almos' time for more-a our big a'venture."

Big adventure, or breakfast at a table? Adventure won. Justin lingered long enough to tell Bess politely, "Thank you for letting me use your bathroom, Ma'am."

The three remaining inside clustered at the window to watch the two alley-sleepers walk away, hand-in-hand. Justin romped with the dog that leaped out when Eddie pulled backpacks from the shell, and all three headed off.

"I'll take you up on that breakfast," Zeke said brightly, moving from his position behind the women.

Haze spun around and pinned him with a laser glare. "Not until you spill the beans, Buster! Every single bean."

Bess took her clues from Haze, though she worded it less bluntly: "You must have stories to tell, Zeke!"

Where to start? "How about if I talk while we eat? We have places to be today, you know," Zeke reminded them.

Receiving only dazed looks in response, he prodded them, "Does SOUP'S ON IN RAVEN CROWLEY'S KITCHEN ring any bells? And how about a certain clerk's job at J Co Drug?"

"Fiddle-faddle!" Haze scoffed, though she did head for the refrigerator.

It's debatable whether eggs have ever been cooked with such speed, or if barely darkened bread is considered *toasted*. But neither woman complained. They couldn't. *They*, not Zeke, interrupted the toaster's cycle; *they*, not Zeke, dished eggs before the timer chimed.

Zeke had hoped for more time to construct his narrative but, lacking that, he rambled on about meatloaf sandwiches, tire swings, and grain elevators. "Each letter of PRAIRIE appears in large letters on a separate elevator. Below the P, they painted a huge rose. The letters for ROSE go below the next four letters in PRAIRIE—"

Haze waved her fork impatiently. "Lovely, I'm sure. Skip to how Eddie got bald."

"That was Justin's doing. He bluntly told Eddie he needed a haircut, and off we went to the barbershop."

Haze gasped, "You met Frank Wilson!"

Bess was even less interested in Frank than she'd been in dogs. "You hear about people with cancer who lose their hair, and friends shave their heads to make them feel less—what's the word? It means stand-out-ish."

"Conspicuous?" Zeke suggested, wondering: *Why can't all of life be as simple as providing the right word?*

Bess found a tissue in her pocket and blew her nose. "You'd think living only thirty miles from Prairie Rose, I would know about a kid there with cancer, but I guess—"

"He doesn't have cancer!" Zeke said firmly. "Justin just wanted Frank to make him and Eddie look like me."

Zeke figured Haze's "*Humpff!*" was directed at her son, not Frank. Given his druthers, he would have run away, shrieking and pulling his hair. Good thing he was bald because shrieking without hair-pulling just wasn't the same.

CHAPTER 26

The canopy was erected again. Zeke debated sniffing the sand-filled-buckets, but decided he really didn't want to know which had served as a cat's litter box. The answer would likely become obvious as the temperature rose. The day already had enough drama and it wasn't even eight-thirty yet. He did, however, discard a cigar someone had extinguished in one of the buckets.

Haze draped the cloth and skirt on the table that Zeke had set up for her, and selected a new pink-ink pen.

Zeke hung the banner and took the tools and stepstool to the car, returning with the lawn chairs.

Together, they organized the display, making quick work of what, by now, was almost a mindless task.

Zeke had to credit Haze with great restraint. She didn't pose a single question until they were seated, awaiting their first customer on their second day in Crosby. Then it came: "How did Eddie get cleaned-up?"

It wasn't the first question Zeke expected, but it was on his mental list of *Likely to Be Asked*, so he was ready. "When Eddie goes to Prairie Rose, he bathes at Justin's house. The clean used clothing came from Luke and Cate Larson; they adopted Justin who is Eddie's son. Luke and Cate collect secondhand items between Eddie's visits, having learned his lifestyle is rough on possessions."

"And all this—the haircut, bath, clothes—happens without a squawk from Eddie?" Haze asked dubiously.

"Not a peep. All three Larsons treat him with great respect. Luke brought out a box of clothes and told Eddie to help himself. He didn't argue; in fact, he was delighted. Nothing's fancy; just basic stuff a guy needs: underwear, shoes, socks, sweatshirt, pants, shirts, a better towel."

"Good example of lending a helping hand, hmm?"

"Yes, and with sensitivity; they work around Eddie's quirks to do what they can. Justin clearly adores Eddie. For that matter, it seemed like half of Prairie Rose called out greetings to him. I was flabbergasted."

"I'm glad Eddie has benevolent people in his life."

"I like Luke and Cate, though I admit I don't completely understand them. In some ways, they remind me of Hank Bedlow. You know: doing things for others, reaching out, all without looking for anything in return."

Each Eden silently contemplated the largesse of kindness which Hank regularly bestowed on their family when he visited Gull in prison. Zeke had not been to China, or the moon, or the bottom of the ocean—but each seemed more doable than trekking from Milford to Draper, Utah, to visit his imprisoned brother.

Zeke cleared his throat and said briskly, "Luke's wise and humorous, and Cate's full of spunk and ambition. Not sure how Eddie found them, but it's a good match."

A car swung into a parking space; doors slammed; two couples exited, ending private conversation for a while for the authors beneath the canopy.

Eddie brought Justin by for a soup sample just as Zeke was bagging their first customer's purchase. But samples were delayed until after they settled one detail: "Tha' red stuff ya ga' me yes-t'day? It don' gots no booze innit, righ'?"

"No booze," Zeke assured him solemnly. "Only fruit."

Eddie leaned down to Justin's eye-level. "Lil' Eddie, ya won' get drunk; it *tas'* like jug wine, but it not."

But it was a moot point. Not because Justin lacked experience with jug wine on which to base a comparison, but because the day's samples didn't include "red stuff."

Justin did, however, give a two-thumbs-up rating to dessert soups. "I'll tell Mama to make this one next out of your cookbook! Thank you for the samples, Ma'am."

Haze beamed. "You're welcome, Justin."

Eddie's verdict? "Tas' good, but ain't soup. Nuh-uh."

"What a polite child!" Haze said, after sending Justin and Eddie off with bottled water and warnings to "Drink it before you get thirsty or you'll get dehydrated."

Zeke grinned. "What makes you think they know the meaning of dehydrated?"

"Are you making fun of me?"

"No, Ma'am."

"Yes, you are. You're impertinent."

"How come when Justin calls you 'Ma'am,' he's polite and when I do, I'm impertinent?"

"Because he's a cute little bald boy."

"Am I a cute big bald guy?"

"*Pfffttt.*"

Announcing its first trip to Main Street with clanging bell, The Goose deposited a gaggle of shoppers by the canopy. But for Zeke and Haze today, the excitement of telling customers about SOUP'S ON IN RAVEN CROWLEY'S KITCHEN took a back seat to discussing the Eddie-Justin-Luke-Cate drama and Hélène/Helen-Frank-Blyss tragedy.

Customers slacked off during the parade, giving Haze, Bess, and Zeke time to talk while machinery rumbled and rolled slowly past the canopy. After the umpteenth smoke-belching tractor passed, Bess said, "I'll go buy treats for us—that'll make this even more fun!" *Even more?* Zeke forced a smile, but didn't comment.

To Zeke's relief, the parade was more than a continuous line of farm machinery and classic cars. Massive draft horses pulled buggies filled with waving dignitaries. Convertibles bore smiling Threshing Show officials, all introduced by the witty announcer sitting on a grandstand opposite the canopy and high above Main Street's parade-watchers. Bess said similar stands and loudspeakers were scattered along the route and at the parade's beginning point out at Pioneer Village.

To Zeke's surprise, Sparky's mysterious duty involved horseflesh. He was one of the hat-tossing, cowboy-booted humans astride an impressive line of curried-to-a-shine horses.   Riders clad in leather and fringes galore kept their steeds prancing in stately formation.

Sparky always caught up with the others after he and his coal-black stallion zigzagged the parade route.   The picturesque partners played their role with flair, posing dramatically so people could photograph or video them.

Several dozen horseback riders of all ages—riding mares and geldings, stallions and ponies, yearlings, colts, and fillies—offered a welcome respite (for Zeke, at least) from engines.   Details about each horse-and-human pair filled the announcer's patter, which also included personal comments:

"Hey, Sally!   Show us what that lasso of yours can do!"   To the crowd's amusement, the teen obliged by skillfully roping a can of Pepsi off the announcer's stand.

Or he teased, "Paul, did your horse stomp on your hat?"   The man flicked an invisible speck of dust off the unspoiled hat (obviously it had never been near any animal's hoof) while his horse whinnied loudly as if also taking offense at such a comment.

Midst all the joshing, the announcer didn't forget education was part of his responsibilities.   He identified standard gaits as the horses demonstrated walks, trots, and canters.   An impressive out-and-back gallop garnered loud applause and ear-piercing whistles.

Barrels quickly set up in the middle of the street allowed for a mini-rodeo performance.   The announcer concluded the outstanding exhibition with an invitation for all to come out to the Pioneer Village grounds to see the complete rodeo later on.   After adding her vote of approval—"The rodeo is good entertainment for all ages"— Bess headed off for a second round of treats: popcorn.

Zeke wondered if Eddie and Justin would enjoy seeing the rodeo. He decided since he was interested, they likely would be, too.   It seemed like a way to spend time watching two people he wanted to observe without appearing to be doing so. He would definitely ask.

CHAPTER 27

Other horses and riders moved along, but Sparky had spotted the canopy. He dramatically reined in his horse next to the curb. Holding cowboy hat over his heart, he bowed low in the saddle. "Hel-*lo*, pretty angel-gal! I mean no disrespect, little honey; just speaking from my heart." *Tap-tap*: His cane against the canopy pole sounded like gunshots to the startled female author.

She cast frantic glances at Zeke who, despite knowing he courted danger, perkily hummed a few bars of *"Hello my baby, hello my honey, hello my ragtime gal . . ."* under his breath.

But not so softly Haze didn't hear. She heard him just fine. A warning growl rumbled in her throat.

"Sparky Johnson. Widower: ten lonely years." *Tap-tap.* "What's your story, Sweet One?"

Haze sucked in her breath. Zeke said quickly, "Mom, this is the fine gentleman who gave me a tour of Pioneer Village. Sparky, meet Widow Haze Eden: two years." Zeke found wicked pleasure in reducing Haze to stunned silence, all the time knowing that if looks killed, he'd be flopping on the ground, breathing his last.

"Will you join me for a cold beverage after the parade, Widow Eden? I'll heft you up here on Midnight," he patted the stallion's wide, shining flanks, "and find us a hay bale where we can hunker down to get acquainted."

Widow Eden kicked the now-whistling Zeke *("Oh baby, telephone and tell me I'm your own . . .")* under the table. It didn't hurt; his prosthesis took the hit.

Sparky viewed Haze's mute stare as acceptance. "Later, angel-gal!" *Tap-tap.* Midnight tossed his beautiful head, reared up in a display of strength and power, and carried his hat-waving rider off in pursuit of the others.

Haze backed up to her chair and sank down. For the first time in any book-signing event for SOUP'S ON IN RAVEN CROWLEY'S KITCHEN, Zeke handled customers for a full ten minutes without any assistance from his co-author.

She sat, eyes closed; occasionally she opened her lips as if to speak, but snapped them shut without releasing a word. Customers and passersby probably assumed she had felt faint and accepted a place to sit out of the sun.

"Mom?" Zeke finally prodded her. "Do you need CPR?"

"No!" Haze regained her hold on feisty. "What I need is a son who will rescue me from people like that . . ." her eyes flashed like a firework display, "*that infuriating man*!"

"Sparky? He's not infuriating, he's friendly. Wow; just think: a horseback ride! Sharing a hay-bale with a handsome widower who calls you 'pretty angel-gal'! What fond warm memories to savor during cold winter months."

Haze snorted.

Not unlike Midnight, Zeke decided, but knew better than to mention it.

"How *dare* you call me 'Widow Haze Eden'? I expect more respect from you!"

"You *are* a widow. Can't have Sparky thinking he's invited a loose woman to ride behind him, right? You know: a hussy like Blyss," he added with faux concern.

Bess returned with popcorn to hear Zeke singing boldly, "If you refuse me, Honey, you'll lose me . . ." and witness Haze whack his shoulder with one good swat.

Luckily the treat was so tantalizing that Haze ceased-and-desisted in her attack, though she did haul her chair as far away from Zeke as the canopy's shade allowed. *Mad at Zeke?* Yes. *Glistening more than necessary?* Not if she could help it. A woman should look her best, though she had no intention of going anywhere with Sparky. *What a crude man! Hefting and hay bales, indeed!*

The Harmonica Band's lively tune as they passed by offered welcome relief from things that went *clink* and *clank* or snorted *"neigh"* and *"whinny."* Yet, it failed to erase uncomfortable thoughts roaming Haze's mind . . . thoughts of hay bales that wouldn't stay relegated to the dark corner to which she had mentally kicked them.

Trying to remember the Band's song title occupied Bess and Haze for at least ten minutes. They hummed bits and pieces, hazarding and dismissing guesses until Bess announced triumphantly, "I've got it: 'The Wabash Cannonball'!"

Zeke jerked. *Cannonball!* Thoughts of *ammo, Quilt Blocks, Haze confronting Hélène* returned with a vengeance. With all the hoopla of getting Eddie to Prairie Rose, Justin and Eddie in the camper overnight, and Sparky-come-a-courting, Hélène had almost slipped off Zeke's radar.

Thankfully, he mused, *the Find-a-Normal-Life Crusade hasn't been mentioned today. Make it one more day and this whole weird chapter of our lives will be over.* Now that was a plan with a single, very feasible bullet:

- Survive one day

How hard could it be? He smiled ruefully, hearing Sage's predictable: *"Uh-uh-uh, Zeke! Don't ask; the answer to that question is never one we like."*

Zeke took care of sales, letting Bess and Haze visit leisurely while the parade began its second time around. When the horses reappeared, the announcer quizzed the crowd. They called out answers which they got right because they knew horses (probably true of anyone growing up on a farm) or they had excellent recall from the parade's first-time-around lessons. Correct answers like "It's a colt!" or "That's cantering!" received the announcer's praise and scattered clapping from those sitting on lawn chairs or perched on pickups' tailgates.

Unfortunately Haze missed her chance to test her memory. At the first sound of horses' clomping feet, she made a beeline for J Co Drug where she hid until the last mane had been tossed, the last horsetail had flicked off flies, and Midnight had carried Sparky Johnson far away.

Haze returned in time to hear The Harmonica Band come by, now playing "Do Lord." Under the canopy, the women broke into an impromptu songfest which Zeke refused to join, despite their calling him a 'spoil-sport':

I've got a home in gloryland that outshines the sun . . .

Zeke's mind wandered in keeping with the song's opening words: *Based on Eddie's questions about owning a home, he must long for one. Don't we all? Wanting a place to call 'home' is an intrinsic part of human nature . . .*

He had no idea how to pursue that discussion without insulting Eddie, but he wished it were possible. The thought of being homeless intrigued, but mostly saddened him. Eddie might be the only homeless person he would ever meet. *And the only one whose word on my character opens doors!* To have a chance to really talk to Eddie about things that matter? It seemed a shame to waste an opportunity . . . *Not that there'll likely be one.*

When he tuned back into the desultory conversation under the canopy, it was as if Bess was privy to the key person in his ruminations. She said, "I think it's amazing how different Eddie is when he's around Justin. Much calmer. It's as if he's more . . . I don't know, *grounded*, I guess, is the best way to put it."

Haze said, "I know what you mean; it seems almost like a physical transformation. He's not nearly as jittery or jumpy or whatever his problem is. Remarkable, isn't it? What's that saying, 'A little child shall lead them'?"

"More than a pithy quote, Mom; it's downright Biblical. Something about lions and lambs. I'd have to Google it to be sure. But I agree: Justin changes Eddie." He fell silent; a phrase in Eddie's "Peace in the Valley" lullaby flitted just beyond reach; something like *". . . and I'll be changed from the creature I am . . ."*

"More like transforms, not just changes," Haze countered. Zeke let her have the last word because he couldn't improve on her assessment. A wise man doesn't argue with his mother, or the Bible.

CHAPTER 28

Zeke and Haze didn't see Eddie and Justin for the remainder of the day. But did that mean they weren't close by? Hardly.

Late in the afternoon, two figures crept along the alley and stealthily climbed the steps behind Quilt Blocks. At the top, they knocked: two fists, striking as one.

The door opened slowly.

The startled occupant looked at her uninvited visitors. She mouthed a silent "Oh my!" while staring from a pint-sized boy to his adult companion. "What happened to you?" she demanded of the man.

"We don' gots head cancer; our heads jus' burn sumpthin' awful. Do ya gots sum beauty-shop stuff to stop the itches?" He leaned close to whisper, "I ain't never say'd nuttin b'fore, but I knows who ya be—"

Hélène blanched and ordered in a raw voice as she pointed inside, "Come in, and don't say another word!"

"Nuh-uh; we sits onna steps, righ' here."

"If you want my help, you come in," Hélène said firmly, still pointing.

The boy reached for the man's hand and whispered, "It'll be okay, Big Eddie. Pretend we're in my house."

Eddie stiffened, but he followed the boy inside.

Hélène dragged a box from beneath the bed and took out a tube and a bottle. Her hand trembled as she read labels. "Who did this to you?" she demanded. Having seen Eddie recently, she knew the damage was fresh. She shook the bottle with excessive force. "Who shaved you bald and then sent you off with no sun-protection?"

Eddie clamped his lips shut, but the lad (completely missing his adult buddy's frantic signals) said, "It was Mister Wilson; he's a barber in Prairie Rose, Ma'am."

Hélène gasped and threw the unopened tube at the bed. It hit the wall, bounced off the mattress, and then slithered along the floor. "That greedy devil!"

Keeping an understandably wary eye on Hélène, the boy quickly retrieved the tube and handed it back to her. "Here, Ma'am. Please don't be mad at Mister Wilson. He didn't know we were going to be in the sun all day."

Hélène snorted and resumed shaking the bottle until she was calmer, though still obviously upset. "You first, Eddie." She motioned him toward the solitary chair at the table. If the boy watching from nearby wondered how this disturbed stranger knew Big Eddie, he didn't ask.

Despite churning anger, her touch was gentle as she used damp soft cloths to clean and spread salve on two stinging, red-hot heads. "Can you sleep sitting up so the lotion won't rub off? I'll give you the bottle. Whenever your heads feel dry, put more on. But," she warned, "wash your hands first, with soap and hot water," though she wondered if such were even possible.

"Thank you, Ma'am," the boy said. "It feels better."

Hélène smiled sadly, but it was a smile. "What's your name?" she asked gently. Now that she was somewhat more composed, she wondered what Eddie was doing with a child in-tow. *And a boy who knows Frank . . .?*

"Justin Edward Larson, Ma'am. I live in Prairie Rose."

Hélène sucked in her breath. Fear filled her eyes.

"Wha' he say'd be right, but I calls him Lil' Eddie. Luke 'nd Cate Larson be his mama 'nd daddy nows."

Eddie's next actions showed an awareness that would have impressed Hélène had she not panicked. He stooped to Justin's eye-level and said, "Lil' Eddie, we jus' gonna tells yer mama 'nd daddy a nice lady fix't our heads, hokey-dokey? We don' tells no names. Nuh-uh."

Justin said, "Sure," not mentioning the obvious: he didn't know the nice lady's name. Eddie glanced quickly at Hélène, as if asking, *"Okay?"* Nodding jerkily, she relaxed for the first time since she'd answered her door.

CHAPTER 29

When she was alone again, The Frets launched an all-out attack on Hélène.   If Eddie recognized her (and she knew that was what he would have said, had she not cut him off) her secret was, well, not such a secret, after all.

Questions droned in her mind like hornets:

How have I been so naïve as to think I can live a mere thirty miles from heartbreak without having it find me again? She chewed a knuckle until it hurt.

Does Frank know I live in Crosby?   And if he does, does he also know where? She paced, tripping on a rug.

Is word out that a phony works at Quilt Blocks?   Am I a laughingstock? She sat, but soon sprang up again.

Do others know I'm Helen Wilson: Frank's clueless-she's-been-betrayed-until-it's-too-late wife? A sigh.

If Eddie actually is *the only one who knows my true identity, can I trust him to keep my secret?   Or has that horse already left the barn?* A quivery moan escaped.

Hearing familiar names like Luke and Cate Larson roll off Eddie's tongue had pierced her soul.   She missed Prairie Rose . . .   Even more, she missed having friends. She could hardly think about them without tears forming:

Al and Joy Jenkins—best friends during our marriages, yet now I hide when I see them in town. The pain of seeing their happiness still intact is too much to bear.

Pastor Tori.   I miss her sermons.   Listening to services on the radio just isn't the same as sitting in a pew, mingling my voice with others on hymns, feeling God's touch in a handshake or hug. Tears burned her eyelids.

Doctor Alex.   I haven't been to a doctor since I left Prairie Rose.   That's not smart, but what if they asked for medical records? Thankfully, I've stayed healthy.

I even miss busy-body Sadie O'Dell, God bless her.

Hélène's conversation with Haze had been a poignant reminder of the hole that running away from friends and neighbors had carved in her life. Loss, loneliness, and isolation loomed even larger after Eddie's alarming visit.

And not just lost friends and neighbors. Family, too. Daughters: once beloved, now estranged because they felt guilty picking sides. *Their dad commits adultery and they call it "picking sides" if they visit me and not him? Their heartbreaking decision says they believe I share Frank's blame for the demise of what they call "Life Before It All Fell Apart."* She pounded fist against palm.

Had she contributed to the death of their marriage? Why couldn't—or wouldn't—someone tell her what went wrong? *Didn't I love Frank enough? Even if I was no longer the carefree skinny-Minnie he married, is that justification for what he did? He's not the jovial, honest, hard-working guy I thought I married, either.* She squared her jaw.

Is it right for my girls to treat me like a deadly virus, sure to take them down with me? Her shoulders sagged.

All the sporting events attended to see Tina perform! All those sweaty uniforms washed in time to get dirty again. Countless pans of brownies made for bake sales. Subscriptions to magazines no one read, all bought to fill quotas. How many hours of Robyn's practicing had she endured?   How many evenings spent fidgeting on uncomfortable chairs at piano recitals or band concerts?

It was what a loving mother did, and Hélène had happily done it all. She had invested her life in her daughters. Now those daughters didn't want to see her. The siblings co-owned a bakery in Minot to which Hélène's last visit had proved so upsetting to all three Wilson women that she had not returned.

At least not to walk through the door.

Several times over the years she parked her nondescript car and stood watching from across the street. Had they missed her, thought about her, tried to find her after she'd fled across the border to Canada?

The purpose of what became that final visit had been to tell Tina and Robyn her new name. She'd found them in the bakery office, putting together a bid on a wedding cake. She had planned to treat them to lunch if they had anyone working who could fill in, but the idea fizzled when they started criticizing her disappearance from Prairie Rose on that bleakest of nights long ago.

When they saw her in the office doorway, there had been no *"Look, it's Mom!"* or *"Are you okay, Mom?"* or *"We miss you, Mom!"* And not a single *"Let me hug you, Mom."*

No, it was: "If you loved us, Mom, you'd do thus-and-so . . ." and "Other parents who divorce live in the same town, why can't you and Dad?" and "When we get married, will you refuse to come to our weddings if Dad walks us down the aisle?"

The ultimately shockers were "Do you want to be a grandmother who doesn't know her grandkids?" from Tina, followed by Robyn's "She's right; when we have kids, we want you and Dad getting along with each other so we won't have to explain nasty things to our children."

Maybe it was the idea of a wedding cake—an all-too-significant reminder of what happens when there's no more *happy* left as a marriage fades into history. If Robyn had been frosting cookies, or if Tina had been working hard to get a jellyroll to roll (a joke from back when they all still laughed together). If all that . . . could the Wilson women have shared lunch and stayed friends?

Their attitudes and accusations so traumatized Hélène she could only sputter. Any self-defense she made, they poo-poo'd and rolled their eyes. She felt dizzy, but willed herself to stay upright. If she fainted, there was no guarantee either daughter would do more than step over (hopefully not stomp) her on their way to sell pastries.

Thankfully she had left the bakery without visible bruises. Was she frustrated, fearful, and furious? Yes, also but she was also unaware it would be the last time she saw her daughters for the unforeseeable future.

Knowing *that* would have done her in even more than the shock she had endured.

Driving away that day with tears streaming down her face, she chided herself for assuming the girls would consider her new name clever. She had envisioned lively smiles on Tina's face, and appreciative nods from the quieter Robyn. *But they didn't even wave goodbye . . .*

Tina and Robyn not only didn't know her pseudonym, they were also unaware Hélène no longer lived in Canada, but in Crosby. To think she had risked moving a mere two hours away, naïvely believing that, by being closer, she could salvage the shaky relationship with her girls.

Two hours: the length of a movie.

Two hours: the time required to cook a pot roast.

Two hours: a volleyball game on the scoreboard.

Two hours: time allotted for church and Sunday School.

Two hours: a dishwasher cycle.

Two hours fly by if fun is involved, or when something is being accomplished.

Two hours literally *loom*, like storm clouds, when only harsh words wait at the far end of the time-frame: words that breed certain sadness, unutterable grief, blinding anger, and deepening loneliness.

Two hours: the measurable distance across which pieces of a Mother's broken heart can scatter.

Rage choked Hélène as she sat in her apartment, weighed by heavy thoughts and burdensome memories. But the years had taught her one safe way to survive an emotional flood: think harshly about Frank. Armed with new ammunition against him, this proved easy. She rose, no longer defeated but empowered by her anger.

"You are one colossal jerk, Frank Wilson! Did you even think about how sensitive Eddie's skin is from poor hygiene and an inadequate diet? Did you pay one bit of attention to his obvious head-sores and insect bites when you shaved him down to nothing but scalp?"

Stomp, stomp.

"So, Frank: What pathetic excuse will you give when you have to explain to Luke and Cate why Justin is burning up with sun-fever? He could end up one very sick little boy, but do you care? Oh no; not you! Not as long as a body in the barber chair means money in the till."

Stomp, stomp.

Good thing Quilt Blocks was closed. She knew the ceiling lights were probably swaying like a circus trapeze down there.

Stomp, stomp.

"Yes, Frank, Eddie's hair was filthy and germy and gross. But you thought it was too much work, too nasty a job to check his scalp for sores, didn't you? Giving him a decent haircut that would allow some protection against the elements didn't fit your time schedule, did it?"

Stomp! Stomp-stomp-stomp.

It felt good to tell Frank off. In fact, so good that Hélène broke the primary rule she had lived by since driving away from Prairie Rose the night she severed all ties to her old life. First, she thought it: *I should go to Prairie Rose and tell Frank off in person.* Then, she said it out loud: "I will! I'm going to Prairie Rose, and I'll look that man in his shifty eyes and let him have it, big-time."

That thought, blowing in from thin air, was so staggering it momentarily knocked the wind out of Hélène's sails. Hearing herself vocalize the thought left her lightheaded. She floundered to the bed and lay down, listening to her pulse pound as erratically as one loose shingle on her former garden shed had in a windstorm.

Her neck throbbed, she touched it gingerly. There, too, her pulse raced. "Frank Wilson, so help me, if I die from a heart attack, I'll never speak to you again!"

A moment passed.

A quavering smile briefly crossed her lips as she realized the absurdity of what she had just uttered. Laughter, beginning as a wild mirthless sound, eventually ended in gulping, exhausting sobs.

Feeling ancient, she swung her legs off the bed, sat for a moment, then slowly stood and walked outside to the landing Eddie and Justin had so recently occupied. No residual odors, which were Eddie's usual trademark, lingered there. "Eddie did look cleaner," she murmured. "Not so raggedy." She sank down on the top step.

If Eddie can change, maybe Frank could, too, she mused, though she hated to let an ounce of hope push a pound of anger off the scale. Anger carried so long had formed clinging tentacles, making it hard to release.

An hour passed while she sat. *Eddie won't be clean for long; he returns to a life where cleanliness is impossible,* she realized sadly. As nervous as he made her, seeming to see right through the barriers she erected against the world, she still wished he had a better life.

Thoughts raced. *Even if Frank changed outwardly, he'd be the same fickle, deceitful Frank inside. And with Blyss still hanging around Prairie Rose, there's no telling what his secret desires really are, or if he acts on them.*

"I want just one conversation with you, Frank Wilson," she said grimly. In the distance, happy sounds from the Threshing Show's evening activities countered her dark and racing thoughts. She rubbed her arms rapidly, feeling chilled despite the day's lingering warmth.

Wiping her eyes with both palms, she said in a voice steely with resolve: "I want to hear you try to justify two thoughtless haircuts. It's one thing for you to ruin my life, Frank, but to make Justin and Eddie suffer? That's inexcusable. I plan to tell you so before this night ends."

Silently, she plotted her strategy: she would begin with his ineptness as a barber and insensitivity toward innocent children and those—like Eddie—whom society ignores or disdains. Next . . . no, there'd be no *next*; she didn't want Frank to think she was looking to reconcile.

For one conversation—one in which she would speak up for those who couldn't—Hélène would give Helen a voice.

CHAPTER 30

"Hey, Dude! Me 'nd Lil' Eddie be ready to go."

Zeke was crouched beside the table, collapsing empty boxes, when Eddie's voice rolled over him. *Right; and I promised Luke and Cate I'd drive you back to Prairie Rose.*

He stood. He gawked. He sucked in air so fast that his nose burned.

Two creatures from a Sci-Fi movie faced him: blood-red scalps dotted with clotting white cream covering blisters. "Living Dead" in the movie title would be fitting.

And I'm among the living dead when Cate and Luke get their hands on me. Until I rolled into Prairie Rose, their son had hair; he showed no signs of molting. Now he looks like a victim of "head cancer." And Eddie looks even worse.

Pricks midst the non-creamed sections on Eddie's head showed evidence of bites. Zeke made a mental note to burn the blanket, rug, and pillow in the camper.

All thoughts of seeing the rodeo evaporated.

"I can't leave yet, but here," he grabbed a five dollar bill from the cash box and thrust it at Eddie. "Go buy cold drinks at a food-stand. Treats, too. Spend it all!"

"Hokey-dokey!" Eddie grinned. "Come on, Lil' Eddie."

"*They* look terrible, but are *you* okay?" Haze asked.

Deep gargling noises weren't much of an answer.

Half an hour later, Haze poked Zeke and jerked her head toward the shady end of the block. There Eddie and Justin sat, sipping drinks and reading. Seeing the short stack of books beside them (*From Justin's bookshelf at home?*) Zeke recalled Eddie's admission: "I don' reads good." That memory—mingled with marveling that an eight-year-old actually had packed books for his "big adventure"—gave Zeke plenty to think about besides sunburned heads as he boxed unsold books.

Bits and pieces of the story in Justin's expressive voice and Eddie's slower echo floated over to Zeke while he dismantled the canopy:

"We looked and we saw him—the Cat in the Hat!"

They had a system: Justin read first and Eddie reread the same page. Justin either nodded approvingly or merely corrected his willing pupil. No mispronunciation was allowed under the youngster's tutelage.

Though Justin was likely beyond the readability level of Dr Seuss books, somehow he sensed Eddie's limited skills and adapted himself without making the man feel ill-at-ease. Justin Edward Larson was rapidly rising to the status of Zeke's first eight-year-old hero.

All the way to Prairie Rose in the beat-up pickup and not-much-better camper, Justin and Eddie talked. Zeke wished he could hear more of the constant chatter about whiskers, candy, belts, and the alley dog they had, at some point, named Doggy-Woggy.

And they read. The supply of books in Justin's pack was limited, but Eddie didn't mind repeats. Zeke heard him say on a rerun of CAT IN THE HAT, "It jus' like this story, Lil' Eddie, so 'member wha' we say to yer mama 'nd daddy." With nearly perfect pronunciation, Eddie read slowly:

Then our mother came in and she said to us two,
"Did you have any fun? Tell me. What did you do?"

In the rearview mirror, Zeke watched Justin nod approvingly. Then the boy gamely recited the prescribed response: "A nice lady gave us lotion for our heads. I don't know her name."

"Tha' be good. It ain't lying, cuz ya dinn't know Helen—" Eddie yelped. "Now I done ruint it all! Cover yer ears, Lil' Eddie, like ya dinn't hear'd wha' I say'd!"

Justin obeyed, but Zeke heard him protest: "It doesn't matter, Big Eddie. I don't know anyone named Helen."

Of course not, Zeke reflected. *You were probably just a toddler when Helen left Frank Wilson and Prairie Rose.*

CHAPTER 31

Zeke figured that Eddie teaching Justin "Ninety-nine Bottles of Beer on the Wall" was a minor offense compared to the transgression that he (the allegedly responsible adult in the threesome heading to Prairie Rose) had committed. He had no defense for delivering a child back to his parents in such a frightening condition.

"But you didn't think about sunburn, either, Luke, when you tossed Eddie's I'M-FAR-FROM-NORMAL cap and didn't replace it! And you could've packed a hat for Justin. That's more important than snacks, Cate!" Wind whipped his puny self-defense away like the fluff it was.

Eddie's face (freckles more noticeable with it so clean) popped up in the window. "Ya say'd sumpthin', Dude?"

"Just talking to myself."

Eddie grinned; the singing resumed: "Seventy-four bottles of beer on the wall . . ."

"At least somebody's having fun," Zeke grumbled, though he voiced his complaint at a less audible pitch.

Luke and Cate called greetings, leaping off the porch when the pickup jerked to a stop. Zeke steeled himself for stern remonstrations and frantic exclamations.

Neither came. Only laughter and joy at reuniting.

Cate hugged her lotion-spackled, blistered son. "You had a grand time on your big adventure, didn't you?"

Justin rattled off activities, seemingly without taking a breath: "I found a dollar when I played Money in the Straw! . . . A *girl* won the Pedal Tractor Pull, Mama! . . . We watched a man make boards out of a log . . . Did you ever see a blacksmith, Daddy? Fire gets real close to their faces and they don't die because they wear masks, but not like my Halloween costume's monster mask . . . I ate three foot-long hotdogs with everything, even onions!"

Luke draped an arm over Eddie's shoulders. "I'm glad you and this excited little guy and your gracious driver," he saluted Zeke, "are in time for supper. Come help me decide if the coals are ready for grilling hamburgers."

That news outweighed any stories of the day. "Hamburgers!" Justin crowed. "Come on, Mister Eden! Daddy makes the best hamburgers in the whole world!"

With self-deprecating humor, Luke said, "No doubt you've read countless articles naming me the winner in that contest, Zeke. Maybe caught it on the nightly news?"

"Yeah; your face was everywhere, man! Weren't you the cover story on TIME MAGAZINE? Hot stuff," Zeke joked, but thought: *Don't you see an eerie resemblance between your son and the red-hot charcoal we're going to check?*

Cate's whole face mirrored her laugh. "You'd better judge Luke's talents yourself! Can you stay for supper?"

"You don't need to feed me two nights in a row," Zeke protested, though not very hard.

"Two rides; two suppers," she quipped. "Come on; your job is cut the watermelon."

"Watermelon!" Justin pumped Eddie's arm. "We love watermelon, don't we, Big Eddie?"

"Can we spit seeds?" Eddie asked Cate hopefully.

"Only if you sit off the porch to do it. I thought I'd never get the seeds cleaned up last time!" she responded.

Zeke was now fully mystified. *What kind of mother ignores sunburn, but has rules about seed-spitting?*

The hamburgers truly merited awards. "Start with good meat" was the only secret Luke revealed. Cate's potato salad led to a discussion of herbs. The watermelon was so good Zeke didn't argue when Luke offered him a second piece even more generous than the first.

Seed-spitting done (and all seeds that didn't quite make it past lips and off the porch steps hosed away) Justin and Eddie headed off on a secretive errand which Eddie insisted needed doing without further delay. "Don' ya be leavin' b'fore we gets back, hokey-dokey, Dude?"

Zeke was secretly glad for any reason which could prolong his time in Prairie Rose, especially when it provided a chance to talk privately with Luke and Cate.

When they were alone on the porch, Zeke faced his hosts and said humbly, "I'm so sorry I didn't take better care of Justin. His head—"

Luke cut in: "Not your fault, Zeke. In fact, Cate and I realized too late we'd sent Eddie and Justin off without sunscreen or caps. I'm sure it looks worse than it is. At least you got ointment for them."

"Wish I could take the credit for it," Zeke said ruefully, "but I have no idea what they used." Having heard Eddie's instructions to Justin about the "nice lady," he decided to let them tell what needed to be told.

"Enough about sunburn," Cate insisted. "We can take care of Justin and Eddie at bedtime, and if anything's needed, we'll give Doctor Alex a call. Meanwhile, since I have the chance, I'd rather talk about soup!"

And so they did, right up to the moment Eddie and Justin returned, giddy and whispering. Zeke was relieved to see that their heads seemed less vivid. It was likely a trick of fading light, but it gave his conscience a much-needed reprieve from self-incrimination not to see blazing scalps. He could only hope Eddie and Justin came through the experience without shedding their skin like the snakes that lived in his Utah woodpile.

"Okay, Dude," Eddie said. "I be ready to go to Crosby."

Zeke's eyes widened. "Crosby? Really?"

Even Luke looked puzzled. "Are you sure you can't stay here longer, Eddie? We've hardly had time to visit."

Cate quickly added, "Luke's right, Eddie. Please stay a few more days! The nights are warm enough to sleep here on the hammock. Oh, and Justin can bring a cot out to the porch; it'll be another adventure for you two!"

Surprisingly, Justin didn't seem at all concerned about Eddie's abrupt departure. A cat spitting out canary feathers couldn't have looked any more self-satisfied than that little boy did as he hugged Eddie.

Zeke couldn't come up with any socially acceptable reason to further delay his departure, and Eddie seemed antsy to get going, so they all headed to the pickup.

"See ya, Lil' Eddie," Eddie said, winking at Justin as Zeke secured the unreliable camper door.

"See you, Big Eddie!" was Justin's so-casual rejoinder. His attempted return-wink was more of a two-eyed blink.

Luke struck out his hand. Zeke shook it, murmuring, "Wish I knew what those two are up to."

"You grill Eddie; we'll tighten the screws on Justin until he squeals. You've got our phone number, so call if you learn anything we ought to know about."

"Hope it doesn't involve Justin hopping trains!"

Luke chuckled. "Now that'd be some big adventure, huh? Whatever they saw at the Threshing Show today would be small potatoes, comparatively speaking."

I have my instructions to grill Eddie, Zeke told himself as he turned the corner. *No reason to delay.* He waited until Eddie had ceased calling greetings through the windows, and the seven silos disappeared from sight in the rearview mirror. He kept his speed low enough that the wind didn't whistle so loudly he would need to yell. "Where'd you and Justin go after supper, Eddie?"

"Walkin'."

"I *know* that. Where'd you go?"

"Places."

Arrgghh! Two calming breaths, then: "Justin seemed pretty happy when you two got back to the house. I thought he'd be sad about you leaving so soon."

Employing a Haze-worthy hedge, Eddie said, "He be happy boy 'most alla times." Silence. A zipper unzipped. A drawn-out note on a harmonica. *The lullaby harmonica.*

Eddie played "Home on the Range" so many times that Zeke lost count. The note for *hoooome* lingered whenever the word appeared in the lyrics. For each repetition, it stretched as long as Eddie could hold his breath.

Finally Zeke interrupted Eddie's one-song concert. "Where'd you get your harmonica?"

"Lil' Eddie ga' me Cris-a-mus gif' long times ago."

What a perfect present. Portable, compact, entertaining. His awe of all-things-Larson bumped up another notch. "Did you see The Harmonica Band in the parade today?"

"Uh-huh." A pause. "They be railroad dudes, huh?"

"Guess so." Zeke caught Eddie's frown in the mirror. "Does that bother you?"

"Nuh-uh; not no mores," Eddie said emphatically.

Zeke eyebrows arrowed. *Bess told Mom that he rides the rails between Chicago and Crosby. So how does "not no more" fit with getting back to Union Station?* "Why do you say that?"

"Don' wanna talk bout tha'. Do yer house be big?"

Talk about non sequiturs! No more talk about harmonicas, and forget trains—I know: let's discuss houses! "It's two little houses joined together, but no, it's not big compared to some homes." He avoided explaining the central arboretum, which was open to the sky and connected the two formerly separate dwellings.

The wind had increased, but Zeke easily heard Eddie's shouted question: "A real house cost lotta money, huh?"

How to explain *matter of perspective* across economic chasms between a homeless man and a successful writer whose wife also had a high-paying profession? "Well," Zeke raised his voice against the wind, "there are expenses like electricity and insurance and upkeep . . ."

Fog cleared; realization dawned: *Eddie wants a home.* "Home, home on the range . . ." *A place where he can relax without constant worries about his possessions being stolen or getting wet. The essence of "private privacy." Oh, Eddie, you need more realistic dreams!*

They drove in silence for a quarter-mile as Zeke pulled his thoughts together. *Owning a home isn't an option for*

Eddie, unless his playing pauper is a façade. But I sense it is fact. Cate and Luke would know, and they trust him. Okay; he can't own, but maybe he could rent. Eddie's getting to me, Zeke ruefully admitted. Again he heard Haze's voice: *". . . he needs you, Zeke."*

"Renting can cost less than owning," he yelled. "Sometimes a landlord pays some of the expenses; sometimes it's part of the rent. But sometimes even a renter has to pay everything, like a home owner does."

Eddie pursed his lips and nodded. Clearly, whatever he was thinking would remain his *private privacy*.

"Where do you want me to drop you off, Eddie?" Zeke finally asked, expecting directions to a curve that Eddie knew from previous trips . . . somewhere along the road where a train slowed enough for a fellow to hop on.

"Main Street," Eddie said succinctly.

So that's what Zeke did. He dropped his passenger right outside J Co Drug. Zeke fussed with this-and-that inside the truck. Nothing in the ashtray. The cigarette lighter didn't work: surprise, surprise. The glove box contained a pair of gloves—now that *was* a surprise.

Finally he realized Eddie had no intention of deserting his odd version of hopscotch (which required no chalk, only a rock he tossed along the sidewalk) which he played while he kept an eye on malingering Zeke. Eddie wouldn't head for wherever he really intended to be until Zeke and the pickup left the scene. So Zeke left.

Sort-of left. Feeling like a cheat, he slowly circled the block, knowing Eddie didn't welcome intrusions. That's what Zeke was: an intruder on Eddie's private privacy.

He was no better than a Peeping Tom; he just substituted furtively turning corners for peering into windows. When he returned to Main Street, Eddie had disappeared with all his privacy still private.

Zeke drove to Bess Green's house knowing more about the inside of her brother's pickup than he did about what was going on inside Eddie's head.

CHAPTER 32

Eddie didn't go far: only across the street. He headed for steps leading from the alley to the efficiency apartment above Quilt Blocks.

Hélène answered his knock immediately because she had been standing right at the door, giving herself a "Go-fight-win" pep talk before driving to Prairie Rose.

She realized her anger with Frank was still so close to the surface that it marked her face when Eddie's first words were, "Don' be mad-like, Helen. I ain't tole no-buddy tha' ya lives here."

"Eddie," she began, "you can't come to see me all the time—"

"I ain't. Jus' two time. Tha' ain't alla the time I could-a come 'nd see'd ya."

Jolted by this unwelcome news, Hélène demanded, "How long have you known I live here?" She stepped back into the room; this time Eddie followed with neither hesitation nor invitation.

He closed the door and leaned against it. She zipped and unzipped her purse, nervously awaiting his answer.

"I see'd when ya movin' in, pushin' yer bed uppa steps 'nd puffin' hard-like: *Wuhh-wuhh-wuhh!* I dinn't help cuz look like ya dinn't want no-buddy no-wheres bys ya."

She eyed him shrewdly. "I moved here a long time ago. Why haven't you, uh, I mean . . . Never mind. Yes, I was mad then . . . and yes I'm mad now—and at the same person." *Now, why did I blurt that out?*

He pursed his lips. "Tha' be Frank, huh?"

She nodded and looked away.

"Ya mad then cuz-a Blyss, huh?"

A startled nod.

"Don' worry bout her. Nuh-uh. She don' gots nuttin to do with Frank no mores. He by hisself alla times."

She swallowed hard. "What did you come to see me about?" she asked curtly. "If it's about sunburn, I gave you everything I had. You'll have to go now; I was just leaving." She raised her purse as if proof were required.

"Nuh-uh; sumpthin' ca'ple'ly diff'rent. It be bout me movin' here." He waved expansively, but his gaze shifted between the bed, the bathroom door, and back to the bed.

"Here? What on earth are you talking about? You can't live here! This is where *I* live!"

"Don' worry; I gots money."

"It's not about money; this place isn't for rent! And I sure hope you don't think you can move in with me!"

Eddie chortled. "I don' think tha', nuh-uh! See, ya gonna be livin' in Prairie Rose whiles I be livin' here."

"What? Why would I want to live . . . *there* again?"

"For yer job. No-buddy cut womens hairs good no mores in Prairie Rose. Tha' be yer job. Uh-huh."

"*My* job?" A pause. "Frank's still there, isn't he?"

"Uh-huh, but he be doin' bad job of ever'-thin'. If'n ya be *there*, 'nd me be *here*, tha' be ever'-buddy bes' thin'."

Dazed, Hélène walked to the window. Behind her, Eddie made shuffling sounds. She turned, and watched him shrug off his backpack. He motioned to her. "Sits on yer bed, Helen 'nd I 'splain hows it be yer bes' thin', too."

She stiffened. "Oh you will, will you? What gives you the right to tell me what to do with my life? And my name's Hélène now. I expect you to remember that."

"Tha' be wha' I say'd: Helen. I jus' say'd it reg'lar, not fancy-like."

Hélène rolled her head back on her shoulders, but did take his advice to sit on the bed. *That*, at least, was a good idea since her legs weren't cooperating.

Eddie swung the chair out from under the table and closer to the bed. "Do ya 'member hows I brung Lil' Eddie to Prairie Rose 'nd he be jus' a lil' baby?"

Puzzled at this odd opening, Hélène could only nod.

"I dinn't know bout missin' sum-buddy. I gots back to Chicago 'nd starts missin' Lil' Eddie. I thinks bout him alla times. B'fore long, I be comin' here bunch-a times. I dinn't min' tha', but nows I gonna be livin' here. No more go 'nd come. Nuh-uh. I stays 'nd lives righ' here alla times." He waved around the room again.

"But—" Hélène's vision blurred; she pressed her thumbs against her temples. Her fingers momentarily blocked her view of this uninvited guest with his cockamamie ideas. "It's fine that you want to see, uh, Little Eddie more, but that doesn't mean I have to go back to Prairie Rose, or that you get to live here, or any of that other nonsense about Frank!"

"It don' *ness-a-sary* mean tha', but it be real good if'n it do." He paused, stared into space, thinking, and then raised his left hand with the fingers wrapped tight in a fist. He released the thumb. "This be bout me livin' righ' bys Lil' Eddie—that be *my* bes' thin'.""

She stared as his bandaged index finger shot up to make a second point: "Crosby be place I gets work-like."

The middle finger's raw cuticle made Hélène flinch when Eddie lifted it for his third point: "Frank not happy; he be real sorry bout wha' he done. He sad-like ever'-day, he say'd. A-course, Dude sad-like, too, 'nd *he* gots house, but tha' don' al-'ays makes peoples happy. Nuh-uh."

Before she could formulate questions on those details, Eddie's fourth finger popped up: "Womens in Prairie Rose don' like hows Frank be cuttin' hairs. It be bad."

Then: "Ya be tired-a hidin' alla times, ain'cha, Helen? The thumb be *my* bes' thin', bein' with Lil' Eddie, but *this* be *yer* bes' thin' if'n ya moves to Prairie Rose 'nd ya don' gots to hides no mores." *What an odd juxtaposition to have the crowning point paired with the smallest finger.*

It was a long speech for Eddie—one to which he'd given much thought; he'd packed it full and heavy. Hélène dissected it mentally, piece by piece:

Little Eddie (Justin, if we're using real names, here) very well may want Eddie to live here, but what do Luke and Cate say about that?

Crosby would be an easier place for a man like Eddie to find odd jobs, or even steadier part-time work than Prairie Rose, so he's right about that.

Why is Frank's happiness, or lack of it, my concern?

Who's this sad Dude with a house?

Frank's sorry? What's that based on? Did he sit Eddie down like some odd-ball Father Confessor and spill his guts? She pursed her lips. *Actually, Eddie does seem like a person who could get someone to do just that. I mean, this is twice he's made his way into my apartment and gotten me talking about things I've left unsaid for years.*

Tired of hiding? Of all that Eddie said, that strikes a chord. Yes, I'm weary of having no friends, no place that feels like home, no garden or birdfeeders to tend . . .

Absentmindedly Hélène swiped a hand across her cheek and was surprised that it came away wet.

Eddie leaned forward, peering into her face. "Dinn't wanna make ya more sad-like, Helen."

"You didn't; I already was . . . *sad-like* . . . to my core."

"Ya don' gotta think righ' nows bout if'n I live here whiles yer be livin' in Prairie Rose. I come back later, okay?"

"Later? No, not tonight. I'm . . . I, uh, have to go . . . somewhere."

Suddenly, the idea of seeing Frank loomed larger than even before when all she had planned to do was tell him off. Now she would be looking at her betraying husband through Eddie's eyes . . . looking for signs of *"sad-like,"* indications of remorse and repentance. In short, cynic that she had become over the past years, she would be seeking solid evidence—and reserving the right to remain skeptical—that Frank Wilson was a changed man.

CHAPTER 33

With Sage's voice in his ear as he sat on Bess' back porch, Zeke was about as happy as he could be without holding her close. They were reviewing his anticipated return flight schedule when he heard a hissed "Dude!" He peered across the yard. *Nothing.*

Just as he thought *I'm losing my mind,* he heard: "Inna alley, Dude!"

"Stay put, Sage; I'll call you right back. Eddie's here."

She chuckled; she'd learned enough to know whatever came next in Eddie's saga was worth *staying put.*

Zeke found Eddie all a-jitter behind the alley-facing garage. Apparently any calming effect Justin had on him dissipated within an hour of lost contact.

"Hello, Eddie. What's up?"

"Hey, Dude! I gotta tell Lil' Eddie sumpthin' real 'portant. Can ya call him on yer lil' phone?"

"Sure, but it's pretty late. Way past a little boy's bedtime. Can you tell Luke or Cate whatever it is you need to say to Justin, and they'll tell him tomorrow?

"Nuh-uh; he don' gonna be sleepin' yet," Eddie said confidently. "See, he know I gonna call so he stay 'wake."

Zeke pulled out the scrap of paper with Larson contact information and punched numbers on his cell. After the first ring, he handed the phone to Eddie.

"Hey, Luke! It be Eddie. Can I talks to Lil' Eddie?"

He nodded at Zeke and whispered, "He be 'wake. Uh-huh," and hopped in place as he waited.

"Lil' Eddie? It be Big Eddie! I talkin' to ya on Dude's lil' phone! Guess where I be! Nuh-uh; I be righ' bys tha' lil' house wheres we sleep'd! . . . Huh?"

He turned his back on Zeke and lowered his voice.

"Not yet. Hey, Lil' Eddie, *tha' idea* we thinks 'nd talks bout? It be gonna happen! Huh? *Soon*-like. G'bye."

Zeke hoped the call made sense to Justin, because he had questions a mile wide and ten feet deep after hearing only one side of this obviously coded conversation.

Still holding the phone (which Zeke watched warily) Eddie did his usual jig in the alley. The phone's safe return came with a second request: "Dude, can I sleep inna lil' house jus' for t'nigh'?" It was followed by an astounding declaration: "T'morrow I gets me a home!"

Zeke's brain teeter-tottered. One end quivered high in the air: a lodging request that was not his to grant. The opposite end bounced against the hard ground of the two-pronged startling claim: *A home? Tomorrow?*

It was a balancing act. He leaned toward *"No more sleeping in the camper!"* but immediately tilted toward *"House? Huh?"* Hovering on the fulcrum of indecision, he skidded toward *"It's not my truck . . ."* but instantly slid back to *"What are you talking about?"*

Eddie ignored all signs of bafflement, continuing blithely, "Lil' Eddie want me close-like, so I ain't never goin' back to Chicago. Nuh-uh. I gonna lives here."

"Here?" Zeke echoed, looking at the garage. "Not here!"

Eddie guffawed. "Not onna truck! Inna lil' room wha' gots water 'nd ever'-thin'. It be wheres Helen live nows."

Zeke gaped, thunderstruck. "Really? With *Hélène*? "

Skepticism didn't discourage Eddie. "Not *with*. She be movin' to Prairie Rose. T'night me 'nd Lil' Eddie wen' walkin' 'nd see'd Frank. He be real happy-like when we tells him Helen gonna work with him. Uh-huh."

Zeke needed to sit. *Didn't I see lawn chairs on the garage wall?* He shoved the big door half-way open: *Yes.* "Sit, Eddie," he ordered, flipping two chairs open behind the truck. "How do you know that Helen, I mean *Hélène*, is going to work with Frank and moving to Prairie Rose?"

"She go see Frank righ' nows. They talk, then she move. Ever'-body be happy-like. Bout time, huh?"

Yeah, 'bout time,' but . . . "You saw Hélène tonight? Since I dropped you off?" *Ah yes: across from Quilt Blocks.*

Eddie nodded, meeting Zeke's penetrating stare head-on. "I say'd wha' I jus' tole ya . . . She be s'prised at firs' but—"

"Slow down: *You* told *her* all this. *She* didn't find *you* and say, 'Eddie, I'm going back to Frank, so why don't you live in my apartment?' *You* started it; isn't that right?"

Eddie nodded, pleased Zeke had caught on so quickly. "Righ'! She not see'd Frank yet, so I tole her."

Zeke frowned. "Why . . .? I mean, what . . . Uh, where did you . . ." Mister Makes-His-Living-with-Words couldn't form a complete thought anymore than he could fly. Eddie, however, looked ready to head for the clouds; all four limbs quivered like hummingbird wings.

"Do you *know* Hélène? Have you been friends a long time? See, what you're saying pretty much turns her world upside-down, Eddie. It's not something a person would suggest to someone they don't *really* know."

"I know'd Helen, 'nd she know'd me from b'fore she lef' Prairie Rose. Yeah, we knows bout us. Uh-huh."

"I see; but all that *knowing* took place several years ago, didn't it? You haven't seen or talked to each other for a long time, right?"

Eddie cocked his head. "Dude! Peoples don' unknow sum-buddy jus' cuz they don' al-'ays be seein' 'em."

Zeke sucked in his breath. Eddie's remark hit a bull's eye: *Gull*—the name of the one person Zeke wished he could *unknow* flashed like marquee lights in his head.

He coughed to unclog his throat, wishing he could dislodge memories as easily. "Did you know Hélène when she and Frank were still together?"

"Mos'ly not. I helps her after tha'. Uh-huh."

"Helped her with, uh, what?" *Prairie Rose isn't exactly Union Station with people needing licensed escorts!*

"Lotta stuff. She al-'ays say'd, 'Yer big help, Eddie.' So I gonna be helpin' more peoples nows."

"Okay, Eddie. I understand that you know Hélène. But still . . ." Zeke shifted uneasily in his chair. "What you've done by going to talk to Frank without Hélène's permission—which you didn't have, right?" A slow shrug. "Letting Frank believe Hélène plans to move back was—"

"She gonna move," Eddie said firmly.

"Maybe so, but you let Frank think *she* wants to work with him before she had said anything of the sort!"

"I jus' know'd wha' she wanna do."

Move on, Zeke! "Talking to Hélène about her moving out and you moving in—all that stuff. You overstepped your boundaries. Do you know what that means?"

A furrowed brow. "It don' soun' good. Nuh-uh."

"It's *not* good. You know how you don't like people to ask *you* questions about some things, or look at your stuff? Frank and Hélène may feel you did that to them."

"Nuh-uh; this diff'rent. See, it be helpin'. It ain't like wha' ya say'd bout lookin'."

"Helping? How can it be helping to interfere like this?"

"It don' be no inna-fear. I be a fren' wha' see'd sad-like peoples wha' don' knows it be good, 'cept if'n I helps."

Say what? This conversation is rapidly becoming a two-Excedrin headache. "Eddie, it may seem like a good thing, but didn't the whole idea *really* start because you want to live closer to Justin . . . *not* because you were thinking mostly about helping Frank and Hélène?"

"It be hook t'gether like this." Eddie's fingers formed a complicated knot. "I helps Frank 'nd Helen; they helps me. Lil' Eddie happy. Ever'-buddy get sumphin' good."

Zeke groaned inwardly, *Admit defeat!* Still, he pressed on: "A better place to start would have been to talk to Luke and Cate. Do they even know about this idea of yours, about you wanting to live near Justin?"

"It be why we calls Lil' Eddie on yer lil' phone. They knows bout it nows. It work out good. Uh-huh."

"Eddie, people like Hélène don't make big decisions like quitting her job here, moving back to work with

Frank: all of that. It just doesn't happen after a short conversation with someone"—*like you? Be nice, Zeke*—"uh, with someone they haven't seen in a long time."

"It ain't been *tha'* long-a times, 'nd we talk pretty long now even if'n at firs' Helen open her door 'nd say'd she be leavin' righ' a-ways. I know'd she be goin' to Prairie Rose cuz b'fore I knocks, she say'd Frank's name bunch-a time like she be practicin'. I hear'd it cuz she shout-like."

"See, that's a problem. You hear one thing and decide that—hold on! You hadn't talked to Hélène about *any* of this before you eavesdropped, right? And you had already talked to Frank? Good grief, Eddie! How'd you get the idea she was heading off to Prairie Rose to tell Frank she wants to work with him again and move back there?"

A shrug. "I jus' knows."

Zeke flashed back on Haze's account of the sordid Hélène-Frank-Blyss mess. "Even if you heard her saying Frank's name, it's pretty unlikely she really wants to work with him again, isn't it?"

"Nuh-uh. She gots her purse on her arm, like she be already gone if'n I dinn't comes. Yes-t'day she real mad bout Frank cuttin' Lil' Eddie and me's hairs so's we gots burned up. See, if'n she work with Frank, he not do dumb stuff. It be real 'portant she move. I tells Frank stuff, 'nd now they talks bout it 'nd sees it be good."

A light flashed in Zeke's head: *Nice lady.* "Hélène gave you and Justin the lotion for your heads yesterday?"

"Uh-huh."

Maybe there is something to Eddie's claim about knowing Hélène if he asked and got her help. But if they really do go way-back, why did Hélène panic and race away when Eddie showed up at our canopy?

"How Frank gonna say he sorry if'n he don' know where Helen be? She not happy hidin' so if'n she know'd Frank be sorry, it work bes'. Nows Lil' Eddie 'nd me gonna lives close-bys. I be ope-nin' a door so lotta peoples walks in a whole-lotta-happy place. Uh-huh."

Zeke stared at moonlit alley ruts, wondering how he—a guy who minded his own business—got involved in such a convoluted maze. *No, it's a confounded mess. A cruel reward for heeding Mom's "Do the right thing, Zeke"!*

"Okay; let's go back to you overhearing Hélène saying Frank's name. Was that when she gave you and Justin the lotion?" *If so, what Eddie told Frank could be true.*

"Nuh-uh; I see'd her two time. Firs' it be me 'nd Lil' Eddie; secon' times, it jus' be me."

"So when did you decide Hélène is going to see Frank tonight? The first time, or the second time?"

"I *tole* ya: she be jus' bout gone when I knocks secon' time. Then I see'd her drive her car." He mimed steering.

"Maybe she went to the grocery store."

"Nuh-uh; she be goin' to see Frank. She mad-like b'fore, but nows she gonna say, 'Frank, wanna be workin' t'gether again? I gonna move back cuz Eddie live in my lil' room in Crosby t'morrow.' Tha' be wha' she gonna say."

"You heard her saying—practicing—those words?"

"Not *zac'ly* them words, but she know'd it be good idea. Uh-huh. No-buddy live in them lil' room in Prairie Rose, so ever'-thin' be fine for Helen 'nd me nows."

Zeke hadn't heard about a Prairie Rose apartment, but it made sense. Hélène would have needed a place to live after Frank's defection, especially if she'd lost the house. It was also logical that she'd live close to where she worked, like her arrangements with Quilt Blocks.

But there were pieces still missing in the giant jigsaw puzzle that was Eddie's story. "This whole crazy idea began because Justin and you want to live closer?"

"Mos'ly. I be missin Lil' Eddie alla times, 'nd he be missin me alla times. We thinks 'nd talks when we t'gether; nows it happen." He emitted a contented sigh, clapped his feet together, and grinned. "Uh-huh!"

"Can you just leave Chicago? Don't you have to get your things?" Zeke tapped the lanyard hanging off Eddie's backpack. "Isn't someone expecting you at your job?"

"Peoples leave alla times, Dude. I gots ever'-thin' righ' here." He nudged his backpack with the toe of a new shoe. "If'n I sleeps inna lil' house t'night, tha' be onliest time. T'morrow I gets bed . . . *prob'ly.* Lil' Eddie 'nd me, we looks inna win'ows 'nd see'd 'em lil' rooms in Prairie Rose gots ever'-thin'. She don' need no two bed. Nuh-uh."

"Eddie," Zeke cautioned, "Hélène rents the apartment over Quilt Blocks. I'm not sure the owner of the store wants anyone living upstairs . . . " *who knows life-on-the-run, but may not understand plumbing's limitations!* He quickly switched to "uh, anyone who doesn't work for her. Speaking of work, how are you going to pay rent?"

"Dude, don' worry! I gots money. When it gone, I jus' gets more. Peoples ever'-where needs helpin'. I helps 'em, they pays me, 'nd I gots more money. See? Tha' be how it go. Uh-huh."

Tune in nightly, folks, for Eddie's Financial Advice!

"Can I sleeps inna lil' house t'night?" he repeated.

"I guess so," Zeke said, resigned to one somewhat comforting thought: *If he's in the camper he's not bothering people!* "When you leave, use the little door over there." He pointed toward the side wall's access door.

The larger door was halfway closed; Eddie was settling in for the night, whistling "Pop Goes the Weasel," when Zeke thought of something: "I'll be right back, Eddie."

If, come morning, Bess or Haze wondered where the leftover chicken and the remains of a quart of milk went, they would probably figure Zeke enjoyed a bedtime snack. But Zeke wasn't snacking; he was hoping a full belly ensured that Eddie would sleep well, and stay put.

The ladies had gone to bed, so he wrote a vague and hasty note which he left on the kitchen table in case either Bess or Haze roamed the house looking for him:

Gone out for a bit. See you in the morning. Zeke

He reached Main Street without attracting any unwanted attention, parked in the alley close enough to watch Hélène's apartment, and began the wait for her return.   Feeling like a Private Eye on stake-out in an unmarked car, he finally reconnected with Sage and tried to communicate all that had transpired when he wasn't calling her "right back."

After the briefest introduction to Eddie's revelation, Sage interrupted with a squawk. "He did what?" Midway through the bizarre tale, she hooted, "I'd love to meet him! What he lacks in wisdom, he has double in gutsiness!"

"You don't know the half of it."

As the story wound down, she advised, "Don't forget about Luke and Cate. The deal was you'd call them or they'd call you if either side learned something the other side needed to know. Don't you agree this qualifies?"

"Big time. So, what do you think? Over all, I mean."

"It's almost as good a plot as what my favorite author comes up with!   For a guy who doesn't read much, Eddie's giving you some stiff competition."

"How he sees it all ending veers into the unbelievable. It's a common problem for storytellers; tying all the loose ends together is tough. Even your favorite author can't figure out a reasonable finish to this one!"

"Well, he's on his way to discovery, sitting in the dark watching and waiting for action to unfold. It's in the '. . . and so the plot thickens' stage, which is where my favorite tale-spinner always shines."

"I'm afraid that tale-spinner's bulb is going dim."

"Nah; just shake it up a little!"

"I've seen enough shaking-it-up in the past few days to last me a lifetime," he said wearily.

"Well, Private Eye Eden, your mission is to bring this story to the finish line in your inimitable style. Then, if you changed the names and places, you'd have another Kiel Nede/Raven Crowley winner to send John and Maggie . . . not that I'm pushing, you realize."

"Wish it were that easy. Eddie isn't as malleable as Raven is. One's a wild fire; the other's a controlled burn. Big difference."

CHAPTER 34

Disconnecting from the call to Sage, Zeke realized he needed to recharge his phone. This required turning on the car, but he had one more important call to make, so he'd just have to live with engine noise. It sure shot holes in any chance of remaining unnoticed in the dark alley.

When he dialed the Larson house for the second time that evening, Luke answered promptly, almost as if he'd been expecting the call. "Zeke here; sorry about the late hour. Heard any interesting news recently?"

A chuckle was not what Zeke expected to hear. "I'll say! Thanks for calling, and don't worry about the time. As you can imagine, Cate and I have plenty to talk about after Justin's call from Eddie."

"I realize none of this is my business, though I did plant myself in the middle of it by driving Eddie to Prairie Rose. If you prefer that I bug-off, I understand, but otherwise, I need to ask: Do you think any of it is true? Especially the part about Hélène giving up her apartment in Crosby so Eddie can live in it?"

"Unlikely as it seems, Eddie believes it, so Cate and I have decided to accept it until facts prove otherwise."

"But he thinks it's all happening tomorrow! He came by where Mom and I are staying in Crosby not only to use my cell phone, but to ask if he could sleep in the camper tonight. 'Only tonight,' he says, because tomorrow he'll be sleeping in a bed—a bed which he seems confident Hélène will leave for him in her apartment here."

"It all parallels what Justin told us." A smile lit Luke's voice. "Eddie's favorite Bible verse is Matthew 7:7—the one about ask, seek, and knock. Pastor Tori said when she told Eddie about it, he said 'Cool!' and made her write it out for him. Talk about childlike faith in action, huh?"

Zeke made an evasive murmur, filing *Matthew 7:7* for future research. He lived more by *work hard, earn what you get* than *ask-seek-knock* . . . but Eddie embraced both philosophies—apparently with great success. *Hmm.* "Uh, Eddie said he and Justin peeked into where Hélène lived in Prairie Rose, saw it was furnished, and decided that Eddie gets her place in Crosby and everything in it!"

"Eddie's mind works differently than ours. Like I said, he has childlike faith, and he reasons like a child, like Justin does. That's part of why they get along so well."

"True, but then Eddie surprises me, coming up with wisdom of the ages." Zeke bit his lip, remembering the most recent such remark: *"Dude! A person don' unknow sum-buddy jus' cuz they don' al-'ays be seein' 'em."*

"I know what you mean. What Cate and I question, over all, is his underlying premise of Frank and Helen working together again. Without going into details, it'll require a miracle of monumental proportions for *that* to happen. Even bigger than Helen—or Hélène, as she prefers to be called, right?—returning to Prairie Rose."

"Yes, it's Hélène now. If it happens, it won't be easy."

"Life rarely is," Luke said. "One thing we've learned over the years we've known Eddie is that he keeps life interesting! Let's see what tomorrow brings."

"You've got it. Well, good night, Luke."

He disconnected the phone charger and turned off the car. Silence returned to the alley.

As time dragged by with no sign of Hélène, Zeke suspected Eddie had told the truth: Maybe she really *was* thirty miles down the road. Maybe she really *was* talking to Frank.

But was she yelling?

Was she crying?

Was Frank sorry?

Was anyone, besides Eddie and Justin, happy-like?

These were tougher questions than what had stymied Kiel Nede's readers sixteen times.

CHAPTER 35

Waiting paid results. Headlights flashed an arc down the alley. The car approached slowly, its driver likely cautious after seeing a strange parked car. Zeke roused from a slouch to check the time on his cell: *Ten-fifty.*

The driver pulled into a shadowy parking spot at the bottom of steps leading up to Hélène's apartment. *Must be her.* Zeke's mouth felt as dry as if he'd licked chalk. Just because he'd been waiting for this moment, didn't mean he had an agenda for what happened next.

Do I call out when she's out of the car? Do I wait until she's at the top of the stairs and say . . . something or other. Argghh! Sage should be here, not a bumbling male like me! Do something before she goes inside—she'll never answer a knock at night . . . at least I hope she wouldn't.

He stepped out of his car, pressing the door shut with as little noise as possible. Hélène paused at the bottom of the stairway, one hand on the railing. In the dimly lit alley, Zeke saw her turn towards him. Gravel crunched beneath his feet, sounding like a hailstorm in the quiet night. He waved—a friendly, non-threatening, *See? I'm a good guy* kind of wave. Bad guys didn't wave, did they? Well, not in Kiel Nede books, they didn't.

But, in Kiel Nede's books, potential victims never lingered in alleys, waiting for strangers striding toward them to come into view or within shooting distance. Hélène would need Raven ASAP if she hoped to survive one of Zeke's scary plots.

"Hélène? Hi; it's Zeke Eden."

"Zeke? What do you want? Uh, is Haze here, too?"

"No, I'm alone," . . . *and freaking you out; sorry.* "I've been waiting to talk to you. I know it's late, but this is pretty important. May I have a few minutes to explain?"

She tensed and glanced up the steps as if wondering how fast she could climb them. "I'm not sure that's . . ."

"We can sit here," he said quickly, motioning at the bottom step. "Or I'll stand, and you sit—whichever you prefer. I just have a couple questions."

"I guess . . . but come up to the landing." Their footsteps created a muffled beat against the dozen or so rubber-matted wooden risers.

She positioned herself in the safest zone: close to her apartment door. Hugging her purse, she held her keys as if ready to open the door . . . or attack him with them.

Glad to see you know that keys can poke eyes out. Maybe you don't need Raven's help. He lowered himself as far away as the railing allowed to seem less intimidating before turning to face Hélène. "I'm here because of a very odd story Eddie told me tonight."

"Eddie." The word was more statement than question, but the expression on her face invited explanation.

"Is it true that you're going to let Eddie move in here tomorrow?" He nodded at the apartment's door. "The *tomorrow* part is why I figured we should talk tonight. He seems to think it's true, and it's all happening tomorrow. I thought you needed to know that, if you didn't already."

She didn't gasp or protest, or laugh or snort. She blinked and audibly inhaled; her exhale was soundless. "I don't know."

"You don't know . . . what? This is the first you've heard about what I said? Or you don't know if it all happens tomorrow? Or . . .? What don't you know?"

She hugged her purse tighter. "Is 'All of the Above' a possible answer?" Her smile was slight, but it was there.

"Here's what I know. I gave Eddie a ride to Prairie Rose to see Justin—" he paused, "You know that Haze has told me about the talk you and she had, right?"

A nod.

"Good. Then you know that I know—sorry; this is more confusing than intended. Anyway, I know you're originally from Prairie Rose. Eddie says he knew you from before, uh, before you left Frank."

Another nod. "He knew me back when I was Helen Wilson. Did Haze tell you that part, too?"

"Enough that I understand why you left Frank. That's why I don't see you moving back to work with him, especially with only *Eddie's* word that Frank has changed. And that's Eddie's story. He says you and Frank are going to work side-by-side again, and you're moving back to Prairie Rose. Even more incredible: Eddie believes it all means he'll move in here tomorrow! See why I'm here?"

She chewed her lip, then: "I saw Frank tonight. Eddie and Justin visited Frank and, this part's pretty muddy, but I gather they did what my daughters used to do."

Daughters. The word loomed in the silence, shaping a sad question in Zeke's mind: *Where are those girls?*

"If they wanted to buy or do something, they let me think their dad approved, and then they let their dad assume I'd said 'Fine; just clear it with your dad.' But with Eddie?" *Is that a smile?* "He doesn't play one side against the other. He sees three sides: his, Frank's, and mine. He truly believes if we all work together—"

Zeke echoed Eddie: "Ever'-buddy be happy-like."

Hélène sighed. "Wouldn't it be wonderful if life really were as simple as Eddie sees it?"

Is this how ask, seek, knock works? "Did you go see Frank tonight just to talk over Eddie's plan? It seems like a decision made too hastily. Sorry if I'm too bold."

"You're not. No; originally I planned to have it out with Frank over haircuts he gave Justin and Eddie. It's one thing for him to treat me the way he did, but the shape they were in when they showed up here," her fist pounded the step between them, "is inexcusable."

"You said 'originally.' I gather something changed your mind *and* your topic before you started talking to Frank?"

"After Eddie began rambling on about me moving back to Prairie Rose and all that, well . . . my anger at Frank lost all its steam. Anger is different than hate. Hate doesn't require steam because it's not going anywhere. Hate just needs a place to camp."

Zeke swallowed hard and stared into the darkness. Eddie- and Hélène-quotes were rapidly replacing anything he remembered from BARTLETT'S FAMILIAR QUOTATIONS.

He knew anger. Anger with Gull sparked, then flared until Zeke thought it would consume *him*. When anger lost steam, it flattened—only to re-inflate as hate.

"I parked across from Frank's house," Hélène paused, adding, "where we'd lived. I watched a long time through the living room window. He read; changed a light bulb; checked the smoke alarm, and jumped when it blared. I heard it, too." She smiled briefly. "He was alone and looked . . . well, I guess Eddie says it best: sad-like."

"Eddie said I'm sad-like, too. He's right."

She recalled: *". . . he gots house . . ."* "You're 'Dude'?"

"Yeah, according to Eddie. Why?"

"He said, 'Dude sad-like,' and I wondered. Go on."

"I know all about anger becoming hate. My brother Gull's in prison for murder, and his method destroyed our bond. Soon after Gull's trial Dad died, making him the second victim. Good thing Death-from-a-Broken-Heart isn't punishable by incarceration, or Gull would have two sentences to serve. I try to purge Gull from my life . . ."

"Doesn't work, does it?"

"Hardly. Like Eddie told me, 'Peoples don' unknow sum-buddy jus' cuz they don' al-'ays be seein' 'em.' That's the kicker. I haven't seen Gull since the trial but, try as I might, I can't *unknow* him."

She sighed. "*Family* is at the center of our sorrows," she waggled her hand between them to clarify the '*our*,' "yet *family* is what Eddie wants. Hopefully if he gets his wish he'll have better luck than we did," she said ruefully. "It's like I'm standing in the middle of a bridge between what's behind and where I want to be. Tonight when Eddie was talking, I finally saw myself moving off the bridge."

"But isn't going back to Prairie Rose a backwards move for you?"

"Wish I knew the answer to that."

"Before Eddie presented this wacky solution to *his* dilemma—involving some pretty major decisions for *you*—you were planning confront Frank. So you drove to Prairie Rose, but *didn't* have it out with him? Why not?"

"After sitting outside the house for a while, I drove to the shop; I've kept a key to the back door all this time. I wandered around the apartment, looking at stuff I'd left behind. Then I went into the shop and just sat there, thinking. And that's where Frank found me. Someone had called him after they saw shadows."

Zeke whistled softly. "You're in the dark; he barges in. Did it become a shoot-out at the Not-So-Okay Corral?"

"No; he was real nervous until he realized I wasn't armed and dangerous. He acted all macho—swinging a baseball bat, talking about calling the sheriff. He turned on lights, but since I look so different than before, he had a lot to process: *A woman burglar?* and *How did a stranger break in without damaging anything?* He was checking a window when truth dawned. All he said was, 'It's you!' and stumbled over to the barber chair."

A swallow gurgled in her throat. Zeke didn't breathe.

"I didn't want to attract interest from anyone outside, so I turned off the lights and we sat there in the dark. It was weird; we had too much, yet nothing, to say after years of silence. I didn't realize he was crying until he blew his nose. There were tears in his voice when he asked, 'Is what Eddie said true? Are you coming back, Helen?' I told him Helen no longer exists."

"What was your answer? Are you going back?"

"I think so. I need hope for my future. If I keep hiding, how can I expect hope to find me?"

Another stellar entry for Hélène's Quotable Quotes.
"What you said earlier about hate finding a place to camp? That's me. I'm one big campground that's so filled up with hate, there's no vacancy for hope." He chuckled.

"Why is that funny?"

"Not funny; ironic. Eddie looked at you, and he looked at me, and saw us for the sorry messes we are. But he isn't content to let either of us stay messy."

"We *be*. Eddie would say, 'Ya be sorry messes'!"

Zeke's grin disintegrated into a yawn. "I promised quick questions; instead we've had quite the chat. Thanks, Hélène. It's been a thought-provoking time."

"I haven't answered your initial question. Yes: Eddie will have a home tomorrow."

"That's a big decision. Why not give it some time?"

"I came up with a workable idea on the way home from Prairie Rose. He wouldn't live here," she waved at the door, "but he can stay in my Prairie Rose apartment. It's near Justin and, meanwhile, I'll work in Quilt Blocks and keep living here while I make up my mind about Frank. He and I will talk again; I promised him that much. He wants to take me to dinner next week . . ."

"Eddie will be thrilled, but why are you doing this?"

"As a parent, I understand Eddie's longings."

I'm not a parent, but I identify with the pain of longings.
"What about work? Are there odd jobs in Prairie Rose?"

"People will find things for him to do. We did when he first came and checked out Prairie Rose. He'd met Harv Thompson in Chicago and heard enough about our little town to decide it was where he wanted his unborn child to grow up. It was quite the experience for everyone!"

"I can only imagine."

"What about you?"

"I gather you mean what about Gull and me?"

"Yes."

Zeke barely recognized his own voice when he finally spoke. "I have a friend in Utah: Hank Bedlow. He drives from Milford to Draper—two hundred miles—every month to see two prisoners; he's Gull's only visitor. Hank hasn't pressured me to go along—not since my heated rejection of his invitation. Any 'Gull-and-me' stuff," his fingers hung quote-marks in the air, "is way, *way* in the future."

"If or when the time's right, you'll know."

"That's what Sage says. Hank, too."

"Haze said you have a wonderful wife."

"I do."

"Maybe someday Frank will say that about me," she said wistfully.

"If not, have Eddie sit him down for a little talk!"

"Eddie makes Frank nervous."

"As well he should."

From a church bell tower, or maybe the courthouse, a clock's chimes resonated. Zeke counted twelve strokes. *So much for quick chats, yet what a productive hour.*

"From what Haze told me, I understand why you hate Gull. He not only killed someone, but stole his method for murder right from one of your books. That's spiteful. Haze said your dad just couldn't deal with it. Hard to see how 'forgive and forget' works in some situations, isn't it?"

"Hank talks a lot about trust."

"Trust?"

"Yeah. Maybe you have as much trouble trusting Frank as I do Gull. He says he's sorry; I suspect any *sorry* he feels is more to do with getting caught than with repenting. Is he sorry enough to change? Hard to say with him locked in a cell—and since I haven't seen him."

"That's precisely what I wonder about Frank. If Blyss hadn't dumped him, would he have sent her away? Sadly, I doubt it. So, yes, he may very well be sorry now; he sure messed up what was a pretty decent life with me. But I need to see evidence of change. That doesn't sound much like forgiveness, I know."

"Hank says forgiveness requires trust in order to survive. He considers trust a fragile thing. He puts it this way: 'Chase trust and it runs; if you catch it and hug it too tightly, it strangles. But let trust come to you and then, if you hold it lightly, it lives.' All that's required of me is that I respect trust like I would any fragile creature. That's when forgiveness comes. I'm just not there yet."

"Aren't we the wise ones?" she quipped, though without humor. "I would have made tea had I known we were going to out-Confucius ol' Confucius himself."

"Sorry to disagree, Hélène, but I think the wise one in this tale of woes isn't on your top step. He's blissfully— please pardon my unfortunate choice of words—sleeping in a battered camper shell in Bess Green's garage."

"Eerie, isn't it? To think about all that Eddie has put in motion . . . Well, today has become tomorrow; I need to get to bed. Thanks for coming by, Zeke. Sorry I wasn't more welcoming when I first saw you."

He stood. "Hey, I'm glad you were cautious. By the way, you can tell Eddie the good news of his dreams coming true. I'll tell him to see you, if he isn't already camped on your doorstep when the sun comes up!"

"Quilt Blocks is closed Sundays, even this weekend, so I'll take him to Prairie Rose and stick around to help get him settled in."

Zeke pulled out his wallet and extracted five twenties. "My contribution toward expenses. Please consider Sage and me as your partners in this adventure. This is payment for some pretty good therapy Eddie foisted upon me. And here's my card with almost every possible way to reach me. Keep in touch, okay?"

She stared at her hand and slowly stood. "You're sure?" She waved the bills. "This seems too generous."

"I'm positive. I want to help make it all work out."

"To return your question, why are *you* doing this?"

From tumbling thoughts, Zeke chose: "He got to me."

She smiled faintly. "Happens a lot with Eddie."

In Bess Green's guest room that night, Zeke slept with no haunting dreams for the first time in several years.

Sunday

Chapter 36

As he walked to Eddie's overnight accommodations, a rabbit scurried from the garden to the alley—a blur that made Zeke feel right at home. Mornings in Utah, he often found places where rabbits had burrowed beneath the garden fence to feast during moonlit nights.

Squinting in the early-morning sun, Zeke opened the garage's side door. Instantly Eddie's head popped up, framed by the camper window like an odd piece of art. Zeke had tried to be quiet, figuring Eddie could use the sleep in a safer, calmer place than he likely ever had back in Chicago. Obviously no one sneaked up on Eddie.

"Hey, Dude," he greeted Zeke sleepily.

"Sorry; didn't mean to wake you. If you were still asleep, I was going to put this where you'd see it before you took off." He held up the note written in block letters on notebook paper: EDDIE: COME SEE ME. DUDE. He had discarded a similar note, signed ZEKE, in a wastebasket.

Eddie mouthed the words slowly, and grinned. "Okay. I sees ya righ' nows. If'n tha' be alls I gotta do t'day, then I jus' sleeps some mores." He flung himself back on his makeshift bed and faked an extended dramatic snore. Soon a chortle erupted and bounced around the camper-shell, ricocheting out into the garage.

Zeke laughed right along with him, and it felt good, though he did wonder if someone walking along the alley wouldn't wonder what could possibly be so amusing inside an old building at the break of dawn.

"What I need to tell you is that Hélène wants to see you this morning. Maybe you should wait a while, like until about nine o'clock, okay?"

"I be gonna sees Helen any ways, even if'n ya don' writes no notes bout it."

That's right; you were. But the results will be much different than what you hoped for! "Good. Okay, I'm going to fry some eggs. If you'd like some, we can eat breakfast together out here. How's that sound?" He took the grin as agreement. "You can grab lawn chairs off the wall and find something to put a tray on. I'll be back soon."

"Hey, do ya gots ketch-up, Dude?"

"I'm sure Bess has catsup in her refrigerator."

"Eggs whats gots ketch-up on 'em be my bes' thin'."

"Then get ready to be a happy man, Eddie."

"I already be happy."

Zeke fried eggs (yes, there was catsup) and reflected on *I already be happy.*

He buttered toast and slathered strawberry jam with a heavy hand and pondered *I already be happy.*

He separated two bananas from a cluster and mused even more about *I already be happy.*

He poured coffee into a thermos, then milk into two glasses, still thinking about *I already be happy.*

Through it all (despite sounds he couldn't control and aromas he couldn't contain that wafted from the tidy kitchen, down the hallway) Bess and Haze still slept. For that minor blessing, Zeke could say: *I already be happy.*

He had not decided how to broach the results of his late-night excursion with Haze whose *"Do the right thing, Zeke"* plea was now being answered far beyond her expectations. He planned to replenish (not only explain) the deep cavity his repeated generosity with Eddie had left in Bess' larder, but it was too early for shopping.

Eddie had opened the big door and set up the lawn chairs, so Zeke put the tray on an overturned box, and they dug in. *I already be happy?*

Sometimes *happy* is wobbly lawn chairs, a dusty alley, and breakfast shared by two men whose life adventures are so vastly different that it almost gives credence to the idea there might be life on other planets.

CHAPTER 37

Zeke returned to the kitchen carrying a tray that no longer held anything edible. He was reading and drinking coffee (second pot) at the table when Bess appeared, sniffing audibly. "Do I smell fried eggs? And cinnamon?"

"Yes to both. I fried eggs for myself and Eddie; he slept in the camper again, by the way. Cinnamon is part of my special French toast recipe, which I'll feed you and Mom for breakfast. Oh, and courtesy of my ravaging your kitchen, you're missing fruit, milk, chicken—the list goes on. Bet you don't go through so much food in a month!"

"Eating's what food's for, not just to look at. 'Eddie,' you say? Where is he now?"

"Heading down the alley, last I saw."

She shook her head, laughing. "That Eddie! As far as I know, he never bothers anyone. Well, he asks for rides to Prairie Rose, but he's not really a pest—just a presence, I guess you could say."

Zeke debated saying *"A presence that's soon to become even more frequently present!"* but decided that story wasn't his to tell. So he opted for "Mom will be up soon; when she shows her face, I'll start the French toast."

"What a perfect Sunday breakfast, and how lovely to be served in my own home! Will you and Haze be going to church with me this morning?"

"I won't speak for Mom, but I'm going to wander around Pioneer Village since we won't set up the canopy until noon."

"That's fine; however, if you're interested, they offer non-denominational church services in Pioneer Village at the historic Daneville Church. Hard to miss; it's across from the parade announcer's stand and has a flag on top of the bell tower, which has a working bell. If nothing else, you'll hear it ring. I believe the service there starts at nine o'clock. That's an important detail, because if you beat the church crowd to the bakery you have a decent chance of getting a fresh and tasty cinnamon roll!"

Nine o'clock was when the religious would gather for worship; nine o'clock was when Eddie would climb Helen's steps. Participants involved in either activity would be blessed.

When Bess returned to her bedroom to get "spiffed up" for church, Zeke resumed reading. So engrossed was he in his book that even Haze's perfume didn't alert him to her arrival in the kitchen. He jerked, bumping against her chin when she kissed the top of his head.

"What are you reading with such concentration that you don't even notice your adoring mother?" she teased.

"It's Mark Kurlansky's book: SALT: A WORLD HISTORY. Fitting material for a cookbook author, don't you think?"

"*Pfffttt!* Time you start thinking like Kiel Nede again. There won't be any more cookbooks from us. At least, *I'm* done. What *you* need to do is dust off some of the many ideas I've sent you over the years. The ones you didn't use yet," she reminded sternly, "and find a good mystery-thriller in them. Plenty there; you just have to look."

"My muse is dried up. Dead. Kaput."

"So water it!"

Zeke closed Kurlansky's book with unnecessary force. He pushed back his chair and left the table. Rinsing his cup at the sink, his eyes lit on a bottle on the sill: his hostess gift for Bess—a jar of Utah Sea Salt from the RealSalt Company. He picked up the container and slowly turned it, reading every word, staring into space . . .

Watching, Haze smiled into her coffee cup. *Ah-ha! I recognize a familiar attention to detail that's been missing. Why, I do believe Kiel Nede is back! Sometimes being a pushy mother can backfire; sometimes it pays big rewards.*

CHAPTER 38

Leaving the life-long friends to their French toast and chatter, Zeke drove to Main Street. He parked near where they would set up the canopy in a few hours, and headed to Pioneer Village. The morning air was fresh; the sun had turned down the heat or, at least, not cranked it up yet. It enervated him to walk along an awakening street and breathe deeply of nature's best medicine: contentment.

Humming a jaunty tune, he passed Bud and Retha's house; he waved in case anyone watched from inside.

He showed his three-day pass at the gate and ambled along a well-trod path that took him toward the buildings. Deep in thought about the book he'd been reading earlier, he barely noticed the flag atop the church's steeple. He stopped short, as if he'd hit a brick wall.

Salt. Salt mines; hmm. My next book was going to be a mining story . . . Stop right there; that's crazy. I'm done with mystery-thrillers. He kicked a stone hard enough to create a miniature dust storm, but ideas weren't as easily dispersed as stones: *Utah has salt; the RealSalt I brought as a gift for Bess . . . No! No more Utah stories; not after the mess* OFF TRACK *made for our family. No more jobs for Raven; it was a good run, but it's over.*

He walked past places that should have interested him, but barely registered: the fully stocked general store, a schoolhouse, two depots, a Post Office, a hardware store, a livery. His mind was consumed with warring thoughts: ideas, considerations that could give John and Maggie heart palpitations and would make Haze ecstatic if the three of them knew.

Somehow he found himself at the same table he'd shared—unwillingly—with Eddie. No beverage this time, just privacy. Privacy, that is, until he heard, "Oh, good, I found you! Bess said you'd headed here."

"Hi, Hélène. What's up?"

"Eddie won't get in my car! He said if he's going to Prairie Rose, you have to drive him. In the pickup."

Zeke buried his face in his hands. "Where is he?"

"Waiting for you at Bess Green's. He's got to be the most stubborn person I've ever met!"

Sighing, he raised his head. "Does he know *why* you want to take him to Prairie Rose?"

"Yes—and he's happy, but he still won't ride with me!"

"*Argghh!* Come on. I'm free for a couple hours; I'll drive him, but you might want to take your own car. The pickup is hardly a lady's dream ride!"

He climbed into Hélène's car. Within minutes they had pulled up next to Bess Green's alley-facing garage where Eddie was bobbing like a Jack-in-the-Box.

"Hey, Dude! Hey, Helen!"

"Hi, Eddie," Zeke said with admirable control, in view of his frustration with Eddie and how his *private privacy* dictated other people's activities. "You heard Hélène has a nice surprise for you in Prairie Rose, right? Seems to me the polite thing to do is accept her offer of a ride."

"Tha' don' soun' po-lite to me. It be *yer* idea of po-lite. If'n I rides to Prairie Rose inna lil' house on tha' truck, it my bes' thin'. Uh-huh."

Private privacy reigns. Zeke decided not to waste time arguing—he had things on his agenda today. "I'll get the keys from Bess," he said wearily. "You okay with driving on your own, Hélène?"

"I am, but when I called to find you, Haze said she wants to ride along with me and see Prairie Rose."

So it was that Bess went to church by herself, while Zeke and Eddie rode out of Crosby for the third time in a rickety pickup (which, this time, Zeke remembered to fill with gas) leaving Hélène to drive an animated Haze to Prairie Rose.

CHAPTER 39

Despite a whirlwind trip through Ekness Super Value, Hélène and Haze still managed to pass Zeke and Eddie on the road to Prairie Rose. They were soon lost from sight.

Eddie knew better than to fuss about their slower pace. Instead, he crowed, "I be livin' inna Helen's lil' rooms in Prairie Rose real close-bys Lil' Eddie. God say'd, 'Ya as't, seek'd, knock'd, Eddie, so I blest ya!' Uh-huh."

"God talks to you?"

"Uh-huh. Some-a times it be sof'-like, some-a times it be loud-like if'n I ain't listenin' good. Then I looks roun' quick-like, won-drin' if'n sum-buddy b'sides me hear'd Him!"

Zeke filed one more thing away for future thought. "So, Eddie: you're getting a special gift from Hélène. Now, I'd like to explain some things to help you show her you appreciate it. Okay?"

He caught a bobbing nod in the rearview mirror.

"Remember when we talked about how it costs money to live in a house or an apartment? Well, there are ways you can make it cost less . . ." For a few miles they talked about turning off lights, short showers, and myriad things a person with a place to call *home* needs to know.

The next ten miles, they talked about food: buying, preparing, and storing it—to prevent food poisoning, and keep from attracting rodents and bugs. Eddie was mostly interested in *eating* food but, to his credit and Zeke's relief, he appeared to listen.

The final ten miles, they discussed being a good citizen, and a friendly (but not-*too*-friendly) neighbor. This, Zeke suspected, might be Eddie's greatest challenge since he viewed everyone as a potential *fren'* regardless of their response to him.

They entered the alley behind the D CURL (a curious detail Zeke still did not understand) and parked behind Hélène's car. The inner door to the apartment was ajar; a screen door separated the inside wonders from jitter-bugging Eddie and his nervous driver. *Will this work out?*

The thirty-mile trip to Prairie Rose had done little to ease Zeke's worries over Eddie. One thing he knew: *If this apartment belonged to me, Eddie is the last person I'd let live here!* Was Hélène a saint or extremely naïve?

He thought about Luke and Cate, and everyone who had waved and called back cheerful greetings to Eddie on their first trip to Prairie Rose. And now, Hélène had stepped beyond her comfort zone to help Eddie. Maybe Mayberry USA was really Prairie Rose and he had yet to meet Aunt Bea and Opie. *Or maybe I have and they're masquerading as Hélène and Justin!*

He followed Eddie into the apartment and got his first view of the place where Hélène had previously lived in quiet desperation and deep despair. As Eddie had said (based on his and Justin's window-peeping) it was still furnished. Simply appointed, yes, but a place Eddie could live, hopefully without destroying it.

Everything in the kitchen was basic: a ceramic sink with no disposal (*One less thing to go wrong*), a four-burner electric stove *(Good; didn't think to explain pilot lights)*, and a no-frills refrigerator. Seeing bread on the counter, Zeke gave himself permission to snoop further.

While Hélène showed Eddie the bathroom, Zeke found a good supply of basics—including catsup—in the refrigerator. The women's hasty trip through Ekness Super Valu—the name on bags Zeke found under the sink—provided enough to feed Eddie until he got used to shopping. *Luke will help, and there's always Cate's Café.*

He opened the cupboard when he heard the others moving to the bedroom. Neatly arranged on one shelf were cans of heat-and-eat staples and a jar of peanut butter. Another shelf held a variety of better soups than

Eddie had probably ever tasted, a box of saltines, a package of cookies, and two kinds of cereal: one healthy, and one sugary enough to get a day rolling.

Zeke wandered down the short hall and leaned against the doorframe while Hélène explained how the heater vents worked, and the basic points of thermostats.

When Haze looked up and saw Zeke, she stepped out into the hallway with him and whispered, "Well?"

"You ladies did a very good job of shopping."

"We divided and conquered the grocery store in record time. Thanks for giving Hélène the money, Zeke." Standing on tiptoe, she kissed his cheek.

"Just trying to Do The Right Thing, Mom." *Though there's still one* 'Right Thing' *I need to do . . .*

He wandered into the bathroom when Eddie and Hélène hit the living room. A radio came on, then the TV as he opened the linen closet: washcloths, towels, bedding—obviously from Hélène's past-life (*Maybe the daughters' beds?*) but still serviceable. Soap, shampoo, deodorant, tub-cleanser and a sponge rested on the edge of the shower-tub. Toothbrush, toothpaste, a nail-clipper, and more soap lined the sink. *Subtle, necessary hints!*

While Eddie learned about the washer, dryer and vacuum, Zeke excused himself, saying vaguely, "I'm off to take care of some things. I'll be back shortly." Thankfully Haze was so engrossed that *vague* passed muster.

His heart pounded as fast as the time he had met an injured badger limping through sagebrush. He muttered, "I ran fast then, I can run fast now if it's a stupid idea."

Blyss' store was easy to find. Zeke saw her through the open door: sitting cross-legged on the floor, reading, with her back to the door. He knocked on the doorframe.

She spun around, still seated; her eyes widened. "Zeke? Welcome!" She rose. *No hands, just leg muscles.* Gulping, Zeke willed his thoughts to shift gears.

A modestly clad Blyss faced him: jeans, a simple blouse, sandals. He thought *Chameleon?* remembering the Bess-and-Haze assessment of her appearance. But something other than attire seemed different about her.

Her hair was twisted at the nape of her neck, held in place with a clip. She wore little, if any, make-up. She looked pretty, without an ounce of *va-va-voom*. He saw her with different eyes today and deemed her *sad-like*.

He glanced around the tidy store. Bookshelves lined the store's walls, with framed artsy posters interspersed. Low tables, surrounded by pint-sized chairs, held children's books and puzzles. Comfortable chairs, floor lamps, and footstools invited guests to find a book and linger. Soft guitar music—*Debussy's Reverie?*—wafted from ceiling-hung speakers. The aroma of coffee drew his eyes to mugs arranged on a rack.

She caught him eyeing the cups. "Would you like coffee? It's pretty fresh—not many customers yet today."

"It smells good, but no thanks. I, uh, came here to ask you something." His mouth was dry and dusty as much of Utah. *Maybe coffee would help!*

"Oh?" Obviously her visitor's words, mannerisms or tone made her as cautious as she was curious.

"When you stopped by our book table in Crosby, why did you flirt with me? Was I sending off signals? If I was, I'd like to know what I did so I can work on quitting."

He paused; she sucked in her breath and held it.

"See," he continued, "I know it doesn't mean much to some guys, but I'm more than just *married*—I'm head-over-heels, totally besotted with my wife. Her name is Sage and she's more than enough woman for me in every way. I love Sage so much, I feel sick thinking I've dishonored her by sending out vibes to any woman other than her. So, tell me, Blyss: What'd I do that encouraged you to act the way you did toward me—you know: flirty?"

First she stared at him, then at the floor. Almost imperceptibly, she shook her head. Her Adam's apple bobbed in a rock-hard swallow. "I was embarrassed when you dashed off . . . because I knew why you'd left."

"It wasn't my finest moment, either."

"You did nothing, Zeke. Even though I know it's wrong, when I saw you I went into action without thinking about anything except how much I wanted, uh, to be noticed. It's ingrained behavior that haunts me."

"The same behavior that brought you to Prairie Rose?"

Blyss flushed and stared at the book she still held. "You heard about that, hmm?" She marked her page and set the paperback on a nearby chair.

Zeke asked softly, "Do you have friends here, Blyss?"

A head-shake. "Acquaintances, and one troubled man who knows me better than he should. Folks leave me alone except to make small talk if they can't escape without being rude. They're so . . . *polite*; I hate polite."

Seconds ticked like heartbeats. "Why do you stay?"

"If I left, I would still be taking the *me* I despise wherever I went. I manage to get in trouble real fast and very predictably wherever I am, as you witnessed. Sometimes, even without trying, I attract men; women hate me for that even if it's not intentional on my part."

"You *do* know males respond to how a gal dresses, to acts—even a simple hair toss or a wink can set us off."

"Yeah; I can pretend it's their problem if men watch me wiggle when I walk, or if they can't handle seeing more skin than is decent, but I know . . ." She chewed her lip.

"Is there still anything between you and Frank?"

Her shock at hearing Frank's name spoken so bluntly showed. "Absolutely nothing," she said firmly. "We both made huge mistakes that we're living with. I don't mean this sarcastically, Zeke, but why do you care?"

"Because I have a question: If you thought there was a chance Frank and Hélène could get back together, after all that has happened, what would you do?"

A long silence. "I'd wish them well and wonder what gives Helen—Hélène—the ability to forgive him. Most of all, I'd hope Frank has changed enough—learned from our mistake—to be an up-front guy, like you. Someone who treasures his wife so much that he confronts me about my inappropriate behavior. You're the first to talk *to* me, face-to-face, not *about* me."

Zeke nodded. "It was something I had to do. I don't want to ruin my marriage. It is my greatest joy."

"I hope Sage appreciates you."

"She does, and she lets me know in countless ways. I have one more question: What keeps you here?"

She laughed without humor. "Money. And don't think it's because I'm raking it in. I guess the answer is really *no* money. Prairie Rose feels like prison to me."

"You remind me of my brother, Gull. He's made many mistakes in his life; he's in prison for the worst one. May I encourage you to look through the invisible bars you think hold you here? Find your way out, Blyss. You are not a prisoner here! Give yourself a chance to succeed at being a different, better *you*."

"I'll . . . I don't . . ." She straightened her shoulders. "I guess if you were brave enough to confront me, I should try to move on. She extended her arms, inviting a hug.

He shook his head, but lessened the silent rebuke with a smile. "Let's just shake hands. Think of it as the first step in your new journey." And they did: each extended one hand. No caressing from her, no wondering from him if there had been a lingering squeeze.

"May I make a suggestion? Luke Larson told me that his minister here is a woman. Do you know Pastor Tori?"

"As much as I know anyone else in town; we talk occasionally. She's pleasant every time; I'm the one who gets my dander up. I mean, my lifestyle and hers are light years apart."

"Enlist her help for the days ahead. She'd make a good sounding board as you dream. Give her a chance and, if the two of you don't click, don't beat yourself up."

"She could have a heart attack if I approach her," Blyss said ruefully. "She initiated the other contacts."

"There you have it: she's already shown an interest. You reciprocate by letting her know you're ready for a friend. Meanwhile, find a Bible and look up Matthew 7:7."

"Someone traded a Bible the other day; I'll find it." She mouthed the note she scribbled on a scratch pad: *Matthew 7:7.* "I'm not religious, but if there's a God, I sure hope that someday I find a man like you when I get straightened out," she said fervently, capping the pen.

"There *is* a God, and He cares. But maybe a man won't be the answer He'll give you. However God responds will be just what you need, when you need it."

"And you know this . . . how?"

"Only because I have a friend in Utah who pulled me through rough patches until I could see light in dark places. Hank says that's God's doing, not his. Actually talk to Eddie sometime about that Bible verse—he's moving into the barber shop apartment, as we speak. I need to get going; I have cookbooks to sell, and you have things to decide. Best of everything to you, Blyss."

"Give Sage a big hug and tell her she's got a wise, brave, loyal husband."

"Will do, though I might edit out all but the hug part!"

"Hey," she called as he pushed against the door. He saw a spark of what the new Blyss could be like when she said, "You have the distinction of being the last guy I will purposely flirt with. How about that?"

"I hope not, though I'm glad to be the last guy you flirt with *inappropriately.* If—no, let's make that: *when* you meet a guy who's legit, in other words, who doesn't have emotional or legal loyalties to someone else, then turn on every bit of your charm. He'll bask in it."

When Zeke left Blyss, both were smiling.

Back at Eddie's new digs, *Will it work?* was the question on three minds. Hélène, Haze, and Zeke bid a jiving Eddie farewell, though for Zeke, the question veered in two vastly diverse directions: Eddie; Blyss. Neither was a certainty, but each had *the stuff* that made success in their potentially different-than-before future lives fall within the realm of possible.

"You sure do love to dance, Eddie," Zeke said with a grin as he watched, leaning against the rattle-trap pickup.

"If'n ya be standin' still, ya ain't movin', Dude!"

Hard to say who stared harder at the ragtag dancing philosopher: Dude/Zeke, Hélène, or Haze.

Zeke checked the time; he and Haze needed to leave very soon or they'd be pushing their luck at getting the canopy ready for this final day's sales. Since she had driven her own car to Prairie Rose, Hélène could work towards getting Eddie further settled in without their assistance.

Haze climbed into the pickup with Zeke. She yelped a nervous "Oh!" when Zeke shifted gears and that action was enough to cause the passenger-side window to drop five irretrievable inches to a place within the bowels of the door's frame.

Zeke grinned.

Haze provided commentary on the day, thus far, at a wind-in-your-face talking speed (which was faster than even Zeke's lead foot could muster from the protesting truck). Meanwhile he cogitated on the day's wild and wide-flung activities (and it not even yet noon) from his perspective, and joined in just often enough with "Uh-huh" or "Really?" to keep from getting swatted.

When Crosby came in view, he decided, *If Pastor Tori's all that Luke claims she is as far as being compassionate, capable, and encouraging—and even half as good as Hank is—then Blyss is in good hands.*

CHAPTER 40

The clock that struck midnight twelve hours earlier, as two people talked on Hélène's steps, now chimed twelve notes signifying noon. Zeke opened lawn chairs under the hastily erected canopy, and Haze shoved empty boxes out of sight. It was Sunday: their last day in Crosby. By sundown, book-signings events for SOUP'S ON IN RAVEN CROWLEY'S KITCHEN would be over.

This time when the parade went by, Zeke saw things he'd missed the previous day: Norwegian Fjord horses, even a mini-rodeo of little kids riding stick horses with yarn manes. Haze wanted to run out and hug them. Luckily she didn't or she'd have met up with a team of impressive Suffolks high-stepping behind the children.

The threshing machines hadn't changed volume levels, but The Harmonica Band sounded even better than Saturday. The crowd willingly sang along:

From this valley they say you are going . . .

Zeke *was* leaving. Maybe not the Red River Valley, but still a place that had provided stimulating experiences.

. . . so remember the Red River Valley . . .

He *would* remember Crosby as where he'd met Eddie and Hélène: two unforgettable people. *As for Blyss? She will serve as a good reminder not to be a fool . . .*

. . . and the cowboy who loved you so true.

When the horses came into view, Haze ducked her head as if that could hide her from the cowboy who might have loved *her* so true. Zeke chuckled; she glowered.

Leading the horse procession, once again, Midnight carried Sparky . . . and a buxom auburn-haired gal clad in beaded leather that caressed each of her feminine curves. "What a fickle fellow," Widow Haze Eden snorted.

~~~

MONDAY

From Crosby to Rochester is 700 miles. Plenty of time for a mother to talk and a son to listen. Point A to Point B is ten-plus hours: sufficient time for a son to speak from his heart; adequate time for a mother to muse without comment. Both of them did.

Their topic? Gull. It marked THE END to *"I need to talk about Gull, Zeke . . . but you won't."* Meeting and talking with Hélène had unleashed Hope in Haze. Despite having friends and a familiar home, she felt lonely in Rochester. Home is where the heart is, right? And her heart was feeling homeless. But what if she were to move to Utah? She'd be nearer Zeke and Sage . . . and could visit Gull.

~~~

TUESDAY

After a good Haze-style breakfast (all the food groups represented) Zeke bid farewell to his mother and left for the Rochester airport where he would return the rental car. He had allowed time for one important stop: a bank. There, he purchased a cashier's check—the usual choice for anyone desiring a gift to remain anonymous.

Moving from the counter to a table where he could work unobserved, he attached a pre-written Post-It note to the check. It said: *"Stretch your wings"*—with no signature. He stuck this in the smaller of two envelopes he'd purloined from Haze's desk, and licked the seal.

This he tucked inside a slightly larger preaddressed and stamped envelope, along with a second Post-It note affixed to the inner sealed envelope. That note gave instructions to the recipient whom Zeke could only hope would be willing to comply with its decidedly odd request.

Dropping the envelope into the airport's postal box, he dithered. *Is this helping or pushing?* he quizzed himself as he let go; the slot's door closed with metallic firmness. "Well, to quote Eddie, 'It be a he'pful push, uh-huh'!"

〰

FRIDAY

In the Prairie Rose Post Office, Pastor Tori thumbed through a fistful of odds-and-ends, pausing to examine a business-size envelope addressed to her in unknown cursive writing. Postmark: Rochester MN 55903.

She moved to the high table opposite the boxes and carefully slit open the envelope, only to find another sealed envelope inside . . . that one addressed to Blyss Hathaway. A cryptic request scrawled on a Post-It note was stuck to the inner envelope:

> *Pastor Tori:*
>
> *We've not met, but I hope you are willing to deliver the enclosed envelope—minus this note—directly to Blyss. Thank you.*
>
> *A friend*

Tori would have soundly trounced anyone she caught doing what she did next, but curiosity is powerful. After furtively looking around, she did the unthinkable: She held the envelope up to the light. *A check? Oh, my!*

"No time like the present," she quipped, and headed for the bookstore, admitting privately that she hoped Blyss would be so curious she would rip open the envelope *right then* and blurt out an explanation for the intrigue. "Not that it's my business, but I *am* involved!"

Half an hour later she was on her way home, none the wiser and muttering, "After all the times I've prayed Blyss would let me get to know her better, only to get the cold shoulder treatment, *today* she offers me coffee and practically begs me to sit and visit for a few minutes— while we're both dying to know what's in the envelope I gave her! An envelope she didn't open!"

She examined the outer envelope with the puzzling Post-It now stuck to its empty insides. "I don't know what God's up to, but I sense it'll be an interesting ride!"

≋ ≋ ≋

LATE SEPTEMBER

Haze called the minute she heard amazing news from Hélène: "Three things, Zeke—all of *great* interest! First, Blyss has moved away from Prairie Rose and is working in a library in Wyoming! Cheyenne, I think. And Eddie helped her pack boxes and load the rental truck!"

Zeke smiled, but only said, "Wow, that is big. Pretty hard to top it, in fact. But you say there's more?"

"Yes! Guess who moved into her store? Never mind," she said quickly, circumventing Zeke's automatic response. "I know you hate guessing, so I'll tell you: Eddie started a handyman business in Blyss' old store!"

"Eddie as a businessman? Wow; that's pretty hard to imagine."

"It's true! Hélène says people gave him things like rakes, shovels, tools—even a wheelbarrow, which he likes very much. They hire him to do odd jobs, like paint a fence, or dig a garden plot, or clean a chimney. Whoever owns the former bookstore building rents it to Eddie, and Eddie earns enough for that *and* the apartment upstairs!"

He grinned. "Who'da thunk it? But why did he move from Hélène's place? Oh-oh, did he mess-up, somehow?"

"That's the third thing! Hélène mostly called to let me know she's moved back to Prairie Rose! She finished working at Quilt Blocks last week and now she's cutting hair with Frank and living in the shop's apartment, which is why Eddie had to move. What do you think about all *that*? I say, it's just one miracle after another!"

"Stop talking long enough to give me a chance to tell you what I think. This is a perfect example of how, if you toss a stone in water, you should expect ripples."

"What's that mean? Oh, I see: you're being philosophical." Then, in typical Haze-fashion, she changed conversational lanes without signaling: "So, tell me, Zeke: are you writing yet?"

≋ ≋ ≋

EARLY OCTOBER

John and Maggie received an e-mail:

Happy to hear that Raven's cookbook sales remain strong. Thought you might like to know this: I've started research for *Lost Ground*. In case you've lost count, *LG* is #17 for Kiel Nede.

Plot summary for *LG*: 2 feuding clans both think they own rights to a Kansas salt mine (actual location left vague, or to be determined? Your call.) As for Raven, he whittles now and he might start playing harmonica (still working on that). One thing's certain: no more soup. (Don't ask; my answer would be a lie, & I hate to lie to friends.)

Key promo line (to be expanded): Raven is called into action when the 2 patriarchs are found dead in the mine.

Do what you want for *LG*'s front cover, Maggie. But on the back cover, I'd really like just a photo of a simple bridge (no reviews by my famous colleagues, no author photo) with this single quote:

"If'n ya be standin' still, ya ain't movin', Dude!"
Eddie (No last name known)

Hope all's well with you 2 KC-MO dynamos, Zeke.

≋ ≋ ≋

MID-OCTOBER

Zeke punched a familiar number on his cell phone. He was actually glad when the call transferred to voice mail this time; it was so much easier to tell a machine this particular message:

"Hank? It's Zeke, here. Just calling to say, uh, that maybe when you head up to Draper again to see Gull, I might, uh, hitch a ride with you. No promises, but we'll see. Talk to you later, my friend."

Discussion Guide

1. Relationships of varying types form the center of this novel—some long-term, some distant, some newly formed. What is required for relationships to begin, last, and survive difficulties or differences?

2. Would you feel most comfortable spending time with Zeke, Haze, Hélène, or Eddie? What would you talk about? Did you choose him/her because of shared experiences, or because you have never known anyone like this person and wonder what makes him/her tick? Is there any character you would prefer to avoid? Why?

3. Discuss the differing situations involving the life-changes several individuals are making at the end of the book. Which, if any, do you think have any chance of long-term success? Why or why not?

4. In nature, ripples exist because of disturbances. What "stones" (some prior to the story's start-point, some within the story's timeframe) dropped into the characters' lives and created ripples? How did the ripples play out? If faced with similar situations, would you have responded similarly?

5. Would Eddie fit in or survive in your community? Would Blyss be tolerated, ignored, or welcomed in your social sphere? Within your circle of friends, what happens to people whose situations parallel these characters' lives?

6. What most influenced the ultimate decisions Eddie, Zeke, Hélène, and Blyss made? What has the most impact on how a person handles grief, despair, or loss?

7. Have you had an "Ask-Seek-Knock" experience in your life somewhat similar to Eddie's? Did hard work figure in the results, or was faith sufficient?

Antique & Classic Vehicles on View

- 1908 Maxwell
- 1910 Overland
- 1912 IHC Auto Wagon
- 1915 Model T
- 1925 Buick
- 1926 Buick 2-door Sedan
- 1927 Ford T-Bucket • Fire Truck
- 1928 Ford Model A • IHC Truck • Model A Roadster
- 1929 Nash • IHC Special
- 1930 Snowmobile
- 1932 Hupmobile
- 1937 Teraplane
- 1938 Coupe
- Early 40s Diamond T
- 1941 Dodge Carryall
- 1943 M2 Aircraft Mover • White Half Track • M29 Weasel with Cargo Trailer
- 1945 Studebaker 6x6
- 1947 Seagreve Fire Truck
- 1949 Chevrolet 2-door sedan
- 1951 Chevrolet 4-Door
- 1953 Studebaker • GMC Cargo Truck
- 1958 4-Door Edsel from Alamo
- 1962 4-Door Dodge
- 1964 Chevrolet C10
- 1965 Cadillac
- 1966 Ford T-bird • Chevy 2-door hardtop • Chevy pickup
- 1967 Dodge
- 1968 Buick
- 1972 Plymouth Duster
- 1973 Thunderbird • Chevrolet Monte Carlo
- 1976 AMC Jeep
- 1977 Ford Ranchero
- 1978 Lincoln Continental
- 1979 Ford LTD Heritage
- 1989 Ford Mustang   [continues]

Details from Past Threshing Shows, con't.

Antique Gas & Steam Engine Driven Tractors on View

- <u>1909</u>: 20 HP Type C Mogul
- <u>1910</u>: 30 HP Hart Parr *[only 1 known to exist]* · 25 HP Fairbanks Morse · 15 HP Type A International Tractor
- <u>1911</u>: 30-60 HP Hart Parr · Quincy Tractor *[only 1 known to exist]* · 40-70 HP Imperial Tractor *[1 of 3 in existence]* · 25 HP type C Mogul · 25-50 HP Geiser gas tractor *[1 of 2 known to exist]* · 40-70 HP Flour City · 25-45 HP Titan · 20 HP Type B International · 25-45 HP Model B Rumley · 25-50 HP Minneapolis · 15-30 HP Model F Rumley · 25 HP type D Titan
- <u>1912</u>: 25-85 HP Nichols & Sheppard side-mount · 80 HP Case Steam Engine rear mount · 15-30 HP Rumley Gas Pull · 15-30 HP Mogul · 40-65 HP Reeves · 110 HP Case steam engine · 25-40 HP Mogul
- <u>1913</u>: 6 cyl Big Four 45 HP *[only 1 known to exist]* · 12-25 HP Mogul · 30 HP Robert Bell rear-mount steam engine *[1 of 2 known to exist]* · 25 HP Garr Scott rear mount steam engine · Big Four 30 · 30-60 HP Fairbanks Morse *[1 of 3 known to exist]*
- <u>1914</u>: 20 HP Rumley double-cylinder rear mount steam engine · 18-35 HP Titan [1 of 3 known to exist] · 15-30 HP Rumley Model F · 20-40 HP Case
- <u>1915</u>: 40-65 HP Twin City · 25-90 HP Nichols & Sheppard double-cylinder rear-mount · 40-80 HP Avery · 27 HP single-cylinder Hart Parr · 30-60 HP Model E Rumley
- <u>1916</u>: Little Devil Hart Parr [1 of 3 known to exist] · 20 HP Advance Rumley rear-mount steam engine · 12-25 HP Bower City
- <u>1917</u>: 30-60 HP Aultman Taylor
- <u>1918</u>: 40-70 HP Flour City · 18-35 HP Rumley Model F · 25-50 HP Avery · 14-28 HP Avery
- <u>1920</u>: 12-20 HP Rumley · 22-44 HP Minneapolis · 30-60 HP Aultman Taylor
- <u>1925</u>: 30-60 HP Model S Rumley
- <u>1926</u>: 35-70 HP Minneapolis

Fic
Hoov

1083148

$14.00

LU00005573 1325